D1275678

# Dressed to Kill

# Dressed to Kill

*Margaret Duffy*

St. Martin's Press
New York

Library of Congress Cataloging-in-Publication Data

Duffy, Margaret.
    Dressed to kill / Margaret Duffy.
        p.    cm.
    ISBN 0-312-11295-5
    1. Women detectives—Fiction.    I. Title.
PR6054.U397D74    1994
823'.914-dc20                                94-32246
                                                    CIP

First published in Great Britain by Judy Piatkus
(Publishers) Ltd.

First U.S. Edition: December 1994
10 9 8 7 6 5 4 3 2 1

To My Parents

# Dressed to Kill

# Chapter One

There was a superstition among the older inhabitants of the Somerset village of Chantbury that if ever the holy and ancient object known as the Chantbury Pyx was removed from the parish church high on the hill above, something terrible would happen. The Pyx – actually only part of one – consisted of a panel from a reliquary, which had been used to hold the Eucharistic host after the relic for which it was made had disappeared. Made of bronze with gilding, it depicted two angels seated inside the empty tomb. It had been found during building work in the late 1960s to construct an extension to the church: a kitchen and a room that could be used for the thriving Sunday school, the children and their two teachers having previously been crammed into the vestry.

The eminent local historian Sir Ninian Hunterstone, who had written at length on the building's past, was overjoyed that the find proved his theory of the church's one-time far greater importance. During the Reformation it had suffered damage bordering on demolition, and what stood today represented only a fraction of its original size. He was less pleased when his suggestion that the Pyx be sold to one of the great museums was turned down flat by the incumbent, the Reverend Harold Forbes, who, with the full backing of the Bishop of Bath and Wells, decided that the treasure should be displayed in a locked cabinet in the church for all to see who so wished. And there it remained for over twenty years.

The Reverend Forbes, now an old man and due to retire in a few months' time, then found himself at the centre of a controversy concerning the possible loan of the Chantbury

1

Pyx to the city of Bath, where an exhibition of medieval artefacts was being staged in the Sheridan Gallery. Most of his congregation were of the opinion that once out of the church it might never return. The affluent times when there was plenty of money to pay for extensions and the like were long gone. The roof needed attention, there was dry rot in the bell tower, necessitating the bells being silenced, and wet rot under the chancel. The fear was that the Pyx would be sold at auction to pay for these repairs. A few thought that the building was more important than a piece of metal some five inches by three and said so, loudly. The Reverend Forbes, having prayed long and earnestly for divine guidance, announced that he would launch an appeal for money to pay for the repairs and gave his permission for the Pyx to be shown at the exhibition, where, he was assured, it would be kept in a glass case protected by every security device known to man. The old priest thought it high time that sanctity and superstition were sundered for ever.

Secular criminal society licked its lips.

The official opening ceremony was held on a late summer morning, when the honey-coloured stone buildings seemed to glow in the sunshine. The exhibition was opened by Lady Amelia Hunterstone, widow of Sir Ninian, who had written at even greater length about Roman Bath and the cult of the goddess Minerva. Having cut the ribbon, Lady Amelia led the gathering of VIPs, reporters on the arts, local dignitaries and sundry others into the main gallery where there was to be a reception. Tables decorated with flower arrangements were laid out with canapés and glasses of wine. Most of the cognoscenti, predictably, headed straight for the Chantbury Pyx in its specially constructed case, the tiny treasure within glinting beguilingly as it lay on draped dark-blue velvet.

'It *has* to be twelfth-century, Joselyn.'

'That's not in doubt, old boy. Probably between 1125 and 1150.'

'German or English, though?' said someone else.

'The Temple Pyx that's in the Burrell Collection is considered to be German.'

'Yes, but this is quite different – rather more primitive in a way. It's English all right.'

2

'Oh, come off it!' protested a lady of generous proportions wearing a large-brimmed red hat. 'It really infuriates me when merely because the workmanship is a little rustic people pronounce that it's English.'

'Yes, Blanche, but if you remember that the standard of English alabaster carving was nowhere as high as it was on the continent –'

'That was the fourteenth century,' the woman snapped. 'And we're not talking about alabaster.'

Standing quite still and alone, wineglass in hand, the conversation ebbing and flowing around him, a slim man of above average height gave every impression of being lost in thought. But while body and features remained passive, the eyes were surveying the assembly in minute detail and with avid interest. Detective Inspector James Carrick was not present in his capacity as a policeman; at least he hoped not. The invitation had come right out of the blue.

The mystery was not to remain one for long.

'You look well, James,' called the woman wearing the red hat when she spotted him through a gap in the throng. No one ever called Carrick Jimmy even though he was a Scot.

Carrick raised his glass in a silent toast. She went over to him.

'You have quite the wrong name,' he said with a smile, looking at the hat.

'Yes, I suppose Blanche does sound a bit washed out. Like veg being got ready for the freezer,' she replied in a bored-sounding voice and then peered at him, eyes dancing with mirth, over the rim of her wineglass as she took a sip.

'Etiolated is the word,' he went on with a slight frown, regarding her with the blue gaze that, on occasion, made criminal suspects squirm.

'How refreshing to know cops who went to school,' she retorted. 'What the hell does that mean?'

'Of pale and sickly hue,' he enunciated carefully.

'Is this revenge for me sending you the invitation, you beastly man?'

'Ah,' said Carrick. 'Yes, if you like.' He chuckled. 'Seriously, though, thank you.'

Blanche Adams was the president of the Wansdyke Fine Arts Society, the sister of the mayor and in more ways than one a colourful local figure. She and Carrick had known one another for at least ten years, the friendship going back to the days when he had been a crime-prevention officer and she had been looking for a 'tame policeman' – her words – to give a short series of lectures to members of the society concerned about the safety of family pictures, silver and other valuables. She had not expected to scoop a born public speaker. Moreover, here was a policeman not merely telling people how to secure their possessions the way he might show them how to lock up their chickens, daughters or collection of World War II milk bottles. Carrick was interested in antiques, china in particular, and Blanche had discovered that he had good taste. Gently, she had nudged him in the direction of small pieces that had come up for auction – Coalport vases, a set of lustre tiles, some early Wedgwood Queensware – and had been overjoyed when he had successfully bid for one or two. She knew he was pleased with what he had acquired, too; not that one was permitted to be made aware of his pleasure. His massive reserve saw to that.

'How are you *really*, James?' she asked gravely.

'I'm okay,' he replied lightly.

'And overworking in order to try to forget?'

'No.'

She shook her head at him sadly. 'Men never tell the truth about things like that.'

'I'm thinking of moving out of the flat – perhaps to somewhere in the country.'

'I'm glad,' Blanche said softly. 'Will it have a garden?'

He nodded. 'I'll be able to grow the neeps to go with my haggis.'

'God, you don't really like that stuff, do you?'

'It depends who makes it.'

'The very idea puts me off – all sorts of bits of innards stuffed into a sheep's stomach.' She pulled a face.

'I'll ask you round on Burns' Night,' he said with a smile. Replacing his empty glass on a tray, he added, 'I must go. Many thanks. I'll make sure that the place is kept an eye on.'

'You're an angel.'

'Not *yet*,' he admonished gently, still smiling. But his eyes were not smiling.

4

Blanche watched him leave. How long would it be before he recovered from the death of his wife?

The security company which had installed extra anti-theft and monitoring equipment in the Sheridan Gallery for the exhibition was also responsible for periodic external surveillance during the hours of darkness, the gallery's own staff being responsible for taking care of what was inside. Inspector Carrick was aware of this, so, apart from ordering passing patrols to keep their eyes open and watch out for anyone hanging around, he only satisfied himself that there was a direct telephone link between the gallery and Bath's main police station. More, he felt, he could not do.

The additional security had been installed after a conversation between the curator of the city's museum, who was organising the exhibition, and an adviser to one of the country's most prestigious auction houses, who was down from London for the day to attend a sale of paintings. The curator asked him what the Chantbury Pyx was worth.

'I really wouldn't want to put a figure on it.'

'Just a guess, Lionel, just a guess. I have to fill in a confounded insurance form.'

'But it's unique, old boy. All the rest – or almost all – were destroyed by those ignorant bastards in the sixteenth century.'

'I must put *something* down.'

'Have they tried to find the rest of it? I mean, there must be at least three other panels and the lid buried somewhere on the site.'

'No doubt, but it isn't really a site in the sense that it's an archaeological dig. There's a perfectly good parish church there.'

'I'm staggered that nothing was done when it was found.'

'So am I, really. Not my fault, I wasn't here in the sixties. Now, Lionel, a figure of some sort. Think of a number, double it and take away the first number you thought of. What are we talking about? Ten thousand? Twenty?'

'Are you mad, man? If it fetched less than three quarters of a million I'd be surprised. As I said, it's unique.'

The curator felt the short hairs on his neck prickling as he thought about the small cardboard box locked in a cupboard

5

in his office. The Reverend Harold Forbes had brought it in himself that very morning and, because his eyesight was not what it used to be and he was a little worried about driving, had come by bus.

On the third night after the exhibition had opened, at a little before ten forty-five, the security van drew up at the side entrance of the gallery for one of the periodic checks to see that all was as it should be. The man who admitted the crew to the gallery was suffering from a headache and ongoing domestic problems. He remembered too late that the knocks to request entry had not been in the pattern agreed upon. This lapse cost him dearly, a pickaxe handle making contact with the side of his head and rendering him unconscious. His colleague, making tea in the tiny staff kitchen, was brutally manhandled until he switched off the new alarms. The raiders made the mistake of battering him to the floor before asking which of the bewildering number of bunches of keys, hanging in the office, opened the case containing the Pyx. They were interested in nothing else. As it happened, none of the keys would have been the slightest use to them because the cabinet could only be opened electronically, using a coded sequence of numbers tapped onto buttons hidden behind a sliding panel in its base. So the thieves smashed the glass, supposedly unsmashable, and moments later the Chantbury Pyx was being stuffed into someone's pocket.

The second of the gallery's security men was not unconscious, despite the battering he had received. He saw them do it, using the same hammer they thought they had knocked him out with.

Then all the other alarms went off.

The bona fide security men were found, eventually, in a ditch in Twerton wearing only underpants and bruises. Their tale of woe – how they had stopped, as they usually did, for a bite of supper at a transport café on the Lower Bristol Road and had been ambushed and overpowered in the almost deserted carpark afterwards – reflected organisation so inept, in Sergeant Bob Ingram's view, that the management should be kicked until their backsides were between their ears. He said

6

as much to Carrick, as they left the Royal United Hospital the following morning, having spoken to the injured gallery staff, one of whom had a fractured skull. The men could tell them hardly anything about their attackers, who had been wearing stockings over their faces. One had been quite powerfully built, the other shorter and slight.

'It was the weak link in the chain,' Carrick said after agreeing with his sergeant's sentiments.

'But we can't do anything about *that*,' Ingrams growled, 'short of going in the john with them and helping them wipe their arses. Some of these idiots put on a pretty uniform and think they can walk on water.'

'And the two men in the gallery paid the price,' Carrick murmured. 'That makes me angry.'

They made their way to their car, Ingrams with his rolling sailor's gait, swinging his arms, slightly too big round the middle; Carrick's longer legs making it appear that he was walking much more slowly than the other.

'You played any rugger lately, sir?' Ingrams asked when they were in the car. 'No, it's the summer, isn't it? Stupid of me.' He only confessed to one sport, darts, and remained in almost sublime ignorance of all the others. His interest was motivated by the fact that he had worked with Carrick for only a fortnight and was still trying to build up a mental fact sheet about him. He wasn't progressing very well. The grapevine had yielded a few spicy titbits that he fully intended to learn more about, but all he knew for certain was that Carrick worked his staff into the ground and had recently lost his wife. Ingrams was trying to find out if the former was a due result of the latter. Somehow, he thought not; Carrick was a bit of a bastard naturally. And he played rugby for a team drawn from police forces of the West Country, the Ferrets. According to the grapevine, he was one of the few from small teams to have scored a try against Bath, and Bath, even Ingrams knew, were good.

Carrick did not look as though he would answer the question, having picked up the handset of the radio. Then he said,'If I was I'd have to start training. I don't know. I might not bother.'

'But they want you, like.'

The chilly blue eyes rested on him momentarily and Ingrams wished he hadn't asked.

'Oh, yes. Now are you going to drive or carry on sitting there like a pregnant penguin?'

I hate you, Ingrams thought as he crashed the vehicle into gear.

'Sorry, Bob,' Carrick said when they had gone a few hundred yards down the road.

# Chapter Two

It was a pity, Joanna Mackenzie thought, two days before the Chantbury Pyx was stolen, that the herbalist downstairs did not sell hemlock. Right then she wanted to put one or two large spoonsful in Lance Tyler's brew of tea, which he always expected her to make.

'Lapsang Souchong,' she sang, operetta-style. 'Warm the pot, make sure the water's boiling, one sugar, no milk.' Savagely, she whacked the metal teapot's lid with the spoon and added, glumly, 'Anyone would think I don't know how to make the beastly stuff.'

No, perhaps hemlock was a bit drastic.

'Or at least senna pods,' she muttered gloatingly. '*That* would keep you busy, boyo.'

The door behind her opened.

'Jo, who on earth are you talking to?'

'No one,' she answered lightly.

'Well, you know what they say – first sign of madness.'

He could be relied upon, utterly, to make the remark. Lance trotted out cliché-ridden comments as inexorably as Big Ben chimed the hours. Worse, he really thought he was being clever.

'Is it ready yet? I'm dying of thirst.'

She poured.

'Preferably in the cup,' said Lance. 'Oh, by the way, did you trace that woman's dog?'

'Bitch,' Joanna corrected, mopping the saucer. 'Yes.'

'Where?' He sounded surprised.

'In the park.'

9

'Well done.' To be fair, she could detect no grudging tone in his voice.

'Being screwed by half the dogs in Bath.'

'Oh, Lord.'

'The old bat didn't know about things like bitches being on heat. Too refined.' She pronounced it 'refained'.

'Jo, I know that many of our clients are elderly – there are a lot of retired people in Bath. But you don't have to make rude remarks about them. They're our bread and butter.'

'How would you know what she's like?' Joanna shot back at him. '*I* get all those jobs. I agree, most of them are old dears. But the one who lost the dog is a snobbish, stupid to the point of mindless, obnoxious old bat.' She held out the tea, only a very little slopped into the saucer.

Lance took a deep breath and smiled thinly. 'Well, let's hope that your disgust didn't show too much and she pays up.'

'She wrote me out a cheque there and then. It's in your tray.'

'Oh, right.' The door almost closed and then opened again. 'There's another little assignment that came in this morning. A Mrs Pryce. She says that someone's stealing plants from her garden.'

Joanna sighed.

'*Valuable* plants,' Lance stressed, eyes watering after taking a scalding sip. He put down the cup and saucer and came over to her. 'Only put in a couple of days ago along with some miniature conifers. You're good at that, Jo. You know about plants and things.'

He'll be saying how much he depends on me in a minute, she thought, bracing herself in anticipation. How the business of Tyler and Mackenzie is kept afloat by my fairly wide knowledge of this and that, attention to detail and ability to work twenty-four hours a day if necessary. She glanced up and looked at herself in the small mirror. Joanna Mackenzie, one-time sergeant of Bath CID, what the hell has become of you?

Lance's face came into focus behind her shoulder and she turned. It had the hurt-little-boy look and any moment he would launch into the words she had heard so many times before. Before he could open his mouth she spoke.

10

'I'll have an early lunch, if you don't mind, and do a bit of shopping. I didn't have time for any breakfast this morning.' He gaped a couple of times like a stranded fish. 'Yes, of course. Off you go then. But you will call on Mrs Pryce, won't you? I said you'd go round and see her this afternoon. Her address is in the case file I made out. It's in *your* tray.'

'Yes, Lance.'

The meek compliance irritated him. 'We're all they have, though, aren't we? The police aren't interested in that kind of thing.'

'I'm not surprised,' she responded dryly.

'Joanna, perhaps you ought to have a really good think about whether you want to carry on being a private investigator.'

Quietly, Joanna said, 'When I went into business with a colleague I seem to remember that there was an understanding that we would share the donkey work. You have just flown back from tracing that couple's daughter in the States. The week before that you were in Hong Kong. Next week San Francisco?' She picked up her bag and walked out.

Joanna descended the stairs, for once oblivious of the ravishing scents of lavender, rose petals, fennel, basil, clove oranges, cinnamon, orange blossom, bergamot and bay leaves. The potpourri was piled in baskets just inside the door of the herbalist's shop and often she lingered just to enjoy and perhaps to buy – she had run out of bowls to put it in at home, she had bought so much.

She walked down Milsom Street and into Union Street towards the Abbey and then turned right up Bath Street. Outside the Theatre Royal the road was completely blocked by a huge theatrical remover's van, men staggering out of it carrying what looked like a Macbeth blasted heath, all of a piece, only the witches missing. It lurched down a side alley, the air in its wake throbbing with modern curses.

Kingsmead Square was peaceful by comparison, the ancient plane tree in its centre completely still in the hot sunshine. Her destination, Oloroso's basement wine bar, was, however, blissfully cool and she sank onto one of the leather bench seats with a grateful sigh.

She did not usually treat herself to what she called a proper lunch on Wednesdays but rather felt that a crisis called for pleasant surroundings in which to think. A tantalising smell of mushrooms cooked with herbs and cream was wafting from the kitchen.

Tony, the waiter, popped up from behind the bar where he had been crashing bottles about. 'Ah, the beautiful Joanna. Sorry, I did not hear you come in.'

'I'm not in the mood for flirting, Tony,' she told him with enough regret in her voice to ensure that he wasn't offended.

'Then it must be a superb fino with ice,' he replied, always practical.

'Lovely.'

The bar specialised in sherries; the walls behind Tony were lined with barrels; amontillado, manzanilla, fino, oloroso and others. There was a short but impressive menu, all the food chosen to compliment a light, dry sherry.

Tony brought her drink. 'You want lunch? Enrico is cooking for the boss right now before we get busy. You like one of his specials?'

'Whatever he's cooking, as long as it isn't mussels or squid. *Anything* but that.'

'I tell him you want cow udder?' Tony asked with a big grin and then roared with laughter when she just glared at him. Over his shoulder he said, 'The boss has gone to Norway?' He knew it infuriated her to hear Lance described like that.

'No. Are you sure you don't mean the States? He's back.'

'No, I am sure I am right. He was in here last night. Norway, he said. A woman's husband has gone away and taken a lot of money from a joint account. She thinks he has left her for a girl they met on holiday in Scandinavia last year.'

'Oh, *that*. Yes, he did mention it to me,' Joanna lied. 'I'm not sure of his arrangements.'

Alone – or as good as; there were two other customers, but they were seated together in an alcove right at the far end – Joanna found that her hands were shaking and she was perilously close to bursting into tears. It was the last straw, to borrow one of Lance's time-expired expressions. Not so long ago, first thing on Monday mornings, they had sat in his office and held a mutual briefing, informing each other of progress, plans, problems and anything else applicable to the business. Lance, for some reason, had recently been involved with

12

something important on Mondays and the meetings had lapsed.

'He's sidelining me,' Joanna whispered to herself. 'I've been too busy finding lost dogs to notice that I've been demoted to girl Friday.'

It was Lance who had suggested that they go into business together as security advisers and private investigators. He had known that she was leaving and was thinking of doing the same himself, not for any particular reason, he was just bored with life as a sergeant in the uniformed branch. It was he who had found the office to let over the herbalist's shop, Savory and Hyssop, in Milsom Street and he had sold his flat in order to raise funds to put into the business, and lived on the premises for a while until finding another to rent.

There had been no question of Joanna inviting him to live with her, though she had taken out a bank loan for her share of the business rather than dispose of her home. She had not known him very well at the time, and she didn't make a habit of that kind of thing. This was not to say that he had never stayed the night with her. These occurrences were becoming rare to the point of extinction because Lance made love in clichés too. Come to that, why had she been attracted to a man with a dimple in his chin and brown spaniel eyes?

After she had eaten – and she was too involved with rehearsing what she would say to him to enjoy it – Joanna did her shopping and went back to the office. She made sure that her tread on the stairs was very determined and the grip on the door handle very firm; she always shrank from picking rows with people. She had a nasty feeling that its outcome would be the end of the little business of Tyler and Mackenzie.

Lance was out.

'Oh, shit,' she said miserably. 'I bet he knew what was coming.'

Disquietening thoughts filled her mind, things she was slightly shocked to find herself thinking; that he really was a bit of a coward, and pompous, selfish and mean. Not to mention deadly boring in bed.

There was no point in brooding about it. Joanna found the details about Mrs Pryce in Lance's tray, put the file in her briefcase and went out.

Beckford Square is situated just north of Royal Crescent and the Circus. The latter consists of three crescents forming a circle. Between one of these is Nash Street, which leads directly to Beckford Square, now, after years of neglect, designated a conservation area and scheduled for massive renovation. The terrace on the western side, actually called West Terrace, was completely boarded up, a large notice fixed to it announcing that it would be restored to its former Georgian glory and converted into retirement flats. In the centre of the square was a little garden surrounded by iron railings.

Mrs Pryce lived at number 3 South Terrace, one of a row of much smaller terraced houses of only two storeys. This side of the square looked as though it had been added as an after-thought, when perhaps the builders had almost run out of money. Here there were no Ionic columns or friezes, no sweeping Palladian curves, just four houses with, even more oddly in such a setting, small front gardens. Whereas most of these had handkerchief-sized lawns, immaculately clipped on the edges and bordered with summer bedding plants, Mrs Pryce had settled for neatly raked gravel upon which stood several stone tubs. The plants in two of these were missing.

Joanna rang the bell and the door opened immediately.

'Mrs Pryce?'

'That's right.'

'I'm from Tyler and Mackenzie,' Joanna said with her best smile. 'I –'

'I wasn't expecting a girl,' the woman interrupted. She had iron-grey hair scraped back into a bun and a complexion that almost matched.

'Mr Tyler and I are partners.'

'I see,' Mrs Pryce responded stonily, as though her visitor had made a slightly obscene remark. 'Come in.'

She led the way into a small back room. It did not look as though it was used all that often and in spite of the sunshine outside it felt cold and damp. In one corner an upright piano was partly covered by a dustsheet. A horsehair sofa and single dining chair were the only other items of furniture.

'Sit down,' said Mrs Pryce in the manner of a headmistress talking to a recalcitrant pupil.

Joanna perched on the edge of the rock-hard sofa and opened her briefcase. The sofa smelled of stale cooking and mothballs.

'If it wasn't for the fact that their garden's very overplanted already, I'd say it was my neighbour.'

Joanna opened her notepad. 'Who took the plants?'

'Of course. What else could I mean?' Mrs Pryce retorted venomously. 'They're not my sort of people at all. Army types. Give themselves airs. Up at all hours of the night playing music. I can *distinctly* hear it even though the walls are very thick. Drinking as well, probably,' she added darkly.

'And the plants were taken from the tubs in your front garden?'

'There are no back gardens. Just a yard behind each house.'

'It's almost the end of the summer and yet you said that the plants had only been put in recently. Why was that?'

'What on earth has that to do with it?' the woman snapped.

'I'm just trying to establish a pattern of events,' Joanna replied patiently. 'Like for example whether the new planting was to replace others that had been stolen.'

'No, nothing like that. The tubs they were in are new. I thought the garden would look better with two more.'

'What were the plants?'

'I've no idea of their names. The same as in the other two tubs.'

'Exactly?'

'You ask the most stupid questions. *Exactly* the same plants. I prefer uniformity. The small conifers had names on labels but I didn't read them – what they're called doesn't interest me. I throw them away before the winter anyway.'

'What, even the conifers?'

'Why not? They look rather boring on their own.'

Joanna changed the subject. 'I would imagine that they were stolen after dark. Have any of the other residents lost plants?'

'I've no idea.'

'There are only these four houses that have front gardens. And you've really no idea?'

'I've just said so, haven't I? I don't tittle-tattle over garden fences.'

'What time do you go to bed?'

'At nine thirty. When the television news has finished.'

'Have you ever noticed anyone hanging about?'

'No.' The woman leaned forward. 'I want this person caught. The police made it clear that they're too busy to look into it. Which is disgraceful when you think how much we all pay in taxes. In the old days the police walked round on foot and caught the likes of petty thieves. And punished them too – with a good box around the ears.'

'So you think the culprit might be a child?'

'Well, of *course* it's a child. Adults – unless they're spiteful old men shell-shocked to the point of imbecility – don't go round stealing plants. He is, you know, the Moffat man next door. Sometimes he thinks he's still fighting the Japs. Shouts and rages about. He ought to be in a secure home for people like that.'

Joanna made a note on her pad. This, she knew, was going to be one of her unsolved cases. Obviously, whoever had taken the plants had done them a favour.

'The wife's of no account,' Mrs Pryce was saying. 'Like a mouse.'

'When were your plants stolen?'

'A couple of days ago. The last day of August.'

'Do you have any suspicions at all? Do any children live in the square who might have done it for a prank?'

Mrs Pryce squared her thin shoulders. Mouth pursed, she said, 'There's Jamie. He's a real nuisance, riding his bike all over the pavements. The kind of child from the kind of background to go very wrong when he gets older.'

'Where does he live?'

'At number 3 on the other side of the square. In the basement flat.'

'What makes you think he's a bad boy?'

With enormously self-satisfying spite the woman said, 'His mother's not married. It's quite outrageous that a woman like that lives here. I told her so – to her face – when I went to complain to her about her son throwing his ball into the front garden.'

And she's only had her plants stolen, Joanna thought, writing 'vicious old bitch' in shorthand on her pad. She rose to her feet. 'Well, I'll see what I can do, but tracing small items that have been stolen is always very difficult.'

'I want them *caught*,' Mrs Pryce repeated. 'Caught and *punished*.'

In the front garden Joanna opened her note pad again and wrote:- eight scarlet, ruffled petunias, two Chamaecyparis Kosteri 'Nana Aurea'. She would have to phone her father about the petunias, which were a hybrid variety, probably a new one. Not that knowing what they were would help at all, she just liked to know what she was looking for.

'I hope you're going to keep watch,' said Mrs Pryce suddenly from behind, making her jump. She had obviously opened the front door again.

'At night? I'm not too sure that Mr Tyler will want –'

'It's not what you or he want. If I hire you and pay your exorbitant fees, then I expect results. Quickly.'

The door slammed.

Joanna went next door and rang the bell. Again, it was answered almost immediately, as though she had been watched from behind the net curtains. She braced herself to be barked at.

'Come to arrest me?' asked the giant of a man, astoundingly quietly.

'I'm not from the police,' Joanna replied, the admission making her just as miserable as it always did. She introduced herself.

He looked disappointed. 'There, my morning's ruined.' The door was flung wide. 'Come in, my dear. Only a silly old man's idea of a joke.' At the entrance to a living room he added, in a loud stage whisper, 'Kettle's on. I'm sure you want to talk about the dragon's missing flowers. I call her that when Alice, my wife, can hear, but she's referred to as something quite different at the Pear Tree, I can tell you. And not fit for a young lady's ears either. Not that Alice is here at the moment but she'll be back directly. Always has her hair done on Wednesday afternoons.'

The room was comfortable, if a little shabby, a small hole in one of the armchairs very neatly darned. The cushion covers were hand-embroidered as were small, lace-edged mats placed beneath the lamps on low tables. One of the first things

17

that Joanna looked at in a room was the mantelpiece, always a good source of information about the people who lived in the house. This one was crowded with homely items; framed and unframed photographs of children, a family of three at various ages, brass candlesticks with new red candles in them, several airmail letters with Australian stamps, a posy of a few garden flowers in a tiny Delft jug, a reel of black cotton with threaded needle and scissors beside it.

Joanna had been on her own for a couple of minutes when there was the sound of a key in the lock of the front door. Peering discreetly around the long curtain at one side of the archway into the hall, Joanna beheld a woman who must be Alice, still a little pink around the ears from the hairdryer. She slipped off a rather smart, light jacket and hung it in a cupboard in the hall.

'A visitor,' her husband boomed from the kitchen where he was rattling cups. 'A young lady private investigator.' He came into view holding a teapot. 'Am I right?'

'Spot on.' Joanna smiled.

'Thought you were. Look as though you mean business.' He pottered away again, whistling a regimental march; Joanna thought it was 'We've lived and loved together'.

'Do please sit down,' Alice said as she came in. 'I hope Jack hasn't been saying all sorts of silly things about Mrs Pryce. Poor soul, she has nothing in her life really. No children or family except her nephew. She just seems to get pleasure out of being horrible to everyone.'

'Is it *Colonel* and Mrs Moffat?' Joanna asked. 'I'm sorry to ask, but I have to note down the people I talk to in case they've seen something and the police eventually press charges against someone.'

'But surely not in this case? Yes, that's right, my husband worked in Whitehall after he was invalided out of the army.'

'Oh no, I don't think it's going to come to a court case this time. Although Mrs Pryce seems to hope it will.'

'She's failed already,' Jack Moffat said with a chuckle, bringing a tray with cups and saucers on it. 'She knows all too well that people don't go to prison for stealing plants. That's why she went to a private eye – hoping that she could unleash an unpleasant sort of nosy parker on us. Not just Alice and

18

me, of course – all the folk who live in the square. The damned woman's paranoid, thinks we're all out to get her. It's her way of getting revenge.'

It wasn't the first time that Joanna had become involved in this sort of thing. People with a persecution complex, usually involving neighbours, were amazingly commonplace. She said, 'Who lives on the other side of Mrs Pryce?'

'Dr Hendricks,' Alice answered. 'But he won't be there now – he has a clinic on Wednesday afternoons. He's hardly at home at all, really, so I don't think he could help you.'

'Got a lady friend,' the Colonel said, nudging Joanna. 'Spends a lot of time at her place.'

'Be so kind as to pour the tea, Jack,' his wife requested. To Joanna she said, 'People do walk through the square. School-children cut through here morning and afternoon. They always have done. The school is only about five hundred yards down Oliver Road at the end of this terrace. I'm sure one of them took the plants just out of mischief. Mrs Pryce is always calling out to them not to be noisy and telling them they've no right to be in the square as they don't live here. It's absolute nonsense. One of them does live here, Jamie, over the road at number 3. He's a nice little boy, a bit wild perhaps, but his poor mother has no husband and has to work to help support them both.'

'And who lives at number 1 on this side?' Joanna enquired.

'Oh, that's the Youngers. But they're abroad – on a cruise, I believe. They've been away for three weeks now.'

'Have you noticed anyone hanging about at night? Is there any trouble with vandals or drunks?'

'No,' Jack Moffat replied. 'Not so you'd speak of. But there's a tramp squatting in West Terrace and I'd like to see the back of him. There's no knowing what he'd do when he's drunk – seems to be stoned out of his skull every time you see him. I reported the fact that he was there to the police but they've done nothing.'

'He's doing no *harm*, Jack,' Alice ventured.

'That's not what you said the other day,' he retorted crossly. 'You said you didn't like strange men lurking about. Nor do I – I think he ought to be sent packing.'

'Why does Mrs Pryce dislike you so much?' Joanna asked.

19

The reply was blunt. 'Because I won't take any of her damned nonsense. She hadn't lived here all that long and it started. First it was complaints about the dog barking. He only barked when someone came to the door and that's what you have a dog for, damn it. Well, poor old Bones died soon afterwards – he was all of sixteen. Then it was the tree out the back in the yard. She said it cut out the light. I'm damned if I'm going to take a saw to a fine birch when all it does is block out the view of the old gas works and factory estate. That's why I planted it when we first came here. After that it was the radio. We have Radio Three on some evenings for the concerts – proms, that kind of thing. But not up loud. She must have listened with her ear pressed to the wall to hear it.'

'It's very difficult,' Alice said and sighed. 'Another cup of tea, Miss Mackenzie?'

Joanna declined, saying she had to be going. She thanked them and left, noting as she walked through the tiny front garden that it was by far the most attractive of the four. There was a clematis growing up a trellis on the wall of the house, standard roses and, around the lawn, a low hedge of rosemary. The borders were crammed with pink antirrhinums, white alyssum – heavily scented – and blue lobelia. Growing over the low wall that bordered the pavement was an unusual variegated ivy, cream and white with pink leaf margins. The overall effect was quite enchanting.

The garden in the centre of the square was less colourful, being almost entirely given over to rather dusty-looking shrubs, the largest of which was a rhododendron, its leaves drooping in the heat. Near it was a large boulder. Joanna went closer, through the gate in the railings, wondering if it served to commemorate someone or something, but there was no inscription or plaque. It seemed to serve no purpose.

'The stake-out,' she said, gazing around with sinking heart.

# Chapter Three

Miss Ethel Braithewaite watched the young woman in the garden in the centre of the square. The stranger was too young to look so severe and thoughtful, she mused, carefully drawing the net curtain aside in order to see a little more clearly. Surely the lass was only in her mid-twenties. She had seen her knock at Mrs Pryce's door, her attention drawn to the car's arrival by the driver sounding the horn accidentally as she leaned over to pick up her briefcase.

The girl was looking at the large boulder. Sometimes, in an idle moment – and Miss Braithewaite, troubled by a heart condition, had all too many of those - she wondered if it covered a grave. Not of a person, of course, but perhaps a horse or dog. She liked to think that; she loved animals but couldn't keep one these days, especially after poor Fluff died so suddenly. Her eyes misted over a little, blurring the slim figure of the auburn-haired girl below. It had probably been that feline enteritis that she kept hearing about from her friend Joyce. Joyce knew a lot about cats. But there had been no warning at all; Fluff had just come in and died.

From where she was standing by the window of her second-floor flat in number 3 North Terrace, Miss Braithewaite could see all of the terrace opposite. Until quite recently, a large elm tree had stood in the garden but it had had to be cut down because it had been infected with Dutch elm disease. She loved trees but now a lot more sun and light shone into the flat, making it much brighter. It was probably the only thing that Mrs Pryce and the other residents had ever agreed about, the need to cut down the dying tree.

21

Miss Braithewaite wondered who the wealthy widow's visitor might be. She appeared to have no friends, which was hardly surprising, she was such an unpleasant woman. Why, the dreadful creature had actually come across to accuse Karen's little boy Jamie of throwing his ball into her garden on purpose. And when Karen had answered her with more spirit than the woman liked, she had gone on to say the most insulting things, more or less called the young mother a slut.

The girl was walking back to her car now and after a quick look round – a move that took Miss Braithewaite quite by surprise, causing her to drop the curtain back quickly – got in it and drove away.

'Bother,' said Miss Braithewaite. She turned, mortified that she had been spotted by that bright, discerning gaze. The girl would think her a nosy spinster with nothing better to do than spy on people. Her living room, she saw in a moment of dispiriting self-illumination, was that of a spinster: little crocheted mats beneath the very boring but valuable china figurines that had been her mother's, a bowl of dried flowers that had faded to a uniform dusty pink, old, dreary but good family furniture . . .

The trappings of a spinster, she thought miserably. Such ugly words.

Two other people saw Joanna get into her car and drive away. One of them, a clerk late back from lunch on account of a dental appointment, who worked at the offices of the insurance company situated over the art gallery at numbers 1 and 2 North Terrace, had no effect on future events so need concern us no further. The other, a nurse folding linen on the third floor of the nursing home that took up the whole of the East Terrace, while gazing out over the square in an effort to take her mind off the tedium of the task, observed the red hair and then turned to stare critically at herself in a small mirror behind the door.

'Sorry, I forgot to mention it,' Lance said. He was standing by his desk flipping through one of their red case files.

'You told Tony about it,' Joanna pointed out.

He seemed to give her his attention for about two seconds. 'Yes, well, I might have mentioned it.'

'Really? I rather resent that I find out about our business matters from a waiter.'

'Jo –'

'You and I are going to have to have a talk.'

'I can't now. I've got to go out. Someone wants to consult me about company fraud. Now you're back you can hold the fort for a while.'

'No, I'd rather come with you. I'm interested in that kind of thing – I thought of joining the Fraud Squad at one time.'

She had not imagined the look of pure irritation that had flickered across his face.

'You can't really, Jo,' he said smoothly. 'I'm meeting someone else as well. Another thing is that although we've an answering machine it does put some clients off if there's no immediate personal contact.'

'Very well,' Joanna said through her teeth.

'Oh, and you might give the place a bit of a hoover,' was his parting remark. 'It doesn't give a very good impression when there are rolls of fluff on the carpet.'

Lance himself had bought the vacuum cleaner, Joanna recalled as she lugged it out of the cupboard a couple of minutes later. State-of-the-art technology, he had informed her loftily when he had brought it in. It did everything: told you when it was full with a chirpy whistle, coiled up the cable all by itself somewhere into its innards, rolled after you on its dinky little wheels. The machine did everything but make the bloody tea for him, she thought viciously. It couldn't suck up the rolls of fluff either; in fact, its award-winning design brush seemed actually to manufacture them as she pushed it over the carpet. In the end she kicked it back into the cupboard and went down on her hands and knees with a dustpan and brush.

The phone rang.

'Mrs Pryce here,' said that hard voice. 'Have you made any progress?'

'I've made some enquiries,' Joanna began. 'But so far –'

'You'll have to act tough to get any sense out of the Moffats – he's not quite all there. Ask the people who live in the flats opposite. Really cross-question them – they're the types who could get up to anything. Except for the Braithewaite woman

23

perhaps, but she's always peeping round the curtains at what goes on so she might have noticed something.'

'I'll keep you informed of any progress,' Joanna promised.

'So I should hope,' said the woman unpleasantly and rang off.

'There you have it,' Joanna said quietly, replacing the receiver. 'Vicious, bitter and not quite all there herself. No, Mrs Pryce, I'm not going to make everyone's life a misery just because you say so.'

All the same, the affair interested her. And surely 'the Braithewaite woman' had been holding aside the net curtain that had been dropped so quickly into place.

The thought crossed Joanna's mind that if, indeed, Mrs Pryce was really spiteful, she might have removed the plants herself. It might be rather delicious to find someone who had witnessed her doing it and confront the woman with her own iniquity. And then ask for a fat fee. At the same time, though, she could not help wondering if some kind of personal tragedy had made Mrs Pryce into what she was.

Whatever the truth, she had to take some course of action.

The prospect of lurking in a small garden square at night, alone, did not worry her. She had kept watch in similar, if more diverting, circumstances when she was in the police. Usually there had been a male companion with her, but this had only been because of possible hazards. CID experience also led her to believe that a passer-by had stolen the plants, someone who regularly walked through the square and had an empty window box at home. There was every likelihood that the window box was not yet full.

She was kept too busy at the office during the rest of the afternoon to have time to interview any more people in Beckford Square. Lance, predictably, did not put in an appearance so at five thirty Joanna locked up and went home. At a little before ten thirty that night she walked silently into the square from the Oliver Road end, making full use of the extra shadow caused by one of the street lights having failed. A quick scan of the front of Mrs Pryce's house revealed that all plants were present and correct. Moments later Joanna had vaulted over the gate into the garden in the middle of the square.

A soft, gentle breeze rustled through the leaves of the shrubs, bringing the sound of a clock striking the half-hour. In the garden all was in deep shade but she could see well enough to avoid blundering about as she stooped to hide herself among the lower branches of the rhododendron. She had chosen the spot in daylight, a vantage point from which there was a good view of her client's home while she herself remained hidden. A black tracksuit with a hood and dark shoes helped with the concealment.

There was a distinct aroma of cats, and soon she could see one approaching her through the dry leaves beneath the bush. She moved slightly, having no wish to be the accidental target of feline territory marking. Moments later a cold nose touched her hand and there was a throbbing purring. The cat cast itself into her lap, weighing at least a stone. It was the Maine coon she had seen sunning itself on a window ledge of the nursing home earlier in the day.

'Go away,' Joanna hissed, trying to push it off.

Soft paws embraced her hand, back feet kicking, the purring now almost drowning out the sound of an aircraft overhead. With great difficulty Joanna stood up, still inside the bush, her face scratched on branches, hair snagged on twigs, and heaved the cat over what seemed to be a strong horizontal branch. The cat decided to go along with this game of tigers and stayed put, still purring.

At a quarter to one the cat was still on the branch, dozing, Joanna thought, and but for a young couple arm in arm, no one had come into her narrow field of view through the leaves. At two thirty-five she heard the footsteps of someone walking quickly. It was a young man with a sports bag of some kind slung over his shoulder. He walked past Mrs Pryce's flower tubs with not so much as a glance in that direction. Then a taxi dropped someone off at the nursing home, Joanna could not see who without making a lot of noise. Another two cars drove through the square without stopping.

The sky was getting light when she awoke with a start, the cat sound asleep in her lap, her legs so stiff she could hardly move. Appalled that she had failed to stay awake, she shifted the cat, which immediately started to purr again. Oh, God, suppose the thief had struck and she hadn't seem him. After carefully looking around, she left her hiding place, climbed out over the gate and went to have a look. No plants had gone missing.

Joanna went home and slept for three hours. She could have done with several more but there was a lot to do. Mrs Pryce's case wasn't the only one in hand, far from it.

Mrs Monica Lang had been matron of the Lord Nelson Nursing Home for eight years. This comprised the whole of East Terrace, Beckford Square, and catered almost exclusively for retired naval officers. Occasionally, if there was more than one vacancy, a member of one of the other branches of the armed services might be admitted, preferably temporarily, but this was rare. The residents did not like it. It must also be said that the owners of the home, two brothers, themselves retired from high-ranking positions in the senior service, were somewhat narrow in their outlook on life.

Mrs Lang had learned to live with this. The pay was good and her quarters excellent, a large flat on the top floor. And being ex-navy and possibly living in times past, the proprietors had no objection to her having her very own ship's cat. Doolally was the second cat she had kept at her present job; the first, a Persian, had disappeared the previous year. This had been an occasion of great grief and distress to her, especially since she had never discovered what had happened to it. A practical woman, she knew as well as anyone that cats are killed on the roads or even stolen, and Cleo had been very beautiful. But never having found her body or learned what had happened, she had spent many sleepless hours agonising about the animal being trapped in someone's shed, lying injured somewhere, or being tormented by children in a thief's home.

Doolally's arrival, a gift from a friend, had healed all the hurts caused by Cleo's disappearance – well, almost all. He had been the largest kitten Monica Lang had ever seen and had soon grown into a massive cat. It was when he was several months old that the feelings of disquiet had begun. First of all Colonel and Mrs Moffat's old dog had died in rather mysterious circumstances; healthy one day, dead the next. Then Miss Braithewaite, on the opposite side of the square to the

Moffats, had lost her cat too. It had come in one day and just died.

No one – unfortunately, Mrs Lang had thought afterwards – had asked their vet to perform a postmortem. She had no evidence, of course, but one person who lived in the square had made it no secret that she loathed animals. The woman appeared to loathe all humanity as well but there was nothing Monica Lang could do about that. But if someone was poisoning pets . . .

She had thought nothing about the subject for several weeks, the job had been too demanding. But when, on this bright, sunny, early September morning, Doolally came in and collapsed, foaming at the mouth, on the floor, Monica knew that she was right. As she had let the animal in through the front door of the nursing home where he had been mewing on the doorstep, she had seen a movement in Mrs Pryce's house. A face at the window, wearing a rare and terrible smile.

Mrs Lang was seized by a very frightening loathing and hatred of her own.

When Joanna arrived at the office there were two policemen waiting to see her. She knew, just by looking at them, that they brought bad news; their faces were carefully schooled into an expression that she herself had had cause to adopt in her police days, the face you wear when something dreadful has happened to someone you don't know.

'Miss Mackenzie?' asked the older, taller one.

Joanna nodded. 'Come in, we can't talk on the doorstep.'

'We tried to contact you last night but you were out.'

'On a case. What's wrong? Has something happened to my father?' Joanna suddenly felt breathless.

They followed her in, the taller one still acting as spokesman. 'Oh, no. It's about Mr Tyler.'

Automatically, she had picked up the post from the floor. 'Lance! What on earth's he been up to?'

'He was involved in an accident last night – some kids joyriding. He's pretty badly injured, I'm afraid.'

'How badly?'

'They're not too happy with his chances at the moment, Miss Mackenzie.'

'So it's head injuries?'

'No, I believe his chest was badly crushed. They had to cut him from the wreckage.'

She had witnessed similar scenes many times, too many, in the pitiless glare of the lights on torn vehicles. The occupants of them had usually stopped screaming by the time help arrived and were dead, unconscious or shocked into silence.

The policeman offered to take her to the hospital, the Royal United, but she declined, preferring to use her own car so that return transport was not a problem. The pair left, relief writ large on their faces. They had done their duty.

The rest of that day and most of the next were remembered by Joanna only with difficulty. At some time during those hours she dealt with post, found someone to go to Norway – a friend of Lance's, retired from Bristol CID, whom they had asked for help in emergencies before – and generally kept the business running. All the while she was aware that her partner was fighting for his life. But when she rang from home at eleven fifteen at night on the second day, the Friday, a Dr Wilding was cautiously optimistic. It seemed more than likely that Mr Tyler would pull through.

Not feeling like eating or sleeping, or anything else for that matter, Joanna decided to take a short drive to Beckford Square.

As she swung round the corner into the square, on foot, having left her car parked on double yellow lines just off Royal Crescent, Joanna was immediately aware of two things. The first was that someone was hurrying away from her towards Oliver Road. Whoever it was paused for a moment, turned and looked directly at her. The second thing she noticed was that the gate in the railings of the square's garden was open. She started to run, heading directly for Mrs Pryce's house. There, she stopped. The front door of the house was ajar.

A trail of earth led across the pavement and into the road. There was no need to count the plants in the tubs or even to look very carefully. The miniature conifers had been pulled up, one lying on its side on the gravel. Several petunias were missing, too.

Joanna called herself a few names under her breath and crossed the road over to the garden. More potting compost was in the road by the gate. She went into the garden but it was too dark to see clearly, impossible to discover whether the plants had been thrown among the shrubs. She turned, having decided to fetch the torch from her car, and tripped over something that was protruding from beneath the rhododendron.

It was a woman's foot.

After a frantic dash for the torch, Joanna plunged into the bush, breaking off a couple of branches to get them out of her way. Moments later she backed out again, taking deep breaths, trying not to be sick.

Mrs Pryce, lying face down but recognisable from her watch, an unusual man's one with a red leather strap, was very dead, the head injuries dreadful to behold.

# Chapter Four

Inspector James Carrick, like most well-educated Scots from Perthshire, spoke with hardly any accent and his English was of a clarity and precision that put to shame most of those who live south of the Border. He would not, Joanna knew already, split an infinitive willingly. He was her old boss and this was the moment she had been dreading, having to meet him again. All those frantic prayers, after she had phoned the police, that he had been transferred somewhere else had come to nought.

He came striding over to the car where she was making her statement to Sergeant Ingrams, his face set into its usual mask of calm efficiency. She waited, hardly daring to breathe, for the moment when he would first catch sight of her. Ingrams was writing busily, the back of his neck redder than usual. It was clear that he had already connected her face with a name he had heard via the grapevine.

Carrick opened the front passenger door and slid in, turning to where Joanna and Ingrams were sitting in the back. He rested one arm on the back of the seat and subjected her to a long, hard stare. Joanna met the look; he had never succeeded in browbeating her.

'I understand you found the body, Miss Mackenzie.' He could have been addressing a stranger.

'That's right.' At least she didn't have to call him 'sir' now.

There was a short silence while police radios crackled. People hurried to and fro, their shadows thrown this way and that by the headlights of several vehicles. An ambulance arrived.

'What time was this?'

'Eleven forty-seven.'

One fair eyebrow quirked but he made no further comment. 'Perhaps you'd care to give me the details.' He got out of the car and opened her door.

Joanna, who had just given her account of events in exhaustive detail to Bob Ingrams, stepped out into the road. Carrick slammed both doors and walked away, over towards the garden. By the gate he stopped.

'Thank you,' Joanna said softly.

He appeared not to hear. 'What were you doing in the square?'

'Mrs Pryce was a client.'

' A *client*?'

'Yes. She'd had some plants stolen.'

'Tell me.'

Joanna told him, keeping to the facts and recounting all relevant information from her interviews with the murdered woman and the Moffats next door.

'And you haven't spoken to anyone else in the square about this?' Carrick enquired when she had finished.

'No, there hasn't been time. And I didn't give it top priority.'

'Pressing business?' he said with a twist to his mouth, noting the arrival of the pathologist.

'Lance is in hospital after a car crash. He may not live.'

'It's been a bad week,' Carrick said after a pause. 'A bad night, come to that. I've just come from the Sheridan Gallery. Someone made off with the Chantbury Pyx and two security guards are in hospital.'

Screens had been erected around the body. Now a section was moved aside to permit the pathologist, who had greeted Carrick with a formal nod, to enter. Carrick made no move to follow, perfectly aware that the man, John Butler, nearing retirement, hated to have people at his elbow while he worked. In a few minutes it would be safe to approach.

'Her front door was ajar,' Joanna said, remembering. 'She must have come out when she heard someone outside. It looks as though she surprised the thief, who dropped one of the conifers.'

31

'Would someone kill for the sake of a few plants?' Carrick asked. 'She thought it was a child, you said. Well, a child certainly didn't kill her. Look, you can see the marks where her body was dragged through the gate – the toe marks of her shoes.'

'It was me who broke the branches of the rhododendron,' Joanna admitted. 'The last thing in my mind was that she'd been murdered. I thought she'd tripped and fallen or fainted.'

'Quite a few people seem to have hated her – that's if the Moffats can be believed.'

'I do believe them. And I think you will when you talk to them.' Another memory returned with a rush. 'I saw someone – I've just remembered. As I turned the corner from Nash Street I saw someone hurrying away.'

'Man or woman?'

'Impossible to say. I didn't get a very good look at them. They were wearing dark clothes a bit like mine. It could have been a tracksuit.'

'Tall, short, fat, thin?'

'None of those. Just – well – sort of average.'

'No other distinguishing marks?' he asked sarcastically.

It had just occurred to Joanna that if she had arrived a few minutes earlier, or kept watch as she had two nights ago, there would have been no theft and no murder. The realisation so devastated her that she made no reply. All around her the smooth, efficient machinery of law enforcement was in motion, a familiar process from which she was now excluded.

Carrick still seemed to be waiting for an answer.

'There was nothing unusual about the person at all,' Joanna said, finding her voice at the second attempt. 'Of medium height and build. I can't really explain it but there was something about the way they were walking that suggested guilt.'

Carrick left her side without replying and went over to where the pathologist was emerging from the screened-off area. A photographer prepared to take shots of the body from every conceivable angle.

Butler was rubbing his knees, he suffered from arthritis. 'Well, she didn't fall and hit her head, that's for sure. It looks like just the one blow – probably something like a hammer but don't quote me until I've done the PM. Thin skull, though – she took no killing at all.'

'Time?' Carrick asked.

'Oh, well inside the hour. The body's still warm.'

'You say she didn't hit her head on anything here, but could she have fallen down the stairs in her own house and then been dragged out?'

Butler peered at him crossly over his half-moon glasses. 'Now you're making life complicated. God knows what happened anywhere else. *Was* she dragged?'

'Yes.'

Butler shrugged. 'Well, death must have been pretty instantaneous. I'll let you know when I know more myself.' And with that he walked stiffly back to his car.

The Inspector made himself go and have another look at the body. According to evidence already accrued, the woman had hated her immediate neighbours and just about everyone she spoke of. And thus she had died, extremely violently, done to death with hatred and discarded as so much garbage.

Discounting the branches that Joanna had broken in order to see more clearly, some damage to the large bush indicated to Carrick that the body had been flung down after being half dragged, half carried face down – the murderer not wishing, for obvious reasons, to get blood from the terrible head wound onto his clothes. The victim's feet had trailed out behind; Carrick had already examined the shoes. The toes were badly scuffed, grass and soil wedged into the crevice between sole and upper.

Had she been dragged from across the road?

Sergeant Ingrams, who had decided to obey the unspoken command to mind his own business concerning their witness – for the present, anyway – was already indoors. He was methodical and had carefully examined the gravel for footprints and other recent disturbance before stepping over the threshold. The only lights on were in the small kitchen at the back and a front bedroom, the latter a lamp with a low-wattage bulb on a bedside table. He was in the kitchen, using his eyes and touching nothing, when Carrick came in.

'I don't think she was killed indoors, sir,' said Ingrams. 'Not a trace of blood, not a thing out of place, no sign of a struggle. And she wasn't dragged from here unless whoever did it smoothed the gravel out again afterwards.'

'There's a nephew,' Carrick said. 'I want you to find him. According to her neighbours at number 2, he's her only relative. They might be wrong, they might be lying. Find him.'

'Now, sir?' Ingrams asked and found himself subjected to a very unfriendly stare. All right, he thought as he left the house. Keep your bloody hair on. So you once screwed your juicy red-haired sergeant and she got kicked out because you were married and the chief super didn't like women in the job. So what? What you need right now, more than anything, is to take her home and . . . . For a couple of minutes Ingrams indulged in somewhat lewd mental images.

Methodically, while he waited for the scene-of-crime team to arrive, Carrick went over the house. Apart from the back room downstairs, Mrs Pryce's home was comfortably and expensively furnished. The curtains in the living room were made of thick, heavy brocade trimmed with silky tassels of the same deep burgundy red as the table lamps in the room. An empty glass stood next to one of the lamps and he bent down to smell it without touching. Gin.

The bed in the pink and white bedroom had not been slept in but the covers had been turned back. Perhaps she had been undressing, having had her nightcap and heard sounds outside that had prompted her to look out of the window. No, the body had been fully dressed. No, again, fool, he cursed himself, women of Mrs Pryce's generation did not rush into the street half-naked, no matter what was happening outside.

'Can I go now?' a voice called up the stairs.

He had not forgotten about her, merely hoped that she would go away.

'I'm up here,' Carrick called, despising himself for three different reasons.

'She hadn't gone to bed,' Joanna remarked, surprised.

'So?' Carrick said in disinterested fashion.

'She told me she went to bed at nine thirty, when the television news had finished.'

'You didn't mention that to me just now.'

'There might be one or two small details that I'll recall,' she retorted. 'Can I go home now?'

'Perhaps you'd be good enough to call in at the station tomorrow and sign your statement. Sergeant Ingrams should have it typed by then. If you think of anything else that you think might be important, it can be added in. And, Joanna . . . .'

She knew what he was going to say.

'I don't want you making any more enquiries. This is a police case now.'

'She was a client.'

'Your client's dead,' he pointed out harshly. 'Rather brutally murdered, in fact.' Then he smiled at her tiredly. 'Besides, I don't want you involved if some nutter's on the loose.'

She did not remember until later that the person she had seen in the square had noticed her.

Later that night, on the second floor of West Terrace, a man watched the scene in the square below. The ground and first floor doors and windows were boarded up to prevent vandals from breaking in, but there was only dirt covering the glass where he had made a home for himself. He had opened the window, with difficulty, in order to clean a small area so he could see more clearly, but he had been very careful; he did not want to draw attention to himself.

Tommy was not a vandal and he had broken in very neatly, round the back. The doors and windows were boarded up there too, but not so efficiently, and it was the work of a moment, when he went in and out, to prise away a few of the planks and tap the nails in a little again, using the hammer that he kept hidden beneath a rock in the overgrown garden.

The front room he had commandeered suited him perfectly. He hated living rough, sleeping in the park, under bridges and so forth. It was bad enough being dirty and hungry for most of the time. Not to have a roof over his head and being prey to the others who lived rough, some of them quite crazy, desperate people, was more than he could stand.

Without taking his eyes off what was going on in the square, Tommy reached out a hand for a can of beer on the window ledge. For a moment his hand caressed the smooth, shiny exterior. The thing was not to be rushed. He had found a pound coin, and afterwards fought two semi-drunk skinheads

35

for it. He wasn't broke by any means, it was just the principle of the thing.

The beer was his only luxury. He didn't dare smoke, not with the entire building being in the state it was, like a tinderbox. And he would be spotted, of course, if he lit up, which was the last thing he wanted. Quite soon, he could leave and never return.

The woman lying dead in the garden below – Tommy could see the police going in and out of her house – had accosted him in the street the day before and shouted that she had complained to the council about him and that he would be evicted. He'd given the silly old cow a piece of his mind that had sent her scurrying for the safety of home. Until then Tommy had thought that no one had seen him.

Well, it was very sad but she wouldn't be able to complain about him again, would she?

Sergeant Ingrams had no trouble in tracking down Mrs Pryce's nephew. His name was Conrad Stacey and he worked as a mechanic at a garage not far from the railway station. The Moffats were the source of this information; they knew his first name and that he drove a battered blue estate car, and Colonel Moffat had seen him at the garage wearing overalls when he had once had his car serviced there. Furthermore – and here Ingrams began to get really excited – Stacey's car had been parked outside his aunt's house during the early evening; the Moffats had seen it at about five and reported that they had, not for the first time, heard raised voices.

Aware that he might or might not be the bringer of bad news, Ingrams drove out to Camerton, where Stacey and his wife lived. He felt that he had been driving round Bath half the night already, having had to get the manager of the garage out of bed and take him there in order to look at his records for Stacey's address. But the night was young, he thought, only a little after one. He was going to enjoy banging on the suspect's door.

There was no one at home, only dogs that barked fiercely.

When he returned with Carrick at nine the following morning, Stacey's car was parked in the weed-covered drive at the side of the cottage, or rather rural slum, Ingrams decided as he gazed around. The long narrow garden was rank with weeds too, the fruit on a couple of apple trees rotting on the ground. The cottage itself, with its moss-filled gutters, slipping slates and peeling paint, looked unoccupied. Carrick pounded on the door. Ingrams thought his new boss had a really godawful way of going about it, enough to raise the dead. He supposed it had something to do with him being a Scot. All Ingrams knew about Scotland was that Glasgow was up there somewhere and that was a pretty tough place, wasn't it? He might have been a bit alarmed if Carrick had told him that his distant ancestors had not been Scots, but Vikings.

After a longish wait, during which dogs barked incessantly, the door was slowly opened.

'Mr Stacey?' Ingrams asked, observing with delight that the man was of medium height and build.

'Yes. Who the hell are you?'

'Police,' Carrick said, showing his warrant card. 'May we come in?'

'Is it about the car?'

'No.'

'I'll have to get rid of the dogs. Wait here.'

The door was closed again.

Carrick said, 'Go round to the back of the house in case he tries to do a runner.'

The deafening barking receded into the distance and a couple of doors were slammed. After a minute or so Stacey opened the front door again. He did not invite Carrick in, just went back inside, leaving the door ajar. Carrick whistled, taxi-summoning style, for Ingrams and followed Stacey down a dark hall.

'You'll have to excuse the mess,' Stacey said when they had both caught up with him in a living room. 'The wife's gone to her mother's in Yeovil for a few days.'

Carrick, obsessively tidy, had never understood those of his own sex who expected women to clear up after them. The room, in his view, was disgusting, strewn with newspapers, used crockery and dirty clothing. It looked as though the dogs had romped right into the inglenook fireplace; there was wood ash all over the hearthrug and grey paw prints on a dark-blue sofa.

37

'Damned dogs,' Stacey said, moving a few things off chairs. 'They're not usually allowed in here.'

It was on the tip of Ingrams's tongue to remark that he was surprised that Stacey was. He kept his mouth shut. They had, after all, come to tell the man that his aunt was dead.

Carrick said, 'Sergeant Ingrams tried to contact you last night, Mr Stacey. I'm afraid we've very bad news.'

'Bad news?' Stacey echoed.

'I understand that Mrs Amelia Pryce was your aunt.'

Stacey nodded dumbly.

'She died last night. We're treating her death as murder.'

The man's mouth opened and closed a couple of times but no sound emerged.

'Where were you last night, sir?'

'She's *dead*?' Stacey sank into a chair.

'Yes, I'm afraid so. Where were you when –'

'Look, for God's sake . . You don't think I did it, do you?'

Carrick perched on the edge of a chair directly opposite Stacey. 'I just want to know where you *were*.'

'I went out – to a pub. I usually do on Friday nights.'

'Which one?'

'Well, more than one actually. The Black Cat. Gus's. The Tea Clipper.'

'They're in Bristol.'

'Yes, sorry, Bristol.'

'Who were you with?'

Stacey's thin, pasty face had gone, if anything, paler. 'No one. I – I went on a bit of a blinder.'

'And why would that be?' Carrick asked very softly.

'No – no reason.'

'What time did you go out?'

'Quite early. Because of having to drive over. About five.'

Ingrams, receiving a glance from his superior, said, 'We have witnesses who say that your car was outside your aunt's house at about that time.'

'Oh. Well, yes. I called in to see her on the way.'

'What did you argue about?' Carrick asked.

'Argue?'

'People heard shouting.'

'If you'd known her you wouldn't ask that,' Stacey burst out. 'Nothing was ever to her liking. I took a bunch of flowers

38

and she threw them back at me. Said I was trying to worm my way into her affections. Affections! She didn't know the meaning of the word. She's always gone on at me, saying what a useless so-and-so I am, how I'm a real black sheep and how ashamed my mother was of me. That's a lie. You wouldn't believe that my mum and her were sisters – like people from different planets.'

'So what was the trouble last night?'

'Just the usual. As I said.'

'Had you gone to ask her for money?'

Stacey's lip curled and, for a moment, Ingrams thought he might actually lash out at his interrogator. 'You're all the same, you fucking cops. Find the weakest person and hang the crime on them. No.'

'And when she refused you went on a drinking bout. It's not unreasonable to suppose that later you returned to Beckford Square. Mr Stacey, who is your aunt's beneficiary in the event of her death?'

Stacey leapt to his feet. 'I didn't kill her! I hated the old bitch for the things she said and did. But I didn't kill her.'

'Answer the question,' Ingrams growled.

'Go to hell.'

Carrick stood up. 'I think we ought to continue this discussion at the station.'

'You're arresting me? You can't. You don't have a shred of evidence. I tell you I didn't kill her.'

'Then prove it. As next of kin I'll also have to ask you to formally identify her body.'

The man shied away from them, his face frozen into an expression of horror. 'I can't. I can't bear death and dead things. Please don't make me do it. Please.'

Carrick just stood there passively, waiting.

Unaccountably, for he thought he was as guilty as hell, Ingrams felt a pang of pity. 'Look,' he said, touching Stacey's arm. 'If you didn't kill her then help us discover who did. Give us a statement of where you were and who you saw last night and then we can check up and if you're in the clear you'll be home in no time at all.'

Stacey made a sound like a whimper.

'We're not arresting you,' Carrick said. 'You're merely –'

'Helping you with your enquiries,' Stacey interrupted bitterly. 'It doesn't make much difference to the one in the hot seat.'

They both went with him to a farm next door where a pleasant-faced woman was given the door key and promised to look after the dogs. God alone knew what she made of Stacey, the sergeant thought, with his furtive, hunted expression. Just like a cornered rat.

# Chapter Five

Joanna, having been informed at the police station that Sergeant Ingrams was out, and declining to wait, went round to see the Moffats instead. This proved to be a worthwhile decision for several reasons, one being that Alice Moffat was far more upset about the murder of a defenceless woman not twenty yards from her own front door than she would admit. She was pleased to ply her young visitor with coffee and talk about her worries. The old couple were also happy to answer Joanna's questions and help her to build up a clear picture in her mind of the entire area.

Beckford Square had only a fraction of the number of people that had lived there in its heyday at the beginning of the eighteenth century. West Terrace was, but for the suspected squatter, completely empty. The Lord Nelson Nursing Home in East Terrace housed, at this time, only fifteen residents and twelve staff including the matron, Monica Lang. South Terrace comprised four two-storey houses; the Youngers, away on their cruise, owned number 1; Colonel and Mrs Moffat lived at number 2, the deceased at number 3 and Dr Hendricks at number 4. This side had been built, Joanna discovered, at a slightly later date to house servants who could not be accommodated at their places of work in the grander houses on the three other sides of the square.

On the opposite side, the Pegasus Gallery (one half devoted to paintings, drawings and bronzes of the horse) was situated at numbers 1 and 2 North Terrace, with the offices of an insurance company above; number 3 was divided into flats, and number 4, the Spa Court Hotel, ostensibly closed for refurbishment, was in fact the subject of a court case involving fraud.

'Sorry to badger you like this,' Joanna said to Alice Moffat, 'but can you tell me who lives in the flats?'

Alice was thoroughly enjoying the female company. 'Well, as we were saying the other day, Karen Williams and Jamie live in the basement flat. The one above that, on the ground floor, is, as you can see, empty and for sale. They were a strange pair, the couple who lived there. Someone said that he left her for a woman old enough to be his mother but I don't know how true that is. I hate gossip, don't you? A Mr Mallory lives on the first floor. I don't really know anything about him. He's rather a noisy person, revs his car and bangs the doors. And he plays the most awful music with the windows open – Mrs Pryce used to complain about it.'

'Do you mean the windows of his flat or the car?' Joanna enquired.

'Both.'

'Heavy rock sort of thing?'

'Heavens, no! Humpleschlacht, my dear. One of those modern composers. It sounds as though the musicians all start on different pages of the score and work their way round to the same place. Quite excruciating if you like *real* music.'

'Terrible if you don't like music at all,' the Colonel rumbled. 'Fella must have something wrong with his ears.'

'And the second floor?' Joanna prompted.

'That's Miss Braithewaite. She's very quiet but does say good morning if you see her in the street. I think she's lonely but you can't really go and knock on her door, can you? It seems so interfering somehow. The woman who lives above her is another odd one. I don't know her name. She rushes out and back as though she doesn't want to be seen. Unless, of course, the poor soul suffers from that fear of going out, I've forgotten what it's called.'

'Agoraphobia,' Joanna said. 'Does she live on her own?'

'Yes, but she seems to have a man friend. I won't call him a boyfriend. I mean, the pair of them must be in their forties. He has a motorbike. Miss Braithewaite said to Karen that. . . .'

'Yes?' Joanna said when Alice stopped speaking and reddened.

'Well, perhaps I shouldn't mention it, but Miss Braithewaite was so embarrassed. Karen told me this, you understand. I think she was quite amused. Apparently this man arrives on his motorbike and clumps up the stairs in all his leathers and big boots. Then, almost as soon as he arrives, Miss Braithewaite said she can hear the springs going in the bed and the woman shrieking away. A little while later he comes down the stairs again. They never go out together and he never seems to bring her anything. Don't you think that's very odd?'

'It's a funny old world, Alice,' said her husband, thinking that with the woman looking as downright peculiar as she did, she was probably having to cross the motorcyclist's palm with silver. Lucky bastard, whoever he was. He probably shut his eyes.

'Who locks the gate at night?' Joanna asked.

'Into the garden?' said Jack Moffat. 'I do. There's a small residents' association. The garden's our responsibility, you see – nothing to do with the city council.'

'Why wasn't it locked last night?'

'Jack forgets sometimes,' Alice said when he didn't reply. She smiled at him. 'One of the signs of old age, I'm afraid.'

'Did you?' Joanna said, not taking her eyes off him.

'I thought you said you weren't in the police,' he said, trying to make it sound light-hearted.

'I *used* to be in the police,' Joanna said unwaveringly.

'I did forget to lock up,' he admitted. 'As Alice said, I'm getting a bit absent-minded.'

As she was showing Joanna out, Alice whispered that her husband occasionally suffered from what she called 'blank-outs'. Being taken prisoner by the Japanese during the war had affected his mind slightly.

That morning Joanna had been allowed to see Lance for the first time. He was still in intensive care, connected up to a frightening amount of medical hardware. It was obvious that, although conscious, he was under heavy sedation. But he had recognised her and had stretched out the hand that was not connected to drip apparatus. She had sat down and held the hand for quite a while, telling him in a quiet voice everything

43

that had happened, including Mrs Pryce's murder. His eyes had widened at this news, and positively sparkled by the time she had finished giving him all the information she had collected. This sort of thing had always been meat and drink to him. .

'It was the least I could do,' she said to Sergeant Ingrams, as she signed her statement.

'The other two were killed,' Ingrams said.

'The joyriders?'

He nodded.

'Good.'

'You're a hard woman.'

'But not a hypocrite,' Joanna said, getting up to leave. 'Is that all you want me for?'

Still seated, he eyed her up and down as a racegoer might a no-hope outsider. 'We've pulled someone in.'

'Clever old you.'

'A good screw, was he – Carrick?'

'Better than you, sergeant, even if you got a new set of everything from the Oxfam shop you were found in.'

She closed the door quietly on her way out.

Unfortunately the serene exit was wasted, for she immediately came face to face with James Carrick as he emerged from an interview room. Very firmly he stood with his back to the closed door.

'You're safe,' Joanna told him tersely. 'I didn't bring the howitzer with me.'

'You've signed your statement?'

'Yes.'

'Remembered anything else?'

'No. Is that Conrad Stacey you've got in there?'

'No comment. I'll get in touch if you're required for an identity parade.'

'Balls. He's in line for all her money if she didn't change her mind and leave it to the KGB. So what? According to Mrs Moffat he's balding and prematurely stooped. No way. Not the person I saw.'

'You just said you hadn't remembered anything else,' Carrick said.

'I said he or she was of medium height and build. But they weren't bald or stooped. They didn't have two heads, three humps or a parrot with a wooden leg on one shoulder either. You'll have to do better than that.'

She had forgotten the way his eyes sort of sparked when he was secretly amused.

'Has anyone mentioned a tramp who's supposed to be squatting in West Terrace?' Joanna asked.

'Yes,' Carrick answered heavily. 'And I know about him. He's harmless.'

'Really?'

'Why don't you go and talk to him?' he suggested with an enigmatic smile.

'I might even do that,' Joanna said, marching out.

Carrick had been about to go to the canteen and have some coffee but instead of doing that he went back into the interview room and asked the constable with Stacey to go and fetch coffee for two. He drew up a chair and sat down. So far the dead woman's nephew had stuck to his story.

Carrick said, 'Tell me the *real* reason why you went out on this blinder.'

'I've told you the real reason. I do sometimes. And I felt really depressed after I'd talked to my aunt. As I said, she threw the flowers I'd taken her back at me.'

It had already occurred to Carrick that Stacey was the kind of man whom most aunts would regard as a living nightmare. On his own admission Stacey had done very badly at school and had been a sickly youth. His only aptitude was for things mechanical and, after private coaching to improve his reading and writing, he had been taken on as an apprentice motor mechanic at the garage where he still worked.

'How long has your wife been at her mother's?' Carrick wanted to know.

'A few days.'

'Does she go and see her often?'

An uninterested shrug. 'Not all that often. They don't get on too well.'

'Tell me again what happened last night.'

'Can I have a cigarette?'

'When you've told me.'

The man sighed. 'I finish work early on Fridays, around four. I went home, let the dogs out and had a bit of a tidy-up.

45

One of them had shit all over the kitchen floor. Then I got changed out of my overalls, shut the dogs in the shed in case whichever one made another mess indoors, and went out. I bought a bunch of flowers from that woman who has a stall by the station.'

'What sort of flowers?'

For some reason this question infuriated Stacey. 'Flowers! I don't know what they bloody well were. Red ones. Bloody red flowers.' He broke off, uttering a sound that could have been a sob.

'Take your time,' Carrick said. 'What did you do with them?' They had been able to persuade Stacey to identify his aunt and, because the blow that had killed her had been to the back of her head, the experience had been less distressing than he had expected.

'Threw them away. Out of the car window somewhere.'

'It was the last straw, wasn't it? Your aunt rejecting your gift after your wife left you.'

'Yeah,' Stacey said after a long, sullen silence.

The constable returned with the coffee and resumed his position by the door.

'What was the row between you and your wife about?'

'We row about all sorts of things.'

'Was it about money?'

'No, as a matter of fact it was about how she keeps going off. She's hardly ever at home now.'

'Someone you can put a name to must have seen you in Bristol – someone who can give you an alibi.'

'I told you, I went to those pubs.'

'I believe you.'

'I don't usually go there – my mates are all here in Bath.'

'I see. So you went where no one would know you because you knew you were going to get so drunk that you'd have been ashamed to be seen by your friends.'

'You've got a mind like a sewer,' Stacey said with contempt.

'What time did you get back?'

'Dunno.'

'Well, you weren't back when Sergeant Ingrams went looking for you at about one fifteen. Presumably you were in a gutter somewhere in Bristol docks.'

46

'I can't remember,' Stacey muttered.

'You must have some idea when you got home.'

'This morning, early. I wandered around for ages – couldn't remember where I'd put the car.'

'Has it occurred to you that you might have come back to Bath a lot earlier, returned to Beckford Square and –'

'No!' Stacey shouted. 'I didn't kill her! I can't kill anything, not even a mouse. That's one of the reasons Jill left me – she said I was just a useless wimp. And I'd be the first one you'd suspect, what with her money and all. Only a fool –' He stopped speaking when he realised the extent of his foolishness.

'Ah,' Carrick said. 'Thank you. Well, it wouldn't have been very difficult to have found out.'

'She kept threatening to cut me off without a penny,' Stacey said, seemingly close to tears now. 'She liked to keep people in suspense. She told my mother when she was dying that she'd pay for a nice nursing home but she never did. I begged her in the end – it would have only been for a few weeks in somewhere pretty like Devon. I'll never forget the way she looked at me and said she'd changed her mind. She said I ought to have provided better for my own mother.' The tears were streaming down his cheeks now, little runnels through the grubbiness of his face. 'She actually looked happy when she said that – happy and sort of triumphant.'

Carrick offered him a cigarette from one of several packets kept in the drawer of the table they were seated at, and lit it for him. Then he said, 'I'll ask Sergeant Ingrams to run you home. Perhaps you'll be good enough to give him a photo of yourself and the clothes you wore last night.'

'You're letting me go?' Stacey asked in bewilderment.

'Just don't leave the area. I might want to talk to you again.'

'But . . . but the clothes. . . . I chucked them in the bath and ran cold water on them. To soak, like. I'd been sick all over myself.'

Carrick had not smoked for years but sometimes, in moments of real crisis. . . . He lit one, drew on it and blew a large cloud of smoke towards the ceiling.

'Get out,' he said.

An hour or so later, after he had taken Stacey home and contrived to have a good look round the cottage, as Carrick hoped he would, Ingrams knocked on the Inspector's door. He was angry, again anticipated by Carrick, not least because of the state of Stacey's sweatshirt and jeans. A fat lot forensic could do with those, he thought as he was bidden to enter. He had wrung the worst of the water out of them, put them in a plastic bag and scrubbed his hands afterwards. A bath or shower would have been more appropriate. Filthy little runt!

'Is that the PM report?' Carrick asked, seeing an envelope in his sergeant's grasp.

'Yes, sir. Just arrived.'

Carrick slit it open. 'Have all the residents of the square been interviewed?'

'All but a couple of old duffers in the nursing home. The world could come to an end for them and they wouldn't be aware of it.'

'Who do you think I ought to go and talk to?'

'Well, all those who live at number 3 North Terrace, for a start. There's a bloke called Mallory who lives on the first floor who admitted that Mrs Pryce had complained that his music was too loud on several occasions. Young Simmonds spoke to him, said to me on the quiet that the guy was pretty offensive. Didn't seem *upset* that the woman was dead, more worried about where he could park his car with all our vehicles in the square. But Simmonds stuck to his guns and got it out of him that he'd been playing CDs fairly late last night. He denied that the deceased had complained then, though.' Ingrams rummaged for his notebook. 'I sort of drew a little diagram of the square, sir, and made a note of all the names.'

Carrick was reading. 'It's exactly what we need. Get a large sheet of white paper and draw it all out. We'll pin it on the wall and –' He broke off with a soft exclamation. 'She *had* been drinking. Not just a wee dram either. There was an empty glass that smelled of gin in the front living room.'

'Getting Dutch courage to have a go at Mallory?'

Carrick looked up. 'Was she the sort who needed artificial courage to tackle anyone about anything? Was his music really so loud that it could be heard right across the square?'

'According to the Moffats, yes. Mallory has his windows wide open – they're big sash things – on warm evenings.

According to them it's terrible stuff. They told me the name of the guy who wrote it but it didn't mean anything to me and slipped my mind. The sort of stuff that sounds as if the musicians make it up as they go along.'

Carrick mentioned the names of a few of the more controversial modern composers.

'Humpleschlacht! That's it, sir.'

'And Mallory just plays his music? No one else's?'

'Got a bit of a thing about it, according to the Moffats. They know about music – listen to the concerts on Radio Three and Classic FM. Mrs Pryce had complained about that, too. It's all Greek to me. Give me country and western any day. Oh, and he has it on up loud in his car too. Roars around in one of those poser's toys with a picnic shelf on the back.'

'Who else?'

Ingrams quickly consulted his scribbled notes. 'There's a Karen Williams lives in the basement. She's got a little boy, Jamie. He's about seven. She's not married. Mrs Pryce really got her knife into her about the boy riding his bike on the pavement and playing ball in the square. She didn't say, but Simmonds got the impression that there'd been some kind of big row not too long ago.'

Carrick returned to the report. 'We'll go and talk to everybody.' He tapped the page he was reading with a long forefinger. 'He was right in what he first said: one heavy blow to the back of the skull. Almost certainly with a hammer, judging by the size of the depression. She had an abnormally thin skull – a fall down the stairs would probably have killed her. He says that the angle and position of the wound suggests that whoever killed her is left-handed. That's really useful.'

'And she'd been drinking?'

'And was healthy for her age, yes.'

'How old was she?'

'Sixty-four.'

'Everyone we've spoken to hated her.'

'I think I'd have hated her too.'

'And you're quite sure about Stacey?'

'No, I'm not sure about him at all. He could have drunk enough to make him forget what he'd done afterwards but still able to drive his car – God help the rest of us – returned to his aunt's house, killed her, dumped her body in the garden and gone back to his pubs in Bristol and drunk himself into a stupor. Did you get that photograph?'

'Yes, sir, but it's not a very good likeness. It was the best he could do. He's not the kind of bloke that people are forever going to be snapping away at with their cameras, is he?'

'Deprived is the word for it, sergeant. Give it to someone and send them over to the places Stacey mentioned. Tell them to drop in at a few other pubs in the same area as well.'

Ingrams was turning the handle of the door when Carrick spoke again.

'But according to Miss Mackenzie she didn't see a balding man with a slight stoop. I watched him as he walked down the corridor. He has an odd gait. He said he was a sickly child – perhaps whatever was wrong with him did permanent damage.'

'She might not have seen the murderer,' Ingrams pointed out.

Carrick stared thoughtfully into space. 'No, but she said there was something about the haste that looked *guilty*. I was always very impressed with Joanna's intuition.'

'It could still have been the plant thief.'

Garrick swore despairingly.

'Who *might* have seen the murderer,' Ingrams continued, experiencing a huge golden glow of pleasure at the realisation that Carrick, astoundingly, had forgotten all about it. Fifteen, love, he thought as they went out.

Karen Williams peered at Joanna over the security chain spanning the narrow gap and then shut the door momentarily to release it.

'I've been interviewed already,' she said.

Joanna explained who she was.

'Oh, so you're not from the press either. They've been around, too. A real smart-arse knocked at eight fifteen – would you believe his brass neck? – and wanted to ask me about Mrs Pryce. Said he was the crime reporter of the *Bath Times*. He got short shrift from me, I can tell you.'

'Benny Cooper?'

'That might have been his name. Sort of smarmy with dark hair and shades.'

'That's Benny.'

'Well, at least he was who he said he was – you never know these days. What can I do for you, Miss Mackenzie?'

'I'd like to talk to you about Mrs Pryce too. She'd hired me to find out who was stealing her plants.'

'And she'd told you that it was my Jamie, I suppose.'

'Was Jamie out in the square last night at getting on for midnight?'

'Of course he wasn't! He was tucked up in bed as he usually is at that time of night.'

'That's what I thought,' Joanna replied, wondering why the woman had fleetingly looked so frightened. 'The truth is I feel partly responsible for what happened here last night. If I'd been keeping an eye on things as I did a couple of days ago, she might not have been murdered.'

'Come in,' Karen said. 'I can't talk long as I work from ten until six on Saturdays. Jamie's at my mum's.'

The basement flat was very untidy but reasonably clean. Toys were scattered over seemingly every square foot of floor space, the living room strewn with brightly coloured plastic building blocks as though a miniature Legoland had been dynamited.

'I won't lie and say I'm upset about that woman's death,' said Karen when they had both seated themselves. 'I felt that she was spying on me all the time. Not just me, though, everyone. I suppose she had nothing else to do and I ought to feel sorry for her. But I don't. It's a relief to know that she won't be banging on my door complaining about Jamie because his ball's bounced into her front garden or he's leaned his bike on her wall.'

Joanna knew that to make notes would be a bad mistake. Karen was already on edge. She appeared to be in her mid-twenties, with green eyes and fair hair looking as though it had not had a comb through it that morning. She might be a nervy sort of person normally, but the business of avoiding Joanna's gaze and wringing her thin hands in her lap was nevertheless interesting.

'You'll be thinking I killed the old woman next,' Karen went on. 'I really could have done sometimes. She said that an unmarried mother shouldn't be living in a place like this.

51

Select, she said it was. I'm afraid I swore at her. I wouldn't
have minded so much but . . .'
'But?' Joanna prompted gently.
'Phil and I *were* going to get married. It was all arranged.
We'd been living together for a couple of years but when
Jamie came along everything seemed different. I told Phil I
hated being called his common-law wife. He said he didn't go
much on it either and fixed everything at the registry office.
Then he went and got himself killed.'
Joanna had been expecting to hear that he had deserted
her.
'It was his own stupid fault,' Karen burst out furiously. 'He
had a mate with a trials bike and they went for a spin on it. No
helmets, no insurance, no nothing. They went out of control
on the Upper Bristol Road and that was that.'
'I'm sorry,' Joanna said. 'Did you hear anything that night,
or see anyone?'
'No. You don't down here. It's like living underground. I
shut the windows at night too. I prefer sleeping upstairs,
really – you feel safer.'
'You feel nervous, then, living alone?'
Karen shrugged. 'A bit.'
'Are there men living around here who you are particularly
worried about?'
The woman thought for a moment. 'Not really. Paul Mallory's a bit of a creep. He lives on the first floor. People say he
drives them crazy with his loud music but I can't really hear it
down here. You can when you're out in the road, though.'
'What does he do for a living?'
'Don't ask me. He seems to be around at all times of the day
so perhaps he doesn't have a job. Perhaps he doesn't have to –
he drives a flashy car.'
'Mrs Moffat told me about the man on the motorbike who
visits the woman in the top flat.'
'God, I wouldn't like to meet him on a dark night! Like a
gorilla in leathers. Poor Miss Braithewaite – she lives above
the Mallory bloke – told me that she bolts and bars her door
when she hears him coming in case his lady friend refuses to
let him in and he goes berserk.'
'Do you know his name?'

'No.'

'What about that of his girlfriend?'

'Bethany Cryon. Apparently she's Canadian. She's probably the only one that Mrs Pryce didn't have a go at, she hardly ever seems to go out and doesn't speak to anyone.'

'So how does anyone know her name?'

'Well, she does have a word with Miss Braithewaite, just now and then. I think Miss Braithewaite takes her up little bits of home baking. She's a nice old lady – a retired teacher.'

'Have you seen the squatter who's supposed to be living in West Terrace?'

Karen frowned. 'Yes, I'd forgotten about him for a moment. Alice Moffat is quite bothered about him. Her health's not been too good lately and I know Jack's worried about her. He reckons that the business of the tramp lurking about at night is preying on her mind.'

'*Does* he lurk about at night?'

'That's what the Colonel says. He sometimes sees him when he locks up the little garden. Drunk – staggering about. Alice is petrified that he's going to get in somehow and attack her. I think she's being a bit silly, really. From what I've seen of men like that they're usually too drunk to do *anything*. All the same, I wish the police would get rid of him.'

Joanna went back to the office and drew a diagram of the square. She pinned it on the wall and stood back and stared at it thoughtfully. All very neat but it didn't really mean a thing. Most important of all was to find the person who had made off with one Chamaecyparis Kosteri 'Nana Aurea' and three 'Fandango' petunias.

She had phoned her father first thing that morning. He had been concerned to learn of Lance's accident but even more upset, she felt, to hear of a woman who despatched expensive, enchanting, light-of-his-life miniature conifers to the dustbin after the first frosts.

'I used to pinch plants when I was a little lad,' her father had finished up by saying. 'There was a big house and the garden was always planted out in the summer with thousands of bedding plants. I'd never seen anything like it. I couldn't take my eyes off them. At home, Mother might buy a packet of marigold seeds in Woolworth's and scatter them around the sides of the yard but that was all.'

'So you *stole* some?'

'I did too. But I couldn't take 'em home because they'd have known where they came from and I'd have been leathered. So I sneaked them down to Grandma and she planted them in a little box she had out the back. She must have known what I'd done but she never gave me away. It was our secret.'

Joanna resolved to find out where Karen's mother lived.

# Chapter Six

Paul Mallory did not regard his first-floor flat in number 3 North Terrace as a permanent address or even as home. Home was in Norfolk, the estate that would be his one day. That was if the old man didn't strike him out of his will. It would be just like his father to do that, they had never seen eye to eye. And until that sublime day when he would inherit or make his own fortune, he was making do with this flat in an area of Bath that he had privately christened the Graveyard.

There was a certain black humour in his choice of name, now that old Mrs Busybody was dead. Life would be far more pleasant now she was gone and not hammering on his door at all hours complaining about the loudness of the music. It wasn't his fault that she was a Philistine and unable to appreciate one of the finest composers who had ever lived.

Coffee mug in hand, Mallory went to look out of his living-room window. The police were *still* in the square. What the hell were they poking around at now? Their vehicles had been using all the best parking spaces since the previous night. They were taking yet more photographs and soil samples from that patch of ground in the middle that the other residents – snob-ridden fools that they were – called a garden. Mallory knew nothing about gardening, in fact he rather despised people who spent hours on their hands and knees dibbing about in the earth. The exercise would probably have done him good for although only in his early thirties he looked older; a pale, puffy face, a soft, flabby body.

Benny Cooper had called in for coffee. They had known each other for some time. Mallory was quite proud to know a crime reporter; he prided himself on several things but mostly that he hadn't been stupid enough to get married. Women were all right, of course, useful in their way. If you bought them a good meal and plenty of drink you could sometimes persuade them to stay the night. Sometimes he and Benny – who was divorced – had a night on the tiles together, went and found a couple of girls in a bar and had a really good time. If the girls got drunk enough, they took them back to Benny's place and Benny took photographs. He did all his own developing – he had to, really, you can't hand that kind of thing over to be done in Boots – and made a very professional job of it. He enlarged the best ones and put them in several albums that he kept in a locked cabinet in his bedroom. Sometimes he'd bring a few of them over and they'd look through them. A bit of a dark horse, was Benedict. Not many people knew it but he also wrote a gossip column for the same paper under another name. He had a nose for finding out things that folk would prefer to remain hidden.

As Mallory stood gazing out of the window, another car drew up. He had seen it before, last night, when he had looked out to see what all the noise and fuss was about. It was the local Maigret, Carrick, Benny had said his name was – Inspector Carrick. Naturally, he had been too grand to come around asking people questions – a little constable had tapped politely on the door and made a nuisance of himself at the crack of dawn doing that – but he seemed to be keeping very closely in touch with what was going on. Must be cursing his luck, what with the Chantbury Pyx being stolen last night as well.

This was not your cosy, pipe-smoking detective, Paul Mallory concluded, taking a couple of steps back from the window as Carrick and the man with him started to walk towards North Terrace. With a bleak sort of face like that he looked as though he might be more at home skinning sheep in the Faroes. Unaccountably, Mallory shivered.

He went out the back way.

Bob Ingrams was with Carrick and as they strolled slowly across the square he said, 'Is it really of any significance that there's a bruise on the side of the deceased's head as well as the injuries that killed her?'

Carrick did not answer for a moment. Then he said, 'It's one of those things that are either of no importance or absolutely vital to the entire case.'

Ingrams felt that he could have worked that out for himself.

'And until some of these people have been questioned again,' Carrick continued, 'we've precious little to go on.' He stopped walking. 'That gate into the garden – is it always open? It was open last night but appears to have a well-maintained lock on it and there are scratches round the keyhole as though it regularly has a key inserted.'

'No one mentioned it, sir.'

'Make a note of it – we'll ask.'

'Whoever dragged the body in there and dumped it took a tremendous risk of being spotted.'

'Yes. And we know now that she wasn't killed in her own house. It's fairly certain that she wasn't murdered out here either. So she was moved because the body was in a place that would have incriminated someone. In other words, she died in one of the buildings of this square.'

'Everywhere's been gone over, though. No sign of any blood.'

'Even West Terrace?'

'As much of it as possible. Sergeant Tomkins fell through the floor in one of the end houses – the boards were just like powder with dry rot. But there's so much dust and dirt everywhere, it would show up any sign of a scuffle.'

'And one has to ask oneself why Mrs Pryce would venture into such a place after dark. I'm assuming she wasn't taken there. There was no evidence that she'd been sexually assaulted. No, I think either she gave chase to the person who was stealing her plants and ended up in a flat or house nearby, or she called on someone, possibly to complain about something, giving it priority over the theft. *If* she noticed the theft at the time.'

'That puts Paul Mallory right in the firing line.'

'I know. I propose we call on him now. First of all, though, get on the radio and find out if they've found anything interesting on Conrad Stacey's clothes. If Mallory's not in I'll talk to Miss Braithewaite. I'll do that alone – two of us might be too alarming for her. Simmonds made a note that she seemed rather nervous.'

57

Miss Braithewaite had been very apprehensive about this interview with the man in charge of the murder investigation. She was not to know, of course, that Inspector Carrick would ring her doorbell first only because Paul Mallory had gone out. Carrick was not aware of it yet but everyone else at number 3 was out too; Karen Williams at work and Bethany Cryon on one of her furtive dashes to the shops.

'Do sit down, Inspector,' said Miss Braithewaite without so much as a glance at his warrant card. 'Can I offer you a drink?' adding quickly, 'Tea or coffee?', appalled that he might think she had been endeavouring to lure him into drinking alcohol while on duty.

'Thanks, but I had coffee just before I came out,' he replied with a smile. He gazed around the living room. 'Such beautiful embroidered pictures, Miss Braithewaite. Did you do them yourself?'

'Oh, er, yes,' she answered. 'It's my only hobby really. I've done them since I retired. You don't get much time in the teaching profession.'

'Indeed no. And how long have you lived here?'

'Just over five years.'

'Was Mrs Pryce living here when you came?'

'By no means. She had only been here for about eighteen months.'

He was still smiling when he said, 'I know you're not a person who gossips but have you any idea what happened to Mr Pryce?'

'I *believe* he was killed in the war, Inspector.'

'Do you mind if I ask how you know that?'

Miss Braithewaite suddenly felt amazingly calm but nevertheless placed her hands carefully together in her lap in case they might shake a little. She said, 'I was talking to the lady who serves behind the counter in the post office. I'm afraid I don't know her name. There had been a little trouble; Mrs Pryce had accused someone of jumping the queue. I think the woman felt sorry for her – Mrs Pryce, that is – and said to me that she had a war widow's pension and was all alone.'

'Were you at home last night?'

'Yes, I don't go out in the evenings.'

'I understand that Mr Mallory below you sometimes has music playing very loudly. Does it annoy you?'

58

'No, I hardly hear it. The walls and floors of these buildings are very thick. When I moved in I had insulating material laid on all the floors and then underlay beneath the carpets. I've suffered before, you see, Inspector. I lived in a flat in Bristol for ten years with *very* noisy neighbours.'

'So you can't hear it at all?'

'Yes, just a little. Especially if the windows are open.'

'Was he playing music last night?'

'Yes, I believe he was. But I couldn't hear it after I'd gone to bed. My bedroom is at the back.'

'What time did you go to bed?'

She knew she was a very bad liar but looked him right in the eye and said, 'At five past ten.'

'So you didn't hear anything at all?'

'No, I'm afraid I didn't.'

'Do you know if Mrs Pryce had ever complained to Mr Mallory about his music?'

'Yes, she had. Karen Williams told me. Mrs Pryce had been very nasty to her too.'

He was not to be sidetracked. 'Have you any idea if Mrs Pryce complained last night?'

'No,' she stated emphatically.

'No?' The one tiny word was like a breath on his lips, a mere zephyr.

Miss Braithewaite's ears roared. 'I – I mean, no, I have no idea,' she stuttered. 'I didn't hear *anything*.'

'Tell me. . . .'

Her hands clutched convulsively. 'Yes?'

'Is the gate to the garden in the square ever locked?'

'Yes, every night. Colonel Moffat has the key. The garden is the responsibility of the residents, you see, and after some vagrants started to sleep in there we – that is, the residents' association – decided to keep it locked at night.'

'What is your impression of Paul Mallory?'

'I really don't know him well enough to comment.'

The fair eyebrows rose. 'Come now, Miss Braithewaite. After a lifetime when it was your job to make judgements about people? Someone like you should be able to write a five-hundred-word essay on a man you'd met on the stairs.'

She *had* met him on the stairs, or, rather, he had raced past her on the ground floor when she had been loaded with shopping. Without speaking, actually knocking her arm. 'He's a product of modern times,' she said. 'Rude, uncaring, selfish, loud, and too fond of the sound of his own voice. Like that friend of his, the man who works for the newspaper. They're birds of a feather.'

Carrick leaned forward, his face intent. 'Who?' he whispered.

'I don't know his name.'

'Describe him.'

'He was round this morning knocking on people's doors, asking questions. He's a crime reporter for the *Bath Times*. He wears sunglasses whatever the –'

'Cooper!' Carrick ejaculated.

Miss Braithewaite, who had just realised that she could very easily write a thousand-word essay about the man facing her, said, 'Police officers have no time for crime reporters, I presume.'

Carrick smiled grimly. 'Some of them. Tell him nothing. If he makes a nuisance of himself, give me a ring.' He wrote down his phone number on a scrap of paper and gave it to her. 'Get in touch with me if you remember anything else.'

To her huge relief, he rose to go.

'There's something you can tell me,' he said, looking at one of her pictures.

'What is that?' she asked, her heart thudding so loudly she knew he must be able to hear it.

'Are those flowers auriculas?'

'Yes, that's right, Inspector. Alpine primulas.'

'My mother had some in pots in the greenhouse.'

When he had gone Miss Braithewaite shakily poured herself a small measure of brandy. Naturally, she only kept it for medicinal purposes.


'Nothing on Stacey's clothes,' said Ingrams, who had been waiting outside. 'At least, no blood. Everything else you can think of, but no blood.'

'But the clothes *had* been soaked.'

'Forensic still reckon there would have been traces because it would have dried on in the time available. All the other stuff had.'

'I don't think there would have been much blood on the murderer,' Carrick said, starting down the stairs. 'Don't forget, she was killed with just one massive blow, not several. Suppose she did come here, having drunk enough to feel really stormy, and raised hell with Mallory. His doorbell – I know because I rang it earlier – is one of those that ring on the back of the door. Would he hear that over the ungodly row going on in his living room? He might even have had the inside doors closed. Even if she'd banged on the door with a fist. . . .'

On the first-floor landing Carrick paused and found a light switch. The stairs were stone, as were the walls, the latter painted dark green up to a height of about four feet, the rest a dirty white. The stairs were uncarpeted and looked as though they might be scrubbed periodically. After Ingrams had fetched a torch from the car, Carrick examined every inch of the landing area.

'It hasn't been washed within the past few hours either,' Ingrams observed, wishing he had the courage to add that the scene-of-crime team had been over everything already.

'I think I'll just check up here,' Carrick said and ascended again. 'Has anyone looked over the ground-floor flat that's empty?'

'No, sir, not yet,' Ingrams replied, furious that he hadn't thought of it.

'Get the keys from the estate agent, will you?'

Sighing, Ingrams went out again. Carrick, he was prepared to swear, was trying to get rid of him. This suspicion assumed copper-bottomed certainty when he saw Joanna Mackenzie coming across the square towards him.

'He's heading for the third floor if you fancy a quick knee-trembler,' Ingrams said with a leer as they passed.

'You'll do,' said Carrick when he caught sight of her through the banisters.

'For *what*?' Joanna snapped.

'The woman on the top floor's just bolted past me like a frightened rabbit. She must have come in through the back. I was about to radio for female assistance – she might talk to a woman.'

'Wouldn't let the cops in this morning, eh?'

'Either that or –' Carrick stood up. 'Joanna, are you all right?'

'No, I'm probably just about to be arrested for assaulting a police officer.'

He switched off the torch and came down the remaining stairs between them, warily.

'James, I will *not* tolerate obscene remarks from your subordinates.'

'Why the hell are you here, anyway?' he asked in the deathly whisper he unconsciously resorted to when angry.

'I rang the nick and they said you were here. I know who took the plants. It *was* Jamie – he gave them to his granny. I've spoken to her and she said he went round with some this morning.'

Bob Ingrams was slowly mounting the stairs.

'Wait here,' Carrick said to Joanna.

'Now we'll see what sort of a copper you are,' Ingrams said. 'Sir.' He had his handkerchief to his nose, which was bleeding heavily.

'Your predecessor was a popular bloke,' Carrick began by saying. 'He was the one who replaced Miss Mackenzie when she was forced to resign for having an affair with her boss. The boss's wife had been dying of cancer for some time and although he loved her very much there were times when he thought he'd go right off his head if he didn't do what comes naturally. Rugby-football changing rooms, I kid you not, are the randiest places on this planet. But despite discretion on the part of the couple involved, someone found out and reported their findings to the chief super. I'll mention no names because he's retired now but a more narrow-minded, woman-hating bigot would be hard to find. He didn't want women in the force at all. My wife is dead now, sergeant, and what I won't tolerate is people making remarks. If you press charges against Miss Mackenzie, the only person who will be happy is the tale-teller, who unfortunately is still in circulation.'

'On the job?' Ingrams asked stonily.

'No, he runs a porn ring. I've been trying to nail him for years and he knows it. He told me openly that if I persisted he'd dig for dirt on me until I was thrown out. Well, he's done it once and scored a point. The fact that you've had your nose bloodied by a witness hardly helps.'

Ingrams turned on his heel and left the building.

'I'm sorry,' Joanna called down when she saw Carrick returning. 'I shouldn't have done that.'

'What did he say?'

She told him.

'That's not *really* obscene.'

'He'd already asked me if you were a good screw. I told him, yes, bloody fantastic – or words to that effect.'

'Joanna –'

'Still thinking of your career, James?'

'I'm leading a murder investigation and it's highly likely that you're an important witness for the prosecution. What would the papers make of that, eh?'

'So you don't want me to come with you to see the Cryon woman after all?'

'We hadn't got her name. No, I wasn't thinking. I don't want us to be seen together.'

'Bethany Cryon. She's Canadian. There's a boyfriend who arrives on a motorbike. Information courtesy of Tyler and Mackenzie, private investigators and consultant advisers to Bath CID, who only screw you when no one's looking.'

For the first time in his life Carrick felt like banging his head against the wall.

'And Jamie?' Joanna went on relentlessly.

'I'll talk to him. Thank you – it might turn out to be an important lead. Now please go. And stay out of it from now on.'

'You didn't really answer my question. How long are you going to let Benedict Cooper run your life?'

'I'm going to crucify him,' Carrick said.

# Chapter Seven

'Miss Cryon?' Carrick said to an inch-wide crack between door and frame, this the result of having knocked loudly three times when the bell did not seem to work.

'I won't be harassed like this,' said a husky voice from within.

'My name is Inspector James Carrick. I'd like to ask you a few questions.'

'How do I know who you really are?'

Carrick offered his warrant card through the slit. It was snatched and then, moments later, thrown back. He picked it up.

'As I said, I won't be harassed.'

'No one's harassing you, Miss Cryon. I'd just like a little chat.'

Suddenly the door was flung wide, actually startling him.

'You'd better come in, then. I know what will happen otherwise – you'll call up people who will kick it down.'

'Do the Mounties kick people's doors in?' he asked, staying where he was.

'All the time,' she snapped.

He went in. The heat hit him in a nauseous wave. It emanated, he saw when he had followed her into the front room, from a bottled-gas heater that appeared to be running at maximum output. The woman herself was dressed in shapeless cotton garments topped by a shawl in a lurid shade of pink. The fringe had become unravelled and she picked at it nervously.

Carrick said, 'Are you aware that a woman was murdered here in this square last night?'

'Now you really are being insulting. You think I'm too stupid to notice police cars and ambulances? Anyone with a –' She broke off and turned away from him, pulling at the edge of the shawl. When she spoke again, all anger had gone from her voice. 'You mustn't take any notice. I had a breakdown and this kind of hassle doesn't improve matters.'

'I'll try and be as quick as possible,' he promised. 'How long have you lived here?'

'Two and a half months.'

She wore tinted spectacles behind which her dark eyes were weirdly magnified. In the extreme paleness of her complexion they looked almost black. The face was triangular in shape with a sharply pointed chin. The overall impression – the mouth small and compressed into a slit – was of a defiant, yet frightened, praying mantis. Carrick found her extremely disconcerting.

'And you left Canada how long ago?'

'Just before I came here. Do you want to see my passport?'

'That won't be necessary. Do you mind telling me why you came to this country?'

She stared at him. 'To get away from the land of endless trees and endless boredom.'

'I see. Did you hear or see anything strange out in the square last night – before the police arrived?'

'No.'

'Did you go out last night?'

'No. I never go out at night.'

'Did you have any visitors?'

'No.'

'Not even your friend with the motorbike?'

'Oh, yes, I'd forgotten. He came in for a little while.'

Carrick had slipped off his jacket. 'What time did he arrive and leave?'

'I can't remember exactly.' She was ripping the fringe from the shawl.

'Please try.'

She came right up close to him. God, Carrick thought, the bloody woman's raving mad.

'I can't remember *exactly*. I think he went home about ten thirty.'

65

'I'd like his name.'

'No. This is no concern of his at all.'

'It is *my* concern. He might have seen something or someone that will help me with my investigations.'

'Harbutts,' she said after a silence during which she stared unblinkingly at him.

'First name?'

'William.'

'Where does he live?'

'With his *wife*,' Cryon hissed.

'All right, where can I contact him at work?'

'He works for the city council, or whatever you call it. You'll find him at the depot. But you're not to tell him I mentioned his name.'

'Violent sort of man, is he?'

She flung herself away from him. 'Mind your own damn business.'

'Did you ever meet Mrs Pryce?'

'Is that the woman who was killed? No.'

'Really?'

'I don't go out much. I meet no one.'

'Just Harbutts.'

'Yes,' she cooed. 'Just my Billy boy.'

He couldn't get out of the flat fast enough.

Joanna walked slowly across Beckford Square, gazing at the ruinous West Terrace. It was early evening and the sun had sunk below the roof with its ornate balustrade. The windows of the second and third floors seemed to stare back at her blindly; how dead and lonely-looking was an empty house, she thought. A careful scrutiny of the boarded-up doors and lower windows gave no indication of forced entry so she strolled back and round the corner into Nash Street, the way she had come. There was an access to the rear of the terrace, about ten feet wide, almost totally overgrown by a privet hedge, unclipped for decades, that hung over a low wall on the right-hand side.

What had been small, narrow back gardens was a wilderness. Rubbish of various sorts had been dumped there and she picked her way carefully over and around old mattresses, a fridge, piles of split and bulging black plastic bags that were very malodorous, and heaps of rotting lawn mowings. Vandals too visited the place, judging by the graffiti sprayed on the walls and the boarding, of which KILL THE PIGS was the only one mentionable. But either there were regular security patrols or damage was repaired as soon as it happened, for the vandals appeared not to have succeeded in gaining entry to the building. All seemed secure.

Joanna was not fooled by appearances and carefully checked each back door and ground-floor window. It was quite obvious that she was following a path of sorts through the long grass and through gaps in the walls and fences that had originally separated each garden. At the last door she was rewarded; the planks had been carefully prised away from the frame. After a struggle, for they were half an inch thick and still securely nailed at the other end, she forced her way in.

It was very dark inside but she had brought a powerful flashlight belonging to Lance from the office. Its bright beam illuminated what had been a scullery many years previously, there was an old-fashioned stone sink beneath the window. Later it had been used as a storeroom; marks on the walls showed where shelves and cupboards had been fitted. Now it was given over to spiders, cobwebs and a large patch of dry rot hanging like a dead suppurating crab in one corner.

Joanna went out through a doorway opposite, crossed a kitchen and continued out into a hallway. This had panelled walls and a black and white tiled floor and opened out towards the front of the house into a wide entrance hall with an imposing curved staircase. She passed doors on her right and left, ignoring them, for whoever lived here now would be upstairs where it was light.

The only signs of real disturbance looked recent, probably as a result of when the police had thoroughly searched the building the previous night. She was startled momentarily when there was a flash of light from the other side of the entrance hall but soon realised that it was the reflection of her own torch in a small mirror.

'No ghosts here,' she murmured to herself. 'Not after Carrick's lot have trampled through like a herd of elephants.'

She went up the stairs, careful where she put her feet, for dry rot was really entrenched in the house, its creeping fingers of platelike growths crumbling all woodwork to dust. On the first-floor landing she came to a large hole in the boards as though someone had fallen right through. She carefully went round the hole, trying not to notice curtains of black cobwebs, rat droppings and a dead starling.

Wan daylight, feeble because it was filtered by filthy windows, met her on the next landing. The air was fresher up here too, even though tainted by a smell she decided was a mixture of methylated spirits and unwashed bodies. She tracked the smell, sniffing, going in the direction of a large room that overlooked the square.

It was actually two rooms, divided across the middle by sliding doors that hung at all angles on broken hinges. She hardly noticed this; her attention was on the fireplace, which had the remains of what looked like a recent fire in it. On the hearth was a small brush and shovel, a blackened kettle and a biscuit tin, also black on the outside as though it had been used as a cooking pot.

In one corner of the room, to the right of the door, was a pile of empty cardboard boxes, orange crates, scrap wood and newspapers. Beneath the window stood a wooden packing case, on its side, giving every appearance of being furniture rather than firewood. Another one looked as though it might be used as a table, a clean sheet of newspaper on the top, and next to it yet another containing a carton of milk, three apples, several bananas and a small packet wrapped in greaseproof paper.

In an alcove to the left of the fireplace was a pile of old blankets and clothing. It was rather a dim corner and it came as a shock to Joanna when she realised that the clothes had a person inside them. This person commenced to snore loudly.

A pair of scruffy trainers stuck out from the blanket. Joanna nudged one of them gently and then again, a little harder when the rhythm of the snoring did not waver. When there was still no response, she left the room and found what had once been an ornate bathroom. There she ran some cold water – marvelling that it was still turned on at the mains – into a plastic mug upended to dry on the washbasin. Returning to the room with the sleeper, she saw that the pile of rags had changed shape slightly and that she was now being regarded by a very keen pair of blue eyes.

'I thought that might make you stop shamming,' she said briskly, placing the brimming mug down on the table packing case.

'That's a very cruel thing to do to an old man,' said the inhabitant of the rags in a nasal whine.

'I want to ask you some questions.'

The pile of rags erupted and Joanna stood her ground grimly as the smell hit her.

'It's dangerous,' said the man, tossing off an old sweater, the sleeves of which had been entangled around his neck. 'Dangerous for a young woman to wander into places like this asking questions.'

'I can take care of myself,' she told him. 'I used to be in the police.'

He glowered at her. 'Friends of yours then, that crap-footed, shit-faced crowd who kicked my little home to pieces yesterday?' he roared. 'What do you do now – work for Social Security?'

'No and no,' Joanna replied calmly.

He started to search the room at a shambling trot. 'Seen a bottle?'

'I *could* get you thrown out, though.'

'Piss off,' he mumbled, still searching.

'How long have you been here?'

'Long enough.'

'*How* long?'

Joanna stood quite still when he suddenly came right up and peered closely at her, his face only inches away. But the angry stare only lasted for seconds and then he was off on his perambulations of the room again.

'I might give you some money for a square meal if you answer a few questions.'

He stopped dead in his tracks. 'Places that cook square meals don't serve the likes of me even if I have the money,' he pointed out, amazed at her ignorance.

'All right, I'll go and get you some fish and chips.'

'And a bottle.'

'No. Two tins of Coke.'

'Then no deal.'

She marched up to him. 'Answer now or you're down the nick. Pronto. I still have contacts, you know.'

He glared at her sullenly. 'I might lose my temper and throw you down the stairs. Or expose myself indecently.' He grabbed suddenly at his dreadful clothing.

'Wow,' said Joanna in a bored voice. 'that would really make my day.'

Astoundingly, he laughed, revealing good white teeth.

'Besides, James Carrick said you were harmless.'

'Is he your contact, redhead?' he asked with a sideways crafty look.

'You know who he is, then?'

'I read the papers. He's heading the murder investigation.'

'What's your name?'

'They call me Tommy.'

'So how long have you been here?'

'About six weeks.'

'Were you here last night?'

'Not until after three a.m.'

'Where were you?'

He subsided onto one of the packing cases. 'Down by the river, in the park by the weir. A few of us meet up if the weather's warm. By the time I got back, the filth had been through here. It took me ages to find my stuff. As if they knew and did it on purpose.'

'People have complained about you.'

'You think I don't know it? The old biddy who was banged on the head came up to me in the street one morning and told me she'd been on to the council about me. Said I was a health hazard. She was the kind of woman who thought all men health hazards.' He spat on the floor.

'Can you prove what time you returned last night?'

'No.'

'There was an empty gin glass in her front room. She might have had a drop more than usual and it made her silly enough to try and get rid of you last night. If you'd shoved *her* down the stairs it could well have proved fatal. You're a strong-looking bloke, you could easily have dragged her body into the garden in the square and dumped it. A bit difficult to explain, after all, a decomposing body on the premises.'

'I didn't kill her,' Tommy said. 'I wasn't here.'

'Have you noticed a man on a motorbike? He visits the woman in the top flat at number 3.'

70

The sullen expression changed to one of interest. 'You should keep away from *him*. He's a no-gooder if ever there was.'

'What makes you say that?'

'I just know, that's all.'

'Be more specific.'

Tommy shrugged. 'I can tell. He threatened me with a spanner one night when I asked him for a fag. Anyway, where do you fit into all this?'

'I was engaged by Mrs Pryce to find out who was stealing her plants.'

'You're a private eye?' he asked incredulously.

'Yes.'

'And that's better paid and more interesting than –'

'I don't have to explain my reasons for leaving to you,' Joanna interrupted.

He waggled a dirty index finger at her. 'You want to know who took the plants? Well, I'll tell you but you'll have to promise to do nothing about it.'

'I know who took them. It was little Jamie. He gave them to his granny.'

'That's right. He plays out here most nights when his mother thinks he's safely tucked up in bed. Probably climbs out of his bedroom window. The kid's lonely and he's not allowed to have any pets.'

'How do you know?'

'Sound carries. I heard her shouting that they couldn't have a cat or dog with her out at work for most of the day. I reckon that's why he sneaks out at night – to play with a big Persian cat that belongs to the matron of the nursing home.'

'It's a Maine coon,' Joanna said. 'I met it a few nights ago.'

'It's been poisoned.'

'*What*?'

'Not dead, though. But it's down at the vet's very ill.'

'Tommy, who told you all this?'

'Mrs Lang. She's the matron. She's the only one in the square who speaks to me. Better than that, if I go round the back I get a big plate of hot dinner. I expect it's stuff that otherwise might be thrown away but it's not leftover food from other people's plates. And dessert. She told me. I met her on the pavement when the vet was taking the cat away. In tears she was – in a dreadful state. I reckon you ought to go and talk to her – she thinks Mrs Pryce poisoned him *and* that it's not the first time she's done it.'

Joanna went out and bought him fish and chips, Coke, cigarettes and a large bar of chocolate. Then she walked right across the square, rang the bell on the immaculately painted and polished front door of the Lord Nelson Nursing Home for Retired Naval Officers and asked to speak to Mrs Lang.

Carrick took Sergeant Ingrams with him when he went to find Bill Harbutts. This was not due to any nervousness on his part, though his excellent memory had brought the man's criminal record instantly to mind. Carrick was simply trying to mend a few fences with his new assistant.

The hunt for the murder weapon had intensified, with frogmen now searching the river. Carrick wasn't optimistic, even though the Avon was low after very little rain for weeks.

Harbutts, it appeared, drove a dustcart. The supervisor at the council depot, looking at his watch after giving them this information, added that the man in question was due back shortly as the crews finished work at five p.m. Normally they would not have been working on a Saturday at all but as there had been a strike the previous week there was a lot of catching-up to do.

Carrick thanked him and left the office, a hut, to sit in the sun on a large stack of kerbstones. Turning to Ingrams, he said, 'Receiving stolen property, taking away several cars without their owners' consent, and GBH. For the last he got two years and was released just over a year ago. Since then nothing that we've been able to connect him with directly.'

'But regularly gets involved in fights at closing time on Saturday nights,' Ingrams remarked. 'And now murder?'

'Filthy temper,' Carrick said, squinting up at the sun. 'And, as we know, Mrs Pryce had a very thin – abnormally thin – skull. I think we're in with a chance here.'

'Did anyone see him last night? Or hear the bike?'

'Oddly enough, no. But the Cryon woman admitted that he'd been to see her. She said he left at about ten thirty, or as near as she could remember. She wasn't very helpful.'

'What's she like?'

'Away with the birds.'

'Eh?'

'Crazy.'

'So what the hell's Harbutts doing there then?'

Carrick pulled a wry grimace. 'Use your imagination. Besides, she appears to be besotted with him. As I said, crazy.'

A few minutes later several dustcarts turned in through the main gates of the compound and parked, amazingly neatly, in a row. The crews, wearing orange overalls, piled out.

'That's him,' Carrick said, shading his eyes against the glare. 'The tall one with the beer gut.'

Ingrams, who was fairly convinced that he had not been brought along as cannon fodder but whose nose was still extremely uncomfortable, walked half a step behind.

'Police,' Carrick said to Harbutts. 'I'd like to ask you a few questions.'

Harbutts slammed the door of the cab with sufficient force to make the vehicle rock slightly and then swung round to regard them both with small angry eyes. 'So I'm not one of those lucky sods who gets a "Good morning, sir. I wonder if you'd be so kind as to –"'

Carrick interrupted him with just a few words, the nature of which made Ingrams blink. They also had the effect of silencing Harbutts.

'Good,' Carrick continued mildly. 'Your full name is William Frederick Harbutts and you live at 37 Elm Tree Terrace, Southdown St Peter?'

'Now, look –'

'I'm conducting a murder investigation and you can either cooperate here or down at the police station. Which is it to be?'

'All right,' Harbutts growled.

'I'm investigating the death of Mrs Amelia Pryce in Beckford Square last night and we're interviewing everyone who was in that vicinity. Your motorbike was seen parked outside number 3 North Terrace. Perhaps you'd confirm that.'

'Yes, I was there. But –'

'What time did you arrive?'

'Quite late – about a quarter to ten.'

'What was the purpose of your visit?'

'To visit a friend.'

'Miss Cryon?'

'Well, since you obviously know all the answers, perhaps –'

Again Carrick cut him short. 'What time was it when you left?'

'Ten thirty.'

'You're quite sure about that?'

'Why shouldn't I be sure?'

'Did you see anyone when you left?'

'No.'

'Think carefully. It's very important.'

After a pause during which Harbutts scowled at Carrick, he said, 'Yeah, that's right. There was a boy – just a kid.'

'Where was he?'

'Look, he was just a little kid . . .'

'I'm trying to find witnesses,' Carrick told him patiently.

'He was just sort of hanging around on the corner by the place that's all boarded up.'

'On the far corner, the one farthest away from you? The one nearest to Mrs Pryce's house?'

'I don't know where she lived.'

'Come now,' Carrick said softly. 'Hadn't she ever come out and spoken to you? Rushed out and complained about the noise from your bike?'

'No.'

'I don't believe you. The woman had complained about everything to everyone.'

'All right,' Harbutts said after another heavy silence.

'She'd had a go at you?'

'Yes – just once.'

'When?'

'A coupla weeks ago.'

'And presumably you apologised in your usual calm, polite way and said you'd be quieter in future?'

Ingrams braced himself for defensive action.

'Did I hell!' Harbutts burst out. 'Meddling old cow. I told her where she could –' He bit off the rest of what he had been about to say, his hatred of Carrick tangible.

'Quite,' Carrick said very softly. 'Did she leave it at that? Threaten you with the police?'

The big man took a deep shuddering breath. 'Look, I *shouted* at her, all right? I didn't touch the woman. I'm not the sort of bloke to hit women.'

'Answer the question.'

'She just shouted back that she'd get the law on me.'

'And you didn't see her in the square last night?'

'No.'

'Thank you,' Carrick said, turning to go.

'I got a hell of a bollocking from Bethany about it.'

'Really?' said Carrick politely.

'She made me promise to wheel the bike out of the square in future and start it round the corner. So I do.'

'How very strange,' Carrick said under his breath as they made their way back to the car.

Ingrams wasn't curious, his nose hurt too much.

# Chapter Eight

Joanna had just got in when the phone rang. She was very surprised to hear Carrick's voice.

'I've been thinking. Perhaps you ought to come with me when I talk to Jamie. It was your case first, after all, and if you're as businesslike as you used to be and intend sending in a bill to whoever's handling Mrs Pryce's estate, you'll have to prepare some kind of report.'

'Where shall I meet you?'

'By the tree in the middle of the Circus?'

'Twenty minutes?'

'Fine.'

Although she was a couple of minutes early, he was there before her, hands in pockets, gazing up into the plane tree, which is of quite heroic proportions. She had a few seconds, moments when he was not aware of being watched, to assimilate the tenseness of his shoulders and stance. She wondered how long it would be before he cracked under the strain.

He had hit the wall once before – his own description of what had happened – in the days when his wife, Kathleen, had been confined to a wheelchair, dying from a rare form of bone cancer. He had handled the situation mainly by working himself and those under him, Joanna included, into the ground. He had treated the first female sergeant in Bath CID no differently from the other officers, but Joanna was a sensitive woman and knew that he was drawn to her. She in turn was attracted to him with his thick fair hair, fine blue eyes and athletic body. There was more to James Carrick than that, however, and he was very good at his job.

On the night in question and after a punishing day that had culminated in a raid on a house in Weston where two bank robbers were hiding, several of Carrick's team had piled into his car and he had driven them all home. The raid, despite the presence of some members of the Territorial Support Group, had not gone completely according to plan. There had been a shoot-out in which one bank robber was killed and a constable seriously injured. No one had escaped unscathed. Carrick was nursing grazed knuckles and a sprained wrist, his subordinates an assortment of bloody noses, split lips and bruised ribs. Joanna had been thrown over a low wall and felt that her body would be black and blue in the morning.

She lived the nearest to Carrick so, naturally, he had dropped her off last. The evening's activities had had a strange effect on her by that time; fear and exhilaration had combined to give her a slightly alarming inclination to think longingly of her boss in Anglo-Saxon verbs and nouns of a very basic nature. By the time they reached the large house in Lansdown where her flat was situated and she prepared to leave his car, she had so wanted the man that her nipples felt as if they might bore holes in her dark-blue regulation pullover.

It had been an odd feeling, walking up the steps to the front door, wondering if he would follow, praying that he would and praying that he wouldn't. She had heard the car door slam and, as she had fitted the key in the lock, quick, light footsteps behind her. She hadn't looked round, not even when she had reached the second floor and was opening her own door. On the other side of it, when it was safely closed, any change of mind on her part would have been pointless.

Joanna was quite sure of that now. She supposed that had she screamed and struggled he might have desisted. As it was, she had gladly kissed him as he was kissing her and then merely yielded to being undressed deftly and urgently. One moment they had been clothed, the next naked, and there, on her hall carpet. . .

'A man who would drive a JCB through the gates of Paradise,' Joanna murmured as she now walked up to him. 'If you ever qualify.'

'Qualify for what?' asked Carrick, who had only heard the last bit.

She smiled like the Mona Lisa. 'I did as you suggested and had a word with Tommy.'

'I spoke to him this morning,' Carrick said quickly.

'I hope he made his feelings plain about the way your mob smashed his little home to bits.'

'No, did they?'

'Ah,' Joanna said. 'So he wasn't really bothered about it after all. Did he say anything about Doolally being poisoned?'

'I beg your pardon.'

'He didn't? No, I don't think it really affects the case either – just another pointer to the sheer ghastliness of the deceased.'

'Joanna, what the hell are you talking about?'

'Pet poisoning. Doolally is a Maine coon cat belonging to Mrs Lang, the matron of the nursing home. He came home on Thursday morning foaming at the mouth and then collapsed. Mrs Lang made him sick by pushing a piece of washing soda down his throat and then called the vet. He's still pretty rough but likely to recover.'

'She thinks Mrs Pryce did it?'

'Almost sure. She said the woman was watching through the window with a really nasty smile on her face. Apparently the Moffats' old dog died suddenly and shortly afterwards Miss Braithewaite's cat came in and dropped dead.'

'Miss Braithewaite's hiding something,' Carrick said as they turned the corner into Beckford Square.

'Surely not.'

'One of the old school. A lady to the last degree but tough as nails. She'll come and tell me about it soon, I should think.'

'Mrs Lang's very fond of her cat.'

'You think she's capable of murder?'

'No, but she's very angry too and was rather vague when I asked her whereabouts last night.'

'No doubt she felt she didn't have to tell you,' Carrick observed, more gently than of late. 'You needn't worry – she's a volunteer for the Samaritans and was on duty from ten last night until six this morning. Someone stands in for her when she's not at the home.'

'What did Paul Mallory have to say for himself?' Joanna asked after a short silence.

'He had gone out.'

'I'm always suspicious when people take a sudden holiday.'

'Me too. And he's a friend of Cooper's.' Carrick stopped, looking up at North Terrace.

'Back at home now, though,' Joanna said, her gaze following his to a lighted window.

'I must talk to the boy first. I rang his mother and told her I'd be along about now.'

'And afterwards – when you've spoken to Mallory too?'

The steps were unlit and they picked their way down them carefully. At the bottom Carrick rang the doorbell before he said, 'I might go home and have something to eat.'

'Or something to drink?'

'Or something to drink,' Carrick agreed.

A light above them came on.

'You used to have a sensible head on your shoulders,' Joanna remarked acidly.

'I still won't be lectured,' he retorted as the door opened. He switched on the friendly professional smile. 'Good evening, Miss Williams. I rang earlier. I think you've met Miss Mackenzie already.'

Karen Williams was not pleased to see them. 'You'd better come in,' she mumbled. When they were all seated in the living room – very tidy – she said, 'This is a terrible fuss over a few plants. I've never heard anything like it – a police *inspector* bothering himself with such a minor crime.'

'Ah, no,' Carrick said. 'I'm not. I'm looking for the person who murdered Mrs Pryce. It's Miss Mackenzie who was asked to find out what was happening to the plants.'

'Worth about twenty-five pounds, actually,' Joanna said. 'Inspector Carrick would like to ask Jamie if he saw anyone in the square last night.'

'My son wasn't in the square last night.'

'He was,' Carrick countered. 'He was seen. And your mother was in receipt of another gift this morning – as you probably well know. There's really no point in denying it. The boy has been seen outside on other nights too.'

The woman had gone very white. 'What will happen to him?'

'The very worst, I should imagine, is that Mrs Lang over at the nursing home will invite him to tea so that he can play safely with her cat indoors. Now, may I please talk to Jamie?'

'He's in his room, I'll fetch him.'

The child had obviously been prepared for this hauling before the law. His face had been washed to shiny perfection, his unruly hair slicked down with water, fairly unsuccessfully, as it happened. He gave Joanna a rather nervous smile, slithered past Carrick and took his place in one corner of a large settee.

Joanna caught Carrick's eye and opened the proceedings. Just like old times when they had interviewed children together, she realised with a lurch of her heart.

'Were you looking for Doolally last night?' she asked.

She immediately had the boy's interest. 'Is that his name?'

'Yes – it's a really good one, isn't it? Well, I afraid he wasn't there because he's been ill. But he'll be back home soon and then you'll see him again.'

'He pretends he's a tiger,' Jamie said shyly. 'We go through the jungle together.'

'I know,' Joanna said. 'He came to see me one night when I was hiding in the garden watching for someone who's been taking Mrs Pryce's plants. But no one came – you must have been in bed then.'

Jamie wasn't stupid. He stared at the ceiling and then back at Joanna. 'Grandma said I mustn't do it again.'

In a low voice Karen said, 'My mother's a little vague – she had a stroke recently. But this morning she realised he'd taken them.'

'That horrible old woman!' Jamie burst out. 'She got hold of me one day when I was on my bike. Her fingers hurt me. She said she'd *kill* my cat.'

Joanna then had a really dreadful thought. Jamie was tall, a big boy for his age, quite a strong child. Her alarming train of thought must have been detected by Carrick because he took up the questioning.

'Did you believe her, Jamie?' he enquired gently.

'No, she was being horrible,' Jamie declared stoutly. 'People aren't allowed to do things like that. But I told Doolally. I told him to keep away from her garden and not to pee in her plants.'

'Did he?' Carrick said, mouth twitching with amusement.

'Oh, yes. All the time. He didn't like her either.'

'Did you see the man with the motorbike last night?'

'Yes, he came out of a house when I was looking for Doolally.'

'What did he do?'

Jamie shrugged. 'Just went away.'

'Started the bike and rode off?'

'No, he pushed it.'

'Did you hear him start it?'

'No. I was counting the clock.'

'On St Margaret's church,' Joanna whispered to Carrick. 'You can hear it very clearly from here.'

'How many was it, Jamie?' Carrick asked.

'Ten!' said the boy triumphantly.

'Then what did you do?'

Jamie wriggled. 'I took some plants.'

'But you dropped one.'

'A car came.'

'Did it stop?'

'No, it just went away again. A man was trying to see the road names.'

'What did you do then?'

'I'd run into the garden, I was scared. So I went home.'

'I want you to think very carefully. Was Mrs Pryce's front door open?'

'No.'

'You're sure?'

'Yes, I looked in case she was waiting for me. It was shut and I could hear her television.'

'Did you see anyone at all other than the man in the car and the one with the motorbike?'

'No, not then.'

Carrick's skin crawled. 'When?'

'I was climbing back in through my bedroom window. I'd put the plants in an old box to take to Grandma and hidden it. Someone came out of the back door. It frightened me and I nearly fell.'

Karen said, 'The ground drops away at the back. His room's at ground level.'

81

'Who was it, Jamie?'

'I don't know – I hadn't seen him before.'

'Tell me as much about him as you can.'

The boy was getting tired and squirmed again, looking beseechingly at his mother.

'Would you like a ride in a police Range-Rover tomorrow?' Carrick said casually.

Jamie's eyes shone. 'Over the high bridge at Bristol?'

'If that's what you want. Now, tell me about the man you saw.'

'He wasn't as big as you. He had a tracksuit on with the hood up. It was dark.'

'The tracksuit was dark?'

'Yes, and it was dark where I saw him. I couldn't see any more.'

'Are you sure the hood was up? Couldn't it have just been his dark hair?'

'No, 'cause his head was sort of funny-shaped – as though he had no neck.'

'Was he carrying anything?'

'A plastic bag. Like you get from the shops. There wasn't much in it, though.'

'Are you sure it was a man? Could it have been a woman?'

'No. Women have big bottoms.'

'Jamie!' his mother exclaimed.

'A very observant lad,' Carrick said to her, smiling broadly. 'Thank you, Jamie, that was extremely helpful. I'll arrange the jaunt for you tomorrow.'

They left, both silent with their own thoughts as they walked the length of the terrace.

'I thought you were going to see Mallory,' Joanna said all at once, jolting him back to reality. He didn't feel too good.

'I am. Merely escorting you back to your car first.'

'Is this person Jamie saw of any significance, do you think?'

'It might be the man you saw later on, after the murder.'

'Yes, I know it's possible. But Jamie saw him leaving the building and I saw someone leaving the square. As far as I could see he wasn't carrying anything. And Jamie's man might have had *long* dark hair.'

'If it was the murderer he would hardly go straight in through his own front door afterwards. I intend to check in a minute whether you can get round the back of North Terrace from Oliver Road.'

'You can. You can get round the back of everywhere. Lanes run from both Oliver Road and Nash Street and they connect with each other.'

'I'll take your word for it. I've just remembered, I haven't a torch with me.' By the car he said, 'Are you going straight home?'

'I'm going to the hospital first, to see how Lance is.'

'Give him my regards.'

'Yes, I will. Thank you. James. . . .'

'Yes?'

'I think you ought to take Bob Ingrams with you when you interview Mallory. Especially if he's thick as thieves with Benny Cooper.'

'He's gone home sick feeling rather sorry for himself,' Carrick said sadly. 'Someone punched him on the nose.'

Joanna spent about a quarter of an hour with Lance. He was still unable to speak to her but looked better and was able to communicate by writing on a pad she held steady for him. His only worry was that his flat might be broken into – he had some very expensive computer and hi-fi equipment – so she promised to contact a neighbour of his who had a key and ask him to keep an eye on the place.

On impulse and troubled by vague, formless worries, she drove back via Royal Crescent. By this time it was just after eight o'clock. Carrick's car was still there.

The sounds of tortured catgut, racked clarinets and howling percussion greeted Carrick as he climbed the stairs of 3 North Terrace to the first floor. He was tired and light-headed with hunger, for there had not been time to eat since the two slices of toast and coffee that he had called breakfast. It was possible that Mrs Pryce had climbed these same stairs the previous night and not descended them alive. But there was nothing to connect Mallory with her death, Carrick had no grounds for requesting a search warrant and no one had seen the deceased anywhere near North Terrace that night. During the first routine enquiries Mallory had been quite helpful in his manner, if infuriatingly condescending.

And yet. . . .

Somehow, in his heart of hearts, Carrick knew she had been there. Finding evidence and proving it was quite another matter.

The music was loud but apparently not set at such a volume that Mallory could not hear the doorbell. 'I was expecting you,' he said, making a play of peering at the warrant car. 'Come in.'

The large living room was like a cave filled with whirling light and noise, the lights moving in time to the music, an acid-house party set to the wrong tunes. Not all the lights moved; some were white and stared relentlessly at pictures of women on the walls, photographs of naked women in the kind of poses that left nothing to the imagination. They were no more explicit than the pictures in magazines that could be bought in most newsagents, but in that setting the effect was powerful.

'That's Sandy,' Mallory said, turning down the music just a little and waving a hand at one picture. 'Juicy, eh? Tickle her fanny for five minutes and she's anyone's.'

Carrick now realised that they were not alone in the room.

'You know Benny, don't you?' Mallory went on. 'He helped me set this up.'

Cooper stood up. 'Inspector Carrick, no less. What can I get you to drink?'

'Nothing, thanks,' Carrick replied. 'I'd like to ask Mr Mallory a few questions.' Like the archetypal plod of detective fiction, he thought savagely. Just as they had intended.

'I was going to pop into your office tomorrow and check progress with this dreadful affair,' Cooper went on smoothly. 'Is an arrest imminent?'

'You know I never discuss cases with you,' Carrick said. He turned his back on Cooper to discover that Mallory had a huge grin on his face. Carrick wanted to wipe the smile off so badly that sweat broke out on his forehead from repressed fury. 'Mr Mallory, what do you do for a living?'

'I'm in publishing,' Mallory answered.

'Are you sure you won't have a drink?' Cooper asked. 'Whisky? There's a Blair Athol eight-year-old single malt in the cupboard.'

'I'm conducting a *murder* enquiry,' Carrick said through his teeth without turning.

Mallory threw himself into a chair, face contorted with mock contrition. 'Give it a rest, Benny. The man's working while we're at play.'

Facing Mallory, Carrick was not spared the blatant message reaching out to him with parted lips and thighs from the walls. By now, for the room was overwarm and there was a strange smell that cloyed in his throat, the sweat was trickling down his back, soaking into his shirt in clammy waves. He swallowed hard and fixed his gaze unwaveringly on the man in the chair opposite him.

'Did you go out last night?'

'No, I was here all evening.'

'Playing music?'

'Yes. Up until about eleven thirty, that is. Then I went to bed.'

'Did you have any visitors?'

'No. No one.'

'Someone of your description left the building by the back way at a little after ten.'

'It wasn't me. And what the hell would I go out the back way for when my car's parked at the front?'

'So you didn't go out the back earlier today when you saw Sergeant Ingrams and me coming over?'

Mallory's pale face coloured; Carrick saw this even through the mind-bending light display. 'No.'

'My mistake,' Carrick said. 'I could have sworn I saw a face at the window.'

'You have to be careful about these things, Inspector,' Cooper drawled from the rear.

Doggedly, Carrick said, 'Had Mrs Pryce ever complained about the loudness of your music?'

'Yes, as a matter of fact she did.'

'When?'

'I'm not sure exactly. Perhaps a few weeks ago. Yes, it was when the weather was very hot and I had the windows open. Then.'

'She was killed by a single blow to the back of the head. Tell me, are you right or left-handed?'

'Don't answer,' Cooper grated. 'You're under no obligation to do so.'

Carrick swung round to him, a manoeuvre that made him dizzy. 'All you're achieving is making him look guilty.'

'I'm left-handed,' Mallory said. 'What of it?'

'So,' Carrick said, suddenly realising that Mallory was being hoist with his own petard, a set of strobe lights repeatedly flashing past his eyes, 'she came up here last night because she was sick to death of this unholy racket and you, because you were either drunk or high after smoking pot – as you have been tonight – grabbed the first thing that came to hand and bashed her head in.'

'No!' Mallory yelled. 'Benny, get this damned idiot out of here.'

'Shut your mouth!' Cooper told him viciously. Then, more quietly, 'It doesn't do to get really offensive with the bill, Paul. You aren't thinking straight. You're upset.'

'Are you worried I might get a search warrant?' Carrick asked Mallory silkily. He felt as though he was swaying on his feet but did not believe it. God, he needed a drink.

'You have no grounds,' Cooper said as though talking to a backward child.

'He's scared,' Carrick said and because of the offerings of Humpleschlacht what he was saying went no farther than Cooper's ears. '*Shitless*. He's got his fingers in your dirty little pie, hasn't he? And when I want him I'll come and get him and the spineless little sod will need no persuading at all to sell you right down the river.'

'Carrick, I've warned you before and –'

'Forget that. It's just one of the charges that I'm keeping warm for you. Forget following me, or getting someone else to, hoping that you'll catch me kerb-crawling or up a back alley screwing a tart. Forget looking for me in clubs or strip shows. I don't belong to your world of instant gratification and the cheap fuck.'

Carrick found his own way out. He hadn't meant to say half of it, he hadn't any evidence. And all this was going through his head as he tried to get down the stairs without falling down them. God, that room had been like the torture sequence in *The Ipcress File* when Harry Palmer had driven the nail into his hand to stop the noise and lights brainwashing him. Carrick leaned on a wall for quite a while.

Outside, on the pavement, he knew he was going to throw up; there were odd booming sounds in his ears and a sort of grey fuzz in front of his eyes. Bile shot into the back of his throat.

Then a strong grip claimed him and steered him remorselessly round onto a rough path and behind a bush. The grip held steady, supporting him while he retched helplessly. At last, he was able to stand upright.

'I've been Humpleschlachted,' he said weakly to his rescuer.

'Rubbish!' said Joanna briskly. 'I know what men look like when they live on whisky and no food.'

By the time they reached their parked cars, Carrick was sufficiently recovered to drive the short distance home. He was followed all the way, the twin headlights in his mirror somehow reproachful. Confound you, he thought, you'll come in and cook my dinner and stand over me while I eat it. Women were like that. But, come to think of it, she had never shown any disturbing signs of domesticity before.

What actually happened was that he cooked dinner for them both while she stood over him, they both ate like horses and then his guest departed, tranquilly wishing him good night. Grimly, Carrick washed up and then fell into bed to sleep like the proverbial log.

Strangely, they had hardly exchanged a word.

Five minutes before St Margaret's church clock was due to strike three, Tommy lurched round the corner from Oliver Road into Beckford Square. He sang a little song under his breath and endeavoured to perform a few dance steps. But no one was in sight to appreciate his efforts so he desisted. For a moment he leaned on some railings. He was exhausted.

'Three more days,' he muttered, hanging on the railings like so many rags.

He pushed himself upright and plodded round the back of West Terrace. There was hazy moonlight but if necessary he could find his way home in the dark, he knew every inch of the place. There were parts of the building that he did not venture into at all, it was too dangerous; floors and ceilings sagging, just waiting to crash down. It was a miracle that none of the local plods had been killed, the way they'd blundered about the place.

By the back door through which he gained entry he stopped. There was no question of absent-mindedness on his part, he *had* tapped back the nails as he always did when he had left earlier. The planks were now loose and had been wrenched farther away from the frame.

Someone had been inside.

He was not unduly disturbed for sometimes children would get in to explore. It was one of the reasons he fastened up when he left, to keep them out. He did not want to be responsible for a child's death. Nevertheless he was very cautious as he went in, groping on the shelf for the candle and matches he used to light his way around the lower floors. He had a torch as well but hid it carefully.

Warily, he lit the candle and made his way to where he had hidden the torch, in a larder just off the kitchen. The batteries were running a bit low but enabled him to see well enough. There was a cupboard under the stairs and the door to it was open. Tommy stood very still, a feeling like ice in his stomach.

He did not have to go any farther in the direction of the cupboard to know that the girl with red hair, dumped inside, was definitely dead.

# Chapter Nine

'Her name was Susan Fairbrother, sir,' Sergeant Ingrams reported, speaking quietly. Ingrams had done some hard thinking over the past few hours and come to the conclusion that although he disliked Carrick intensely, a feeling that he was sure the Inspector reciprocated, there was a job to do. And right now he was handling his boss with uncharacteristic sensitivity, for on beholding the body for the first time Carrick has almost fainted.

The girl was lying face down in a slightly curving position, one knee drawn up, the wonderful red hair spilling over the floor in a silken cascade. Ingrams had found himself holding his breath when she had eventually been turned over, revealing that she had been lying on her handbag and also that the body was not that of the girl with the devastating right hook.

'Does it look as though anything was stolen from her bag?' Carrick asked. He had known it was not Joanna before he had gazed down on the dead face. She had never worn this sort of clothes or high-heeled shoes with the backs scuffed and worn. The hands, too, could not have been Joanna's; the nails were bitten right down to the quick, and the right hand had some kind of purple birthmark on the back. But when he had first seen that hair. . . .

'There's no purse or chequebook,' Ingrams reported, still going through the bag. 'Her name was on a couple of library tickets – if they're hers, that is.'

'Why the hell was she dragged in here? To make it look as though Tommy had killed her?'

'Didn't he? It looks as though she was definitely killed inside the building. I had a quick look round before you arrived – there are signs of a struggle in the room next on the right.'

'Are you holding him?'

'Too right. He's in a van outside.'

'Who called the police?' Carrick asked wearily.

'Well – well, I think he did.'

'Perhaps you'd be so good as to go and have him released. I'll talk to him here.'

Lights had been rigged up in the downstairs rooms. Rather than dispelling the horror of a corpse in a darkened building, the illumination somehow heightened it, the glare revealing cobwebs moving as though ghostly hands were brushing through them and walls and ceilings stained with moulds and fungi.

'Any evidence so far?' Carrick asked Ingrams when he returned, raised voices in his wake.

'One good footprint over by the wall in the next room, sir. There's a lot of disturbance in the dirt and dust on the floor, of course, but one clear footprint, a size eight or nine, I'd say, made by a plain-soled shoe. That does let the tramp out – he's wearing filthy old trainers.'

The pathologist, John Butler, emerged from the cupboard, puffing and blowing. 'Confounded knees.' He glanced up to see Carrick and Ingrams standing a few yards away. 'She was strangled, about two hours ago. But put up a good fight – there are marks all over her where he knocked her about. Heaven forfend that I should teach you your job but that might mean that you're not looking for a big strong man. I'll tell you if there are any similarities with the first murder. I don't know what our lovely city's coming to – two murders in so many days. This square is a gloomy hole if you ask me – should have been demolished years ago. Neither Wood nor his son had anything to do with it. Did you know that?' And with that he stumped out.

'Architects,' Carrick explained, seeing Ingram's puzzlement. 'John Wood the Younger designed Royal Crescent and Brock Street which links it to the Circus – the work of his father. Beckford Square came afterwards – I'm not sure who the architect was.'

'Next time I'll mind my own business,' Tommy shouted to someone to his rear as he shambled up. 'You want me?' he said to Carrick.

'Did you go in any of the other rooms?'

'Tonight? No.'

'Take a look at her, Tommy. Tell me if you've seen her around here.'

Tommy looked surprised. 'So it's not the lovely bit of crackling who called in to see me?'

'You know it isn't.'

'Sorry, guv,' Tommy said quietly.

Together he and Carrick went to where the body lay.

'She worked over at the nursing home,' Tommy said after several long moments had elapsed. 'Nursing assistant or maid, something like that. I don't know her name, of course. Nice girl – she was sometimes in the kitchen when I was given something to eat.'

'According to library tickets in her bag, her name was Susan Fairbrother.'

'That other girl – Mackenzie. She didn't say so but something tells me that she might have been around when the old woman was killed. And now this. A case of mistaken identity?'

'It *had* occurred to me.' Carrick beckoned to a constable standing looking as though he had nothing to do. 'Go over to the nursing home in East Terrace and knock them up. Ask to speak to the matron, Mrs Lang. Tell her what's happened and that I'll be over directly.'

'D'you need me any more?' Tommy asked.

'What time was it when you found her?'

'A little after three.'

'And you saw no one on your way who could have come from this building?'

'Not a soul.'

'Okay, you can go.'

'Go I will, guv. Moving out. What down-and-out in his right mind would stay here now?'

'If you like, I'll ask Mrs Lang if there's an outbuilding you can sleep in over there.'

'Thanks for the offer but no. People like me have been known to wake up with knives in their ribs if they're even in spitting distance of the fuzz, and you lot are going to be crawling all over this square for days.' He gathered his tattered coat around himself and made as if to leave but, seeing Ingrams, said, 'Dear oh dearie me, officer. It looks as though someone socked you on the conk. I wonder who that could have been?'

'Sod off, you filthy little git,' Ingrams snapped, 'or I'll run you in for being a public nuisance.'

'A nice warm cell for the rest of the night.' Tommy sighed. 'What a shame!' He wandered away, shaking his head sorrowfully.

'God, he stinks,' Ingrams said, nostrils flared.

Carrick gave permission for the ambulance men who were waiting to take the body away and he and Ingrams crossed the square, leaving the scene-of-crime team to go over the rooms inch by inch to try to piece together what had happened.

Mrs Lang was getting dressed and would be down directly. She came down the main staircase moments after Carrick and Ingrams had been given the information by the constable.

'I was awake,' the matron said. 'I heard all the vehicles arriving. It's so quiet here normally.'

Carrick supposed that people in the nursing profession, like police officers working for the CID, had to cultivate the ability to be instantly awake. He apologised for having to disturb her and broke the news.

'Susan! Oh, no! I simply can't believe it. Are you absolutely sure?'

'According to a couple of library tickets found in a handbag that was with the body. Will you describe the girl, please, Mrs Lang?'

'Oh, dear,' said Mrs Lang. 'This is ghastly. She was about five feet seven inches in height and had long red hair that she usually wore in a ponytail when she was working. Yes, and there was a scar or birthmark on the back of her right hand – I've never liked to ask her about it.'

'Then there's no doubt,' Carrick said. 'Who is her next of kin?'

'Her parents. They live in York – that's why Susan lived in. Frankly, I prefer the single girls who work here to live on the premises, especially when they're only young.'

'How old was she?'

'Nineteen. Oh, my goodness, I shall have to break the news to her parents. She's an only child. What a terrible tragedy for them!'

'It would be better if you spoke to them rather than the local police calling round. Mrs Lang, I was wondering if you would formally identify the body.'

'Yes, I will. Especially if it saves her parents the task. They're rather elderly and none too strong, from what Susan told me. Do you want me to come now?'

'No. Some time mid-morning will do. I'll give you a ring if I may. Tell me, do you know if she was with anyone tonight?'

'I'm not sure but I think the girls off duty were going to a dance at the Assembly Rooms. Susan wasn't on duty tonight so it's possible she went. I can easily find out for you by talking to the others.'

'It's all right. I'll have to talk to everyone to discover her movements. Do you know if she was on duty on Friday night?'

Mrs Lang frowned. 'Do you mind coming to my office? The duty rosters are on my desk.'

The office was only next door. Monica Lang switched on a light and picked up a thick exercise book. 'As you probably appreciate, the care has to be round the clock. A couple of the old gentlemen here have a very tenacious hold on life but it's all willpower, Inspector, there's no real medical reason why they're still alive. Here we are. Yes, Susan was on duty.'

'Have you any idea at all what she was actually doing between about eleven fifteen to a quarter to midnight?'

Monica Lang sat in the chair behind her desk. 'That's rather difficult without talking to the night sister. Susan wasn't an SRN, you understand, she wasn't qualified to give medical attention. But most of our patients' needs don't come into that category. They want cocoa if they can't sleep, or wish to be assisted to the toilet, or perhaps simply want their pillows shaken and someone to talk to for a few minutes. If Susan was working at night, those would be her duties. During the day she changed beds, helped some of the more infirm to eat their meals and generally fetched and carried.' She picked up the phone. 'I can find out for you straight away.'

In an undertone Ingrams said, 'You're trying to find out if the girl came face to face with Mrs Pryce's killer?'

'Yes, but that would only have happened if the murderer works here and she saw him come in with blood on his clothes or whatever. We already know that she was on duty so it's unlikely that she would have been out in the square. I'm just trying to narrow down the options.'

'She might have seen what went on from a window.'

'That too. But the vital thing, don't forget – if the theory is to hold water – is that he saw *her*. Get some people over here, will you? We'll talk to all the staff now.'

'There was a small emergency,' Mrs Lang said, putting down the phone. 'One of the patients soiled his bed and Susan was involved with bathing him and remaking the bed.'

'Whereabouts would that have been?'

'On the second floor. In a suite of rooms at the back.'

'Is that anywhere near a staircase that other members of staff might use, having just entered the building?'

'No, not really. But she would have had to go to the linen room. That is.'

'Did Susan have a boyfriend?'

'No one that she spoke about to me. That's something else you'll have to ask the others about.'

'I'm sorry but I'll have to ask you if there are any members of staff, male, whom you're not happy about.'

'No, no one,' she answered immediately. 'I have a very good team.'

'Have you had occasion to fire anyone recently?'

'No. I know what you're getting at. The only men here are Danny, the porter, who has been here for twenty years, and Chris, a student who helps in the kitchen. We have a succession of students, both male and female. Most of them seem to be studying to be nuclear scientists and dreadfully difficult things like that. I make it perfectly clear to all of them that work is on offer, not skylarking and sex – if they want that they can go and work in a pub or club. Don't get me wrong, this is a happy place. Or was,' she finished by saying sadly.

'Thank you,' Carrick said. 'We'll try not to disturb your old gentlemen.' By the door he paused. 'How's Doolally?'

Monica Lang's face broke into a smile. 'Almost recovered. I might get him back on Monday.'

'You really think Mrs Pryce poisoned him?'

'He vomited a piece of meat that *I* hadn't fed to him. Fresh meat – what looked like a piece of steak. The vet had it analysed and there were traces of the sort of poison that gamekeepers use on bait to kill foxes.'

'Strychnine?'

'I believe so.'

Where would she have obtained that from? Carrick wondered. Well, her nephew did live next door to a farm.

No one, it appeared, had seen Susan Fairbrother that evening. She had not gone to the dance, although she had initially shown interest in buying a ticket. Saturday had been her day off and she had not been due to resume her duties until two o'clock on Sunday afternoon. This much was established during the staff interviews which followed, Carrick utilising his technique commonly referred to as 'saturation bombing', flooding the establishment with all available personnel to conduct interviews in the shortest possible time. Often, this provided useful information very rapidly. Not on this occasion, however.

At seven on that Sunday morning, Carrick and Ingrams left, the latter with orders to go home and rest for a few hours. Both his eyes were now blackening noticeably, but he felt a little better.

Neither of them was aware that Tommy watched them from his old haunt on the second floor of West Terrace. He had returned when the police had left. Home was home, after all, and it was only for another three days.

Carrick had every intention of going to his office to note down certain points and theories while they were still fresh in his mind. He was used to talking things out with his assistants but Ingrams, in addition to feeling slightly unwell at present, was not, frankly, of the calibre that Carrick had been fortunate enough to acquire before. He wanted, desperately, to share his thoughts.

He couldn't manage without her after all.

He was not even admitting to himself the real need, the overwhelming yearning that was the underlying reason why he drove past his own home and stopped outside a house half a mile up Landsdown Hill. But it was no surprise to the girl who answered the door. She had been hoping, for several good reasons, that matters would progress precisely along these lines.

'I told him,' Carrick said after the first few seconds' silent appraisal of one another.

'Cooper?' Joanna asked, slipping off her cotton dressing gown.

He kissed her avidly. 'Mallory is involved in Cooper's sideline.'

'Is that why he Humpleschlachted you?' she asked, smiling.

Common sense broke through for a moment. 'I mean it, Joanna. Mallory's flat is full of porn. Cooper was *there*. Mallory had got him along to hold his hand.'

Joanna divested herself of her silk pyjamas, removed his jacket and thereafter James Carrick's common sense deserted him. She had no fears. Desperate he might be but, as before, there was consideration and, after the first wild coupling, tenderness. She kept him with her all that day, despite his protests that he ought to be at work – he had not yet told her why. They slept, made love again, and at last he opened his eyes and gazed upon her, smiling self-consciously, and was at peace.

'Joanna, is it possible that the person you saw leaving the square saw *you*?'

'Yes, he did. I remembered afterwards. I meant to tell you.'

That night the Reverend Harold Forbes had a dream in which the Chantbury Pyx was cast into a bottomless pool in a pagan temple.

# Chapter Ten

On Monday morning Miss Braithewaite came to a decision. Certainly, something had to be done, she could not eat or sleep for the worry of it. She had never in her whole life had such a burden on her mind and she knew that if she did nothing about it her health would break down. It had been all she could do not to blurt out her wretchedness to the pleasant woman police constable who had come to ask her questions following another dreadful murder the previous day.

Miss Braithewaite dressed suitably, putting on the small blue straw hat which she knew looked well and which she hoped would give her confidence, then gazed around sadly at her home and went out. Truly, nothing would ever be the same again, nothing in fact had been sane and normal since the night Mrs Pryce had died.

'I should like to see Inspector Carrick,' she said in a low voice as she placed her bag, clutched in gloved hands, on the reception desk at the Manvers Street police station.

'I'm afraid he's not here just at the moment, madam,' said the duty sergeant, Woods. 'Can I help you at all?'

'If you don't mind, I would far rather speak to Inspector Carrick,' whispered Miss Braithewaite, her courage ebbing fast.

He leaned both arms on the desk and spoke equally quietly. 'Is it really important?' Many old and well-intentioned ladies sought to talk to CID officers about lost dogs – or lost causes, for that matter.

'Very.'

'Give me *some* idea and then I can contact him if necessary,' Woods said patiently.

'It's about Mrs Pryce's murder.'

'Thank you,' he responded briskly. After taking her name he directed her to a waiting area, a few chairs set at the side of a wide corridor.

Gingerly, she sat next to a youth with rings in his nose, his hair dyed green with bright pink stripes running from his forehead to the nape of his neck. There was no choice in the matter, for an immensely fat woman took up three of the chairs with herself and several carrier bags full of shopping. She wore a long, grubby cotton dress, once pleated, now shapeless, that looked as though it might have been bought at a jumble sale. Miss Braithewaite, after one horrified glance, tried not to look in the woman's direction at all, for it appeared that beneath the dress she wore nothing what-soever, the thin fabric clinging to her enormous breasts and, damply, to her tree-trunk thighs. She sat, legs spread apart, fanning herself with a newspaper. Then, she spoke.

'Bleedin' 'ot, ain't it?'

Ethel Braithewaite agreed that it was.

'We'll have thunder next, you mark my words. If there's one thing I can't abide it's thunder. Me and the dog go and hide under the bed together – he can't stand it either.'

'There's nothing to be frightened of, really,' Miss Braithewaite offered tentatively, wondering about the prac-ticalities of what she had been told.

'Don't you believe it,' the woman said scornfully. 'My uncle Josh was killed by lightning. He 'ad a few too many one night and fell asleep on the hearth rug. Lightning came right down the chimney, struck the grate and blew it clean into the room. Stove 'is 'ead in somethink 'orrible. Auntie Vi was never right afterwards.'

The youth snickered, and received a shove that almost pitched him onto the floor.

'You can shut your filthy little trap too. If it wasn't for you behaving like a bleedin' tomcat I wouldn't be sitting here now.'

Miss Braithewaite was saved from further family history by Woods calling out to her, 'Inspector Carrick won't be long, if you'd care to wait through here.'

He led the way down another corridor and showed her into a room. It was furnished with only a bare table and two

98

wooden chairs. She sat on one of them after the door had closed, hoping that the choking feeling did not mean that she was about to be ill. A couple of minutes later, when one of her little white pills had taken effect and she was feeling much better, she realised that this was precisely how it should be. There were even bars on the dirty wired-glass windows. Echoing footsteps came and went along the corridor outside. This is what prison must be like, she thought. The officer at the desk, not a young man, had known she had something to hide or was mad, or both, that was why he had shut her in here. Policemen must have a wonderful intuition about people's characters.

After an eternity had gone by, probably only ten minutes, the door opened and Carrick came in. Miss Braithewaite hoped that her surprise did not show as she beheld a man seemingly five years younger than when she had last seen him. How old was he now? she found herself wondering. Yes, thirty.

'Woods said that he'd rescued you from rather alarming company,' Carrick said, pulling up a chair. 'We could go in my office but Sergeant Ingrams is on the phone in there. Now, Miss Braithewaite, what can I do for you?'

She took a deep breath. 'This is all such a shame, Inspector,' she began in a whisper. She had not intended to speak thus but her throat was suddenly very dry. 'What I mean is, you've been so kind. But I'm afraid I've come to confess.'

Carrick sat down. 'Confess?' He was never to know how grateful she was that he had not smiled patronisingly upon her.

'I killed Mrs Pryce.'

'Ah,' Carrick murmured. 'And I'll be honest with you. I was going to come and see you this morning.'

'You *knew*?'

'That something was really worrying you, yes.'

'I . . . I think you're the first person I've ever lied to in my life, Inspector.'

He had difficulty in making sense of this for, by this time, Miss Braithewaite was in tears. He gave her his clean handkerchief, excused himself and went out for a couple of minutes, leaving the door ajar. When he returned he brought a tray with two cups of coffee and a plateful of toasted teacakes, thickly buttered. He even remembered a knife to enable his guest to cut hers into polite-sized pieces and a paper napkin.

'You haven't had any breakfast,' Carrick said. 'Neither have I.' And when she gazed at him in amazement, he added, 'I'm a seventh child of a seventh child so I *know*.' He placed one of the cups of coffee before her and a plate.

In spite of everything she said, 'I rather thought you were an only child.'

He smiled, an eyebrow quirked. 'I am. Now, drink that coffee while it's hot and then tell me about it.'

Miss Braithewaite began straight away. 'Mrs Pryce came to my flat that night saying that she had knocked on Mr Mallory's door to complain about the noise but either it was so loud that he couldn't hear or he was ignoring her. She wanted me to bang on the floor with a broom or something. I refused because, for one thing, all the rooms but the kitchen are carpeted. We had an argument and I said things I shouldn't have done. I accused her of delighting in making trouble and of assuming she had some kind of right to say offensive things to people. She tried to force her way in to bang on the floor herself. I was very annoyed with her by this time and also rather frightened. She was beside herself – I've thought since that she might have been drinking. Her nasty clinging fingers were hurting my arm as I tried to stop her coming in. So I gave her a big push – we were standing near the top of the stairs by that time. Then I ran back inside. She must have fallen down the stairs. I was too frightened to go back outside and look. I killed her, Inspector.'

Carrick swallowed the piece of teacake that was in his mouth and said, 'Eat something. Drink your coffee.'

The ex-schoolmistress did as she was told, feeling too weak and shaky to do otherwise.

'There are certain aspects of the case that haven't been made public knowledge,' he continued gravely. 'No matter. What time was it when she rang your bell?'

'At half past eleven. I did stay up late – there was an opera on BBC 2. It was just finishing, actually, so perhaps it was a few minutes earlier than that. I was rather annoyed at missing the very end.'

'Could you hear Mallory's music above the sound of your TV?'

'Yes, during the quiet passages.'

'What did Mrs Pryce say when you opened the door?'

'She shouted at me. Something like "Something's got to be done about him! Get a broom. I'll show him what noise means. I'll teach him not to answer the door."'

'And?'

'I refused. I don't do things like banging on floors. All I wanted to do was see the end of my opera. So she said she'd do it if I wouldn't. She called me a silly old ninny and tried to push her way in.'

'She was really agitated, then?'

'Very. I've never seen anyone so unreasonable and rude.'

'And you tried to bar her way?'

'Yes. We sort of jostled in the doorway. She hung onto me in a frightening way. I managed to push her backwards out onto the landing. But she still hung on – she was very strong.'

'Was she saying anything while this was going on?'

'I think we both were. Things like, "Let go. Don't be silly."'

'So by the time you managed to shake her off you were both near the top of the stairs.'

'Yes, but neither of us, I think, realised how close we were. And when I gave her this big push. . . .'

'Take your time,' Carrick said gently. 'This is very important. Did you actually *see* her fall?'

'No. But I saw her overbalance as I turned to run back into my flat. I was absolutely terrified by what I had done.'

'Did you hear anything? Her bumping down the stairs? Screams?'

'No. Nothing. But I think she hit her head on the wall as she overbalanced. I can't really be sure about that now. I'm a coward, I know, but she was so strong and I was scared too that she'd run after me and hit me or something.'

'But that would be unlikely if she'd fallen down the stairs.'

Miss Braithewaite drank a little more coffee.

Carrick was staring at her intently. 'Think very carefully. As you ran back into your flat, what was the real fear uppermost in your mind? That she had fallen down the stairs

101

and was seriously hurt or had merely overbalanced, banging her head on the wall, and was right on your heels, bent on revenge?'

'But she was killed! She had dreadful head injuries and was found in the garden! She must have dragged herself there and –'

'Answer the question,' Carrick ordered bleakly.

Anything to gain respite from those icy blue eyes. 'I ran back in and slammed the door because I thought she'd hurt me. But I was wrong, wasn't I? She couldn't possibly have been after me.'

'Do you possess a hammer?'

'Yes, just a small one. I use it when I put my pictures up.'

'Where is it kept?'

'In a drawer in the kitchen together with a few other tools. Why do you ask?'

He ignored the question. 'Did you see anyone else on the stairs?'

'No. No one.'

'Sounds of footsteps? Doors closing?'

'No.'

'You didn't kill her, Miss Braithewaite. She had a small bruise on her temple but the injuries that proved fatal had not resulted from falling down the stairs.'

'But I *must* have been instrumental in her death.'

'No. Not even that. I can't charge you with acting in self-defence. What I can tell you, and I'm sure you'll keep it in strict confidence, is that she *had* been drinking. I'm sure that so unpleasant a woman sober must have been extremely frightening when angry and a little drunk.'

Tears of relief brimmed in Miss Braithewaite's eyes.

'All I wish is that you'd told me this before.'

'I'm sorry,' Miss Braithewaite said stiffly.

He smiled. 'Do you have any friends or relatives you could visit for a short while?'

'You want me to go away?'

'I think you need a break.'

'Well, I could go and see my sister in Cornwall, I suppose. She's always nagging me to visit her.'

'One thing before you go. What do you make of Bethany Cryon?'

She knew it was impolite but helped herself to the last piece of teacake. 'I've never actually been in her flat, you understand, Inspector. She doesn't want visitors. But I take up little bits of baking and they always seem very welcome. She's a very strange woman, though. The only time I've seen her smile is when I gave her a syrup tart. Most effusive with her thanks. Not many women have such a sweet tooth.'

'And the boyfriend?'

'The kind of man whom maiden ladies have nightmares about.' Struck by a thought, she actually waggled a finger at him. 'Don't misunderstand me, I'm not narrow-minded by any means. Maiden ladies have plenty of dreams about men that aren't nightmares at all. But that man is violent, a thug, the kind who would be involved with rape and pillage.'

He could do with her on his team, Carrick thought as he showed her out. She was one of the Miss Marples of the world, a rare and dying breed.

'Right!' he said loudly, bursting into his office and making Ingrams and a WPC, whom he had been endeavouring to charm for days, start guiltily. 'We have a breakthrough, a witness, Miss Braithewaite, no less, who now has admitted that Mrs Pryce called on her at just before eleven thirty on Friday, having failed to gain entry to Paul Mallory's flat. The ladies tussled and Mrs Pryce, it seems, banged her head on the wall at the top of the stairs. I think that then, even more furious, she went back downstairs and forced Mallory to answer the door. Has anything happened since we started to watch the place?'

'No, sir,' Ingrams said. 'At least, not what you were hoping for. No one has attempted to remove any boxes or so forth from the flat.'

'All the better. We'll go and grill him medium rare.'

Ingrams cleared his throat. 'Have you seen the paper this morning, sir?'

'No.'

The sergeant gestured towards Carrick's desk. 'I bought a copy. I think you ought to see it.'

Slowly, Carrick went across and picked it up.

The article was not particularly libellous as such things go. Benedict Cooper had written a fairly accurate account of events over the past few days concerning the murders in Beckford Square, embellishing it with such headlines as WILL THE BEAST STRIKE AGAIN? and, over the page, POLICE NO NEARER FINDING THE KILLER. The story mentioned the name of the officer in charge of the investigation, adding that he was 'Scotch' (which of course is whisky or tape but not people) and had had plenty of experience finding murderers in his native land. (Carrick had come south just after his tenth birthday.) Cooper somehow suggested that Carrick's very uncouthness might be a little misplaced in such a refined city as Bath and perhaps the case might be solved more quickly if the Bristol CID were brought in. The story also hinted in the most careful way that the Inspector's efficiency might be impaired by the death of his wife some months previously, not to mention losing his sergeant Joanna Mackenzie, dismissed from the force for improper conduct.

'She wasn't,' Carrick said.

'I know,' Ingrams replied, knowing precisely what Carrick was referring to. 'She can sue.'

Carrick dropped the newspaper into the wastepaper basket.

'Be careful, sir,' Ingrams risked.

'You think it's a warning?'

Ingrams opened the door and shooed out the WPC. 'Can he really do you harm?'

'All clever journalists can do harm. To anyone. He can swear on oath that I accepted bribes, had him done over, threatened his friends. Make no mistake about it, Cooper's *bent*.'

'We'd better tread lightly with Mallory then.'

'That's what Cooper wants. Mallory might be a murderer or he might not. What I really want to know is why Cooper's bothering with him. And in view of the fact that Mallory's pretty stupid it can only be because of one thing – money.'

Joanna also had a visitor that morning. She was very surprised to see a clergyman coming up the stairs as she left her office en route to the kitchen at the back.

Still ascending, the priest said, 'I'm all too aware that I should have contacted you by telephone first. Many apologies. But I was passing. Perhaps I may make an appointment.'

104

'We're terribly chaotic at the moment,' Joanna said. 'Mr Tyler's been involved in a road accident and is in hospital. I really can't take on any more work just now.'

'What a blow! Never mind. I suppose you wouldn't know of another firm I could contact?'

There was something familiar about the man. 'Have we met before?' Joanna asked. 'I feel sure that I know your face.'

He beamed. 'It's quite possible we've met but I know you're not a member of my congregation. My name is Harold Forbes.'

'The Chantbury Pyx! You had your picture in the paper. Please come up.'

Obviously delighted, he followed her into the office. 'I've been on to the insurance company and they're perfectly happy for me to hire private detectives. Such is the value of the Pyx that even if your fees amount to a considerable sum it will have saved them a great deal of money. And I assure you I've been in touch with the organisers of the exhibition who also had the Pyx insured and they've told me to go ahead and –'

'You want *me* to find the Pyx?' Joanna said. She did not usually interrupt clergymen in mid-sentence.

'But yes! I'm more than aware that the police are fully stretched with these awful murders – I really don't know what Bath is coming to. At one time . . . No, I must not digress, it's a very bad habit of mine.'

Joanna sat him down and gave him some coffee, her brain in overdrive. She had told Carrick that under no circumstances could she go away on holiday, not with Lance in hospital. The business would simply fold. Carrick's theory that Susan Fairbrother had been killed because Mrs Pryce's murderer had seen a red-haired woman watching him did not warrant such evasive action. Unless he obtained very good evidence that gave credence to his ideas, she did not want a minder either, bound to be, as she had put it, 'an oafish rookie as big as a barn door and wearing size eleven Doc Martens'.

She said, 'I'm afraid it isn't just going to be a matter of tracking down a local thief and finding the Pyx hidden in a cardboard box under his bed. It's quite likely that it's been spirited abroad by now.'

'Oh, dear. Such a thing hadn't occurred to me. But surely, it's so well known that it would be recognised immediately someone tried to sell it?'

'Yes, but some collectors don't buy the things they really want, they arrange to have them stolen.'

'Stolen to *order*?'

Joanna nodded. 'And probably not seen for many years, remaining hidden in the house of a collector in, say Japan or the States.'

Earnestly, the Reverend Forbes said, 'Can you contact the police? Ask them if they've made any progress? I hate to badger people when I know they're worked off their feet but I must confess to feeling a little desperate.'

'Of course.' She reached for the phone. 'Do you have a picture of it? I like to know what I'm talking about.'

After looking in every pocket, the incumbent of Chantbury found a photograph of the Pyx in his wallet, one of the postcards on sale in the church.

'*That* small?' Joanna exclaimed, reading the information on the back. 'Five inches long by three wide? But someone could just put that in their pocket.'

'Alas, yes. You understand that it was only one panel of a pyx, though. The original complete article must have been a very nice little casket.'

Dialling Carrick's number, Joanna had not really expected him to be there, but he answered almost immediately. His tone suggested that he had just been on his way out.

'The Chantbury Pyx,' Joanna said. 'I've the Reverend Forbes with me.'

'You'll have to speak to Sergeant Evans about that – he's handling it at the moment.'

'A little bird told me that due to a chronic shortage of staff you're in overall charge.'

There was rather a long silence on the other end of the line. Then he breathed out hard and said. 'Okay. I take it he's worried, wants a progress report and doesn't like to hound me.'

'Precisely.'

'There's someone coming down from the Met, from the Arts and Antiques Squad. One Sergeant Declan O'Connor.

There might be a link with a big bust they did on a warehouse on Saturday night in Chiswick. They've had someone inside the gang for months, apparently. I'll keep you posted.'

'You mean a link with the Pyx?'

'Yes, it was listed on a suspect's computer.' Carrick said he had to go and rang off.

Having conveyed this information, Joanna said, 'Has anyone ever offered to buy the Pyx?'

'Yes, a Japanese collector showed an interest a few years ago.'

'Did he approach you directly?'

'No, through an agent – an antique dealer here in Bath. A highly reputable one, I must add.'

'Do you mind telling me how much was offered?'

'No figure was mentioned. The discussions never reached that stage. I made it clear that it wasn't mine to dispose of – it belonged to the Church. He politely took no for an answer and went away.'

Joanna requested the name of the dealer and wrote it down. 'I'm not quite sure why the Pyx was stolen from the exhibition and not from your church, where it's been on display for many years with nothing like the security arrangements that there was at the gallery.'

'Publicity, I would have thought, young lady. That is why I do not really suspect the man who made enquiries for his client. We are an obscure little village in a corner of Somerset not visited by many tourists. Only simple souls interested in church architecture and holy works of art would risk the suspension of their vehicles on our lanes. There are no gift shops and the village doesn't even boast a public lavatory. I blame myself alone for the loss of the Pyx – it seemed greedy to keep it all to ourselves. Perhaps we should have obtained permission to sell it and given the money to the poor.'

'Didn't Jesus say that the poor will always be with us?'

The Reverend Forbes gazed at her in surprise. 'Yes, you're right. He did. I wanted to counter local superstition too. People had always said that something dreadful would happen if the Pyx left the church. Ah, well, who's to say?'

'I'll pass on any information that comes my way,' Joanna promised.

'Please do a little quiet checking as well,' the priest requested in a conspiratorial whisper. 'If you can. I have every faith in the police here but the loss of a small piece of church property can hardly take priority over finding murderers. I'll arrange for your expenses to be met as soon as they're incurred.'

He had wished her good day and was on the way out when he said, 'Oh, I almost forgot. Such a shocking memory these days. You might like to talk to one of the security guards. I visited him in hospital and he mentioned that he had remembered a few more details of the robbery. He was hit about the head with the hammer one of them used to break the glass case, you know. Quite dreadful. I'm afraid I've quite forgotten his name.'

# Chapter Eleven

'I've told you three times now,' Paul Mallory protested. 'Mrs Pryce did *not* complain to me on Friday night about the loudness of my music.'

Carrick said, 'A witness has come forward who saw her, upstairs on the second floor, at eleven thirty. She was shouting at Miss Braithewaite that you wouldn't let her in.'

'Well, perhaps I didn't hear the doorbell. It's quite possible during the more robust passages of Humpleschlacht that one wouldn't.'

'Or a bloody airliner crashing on the terrace opposite,' Ingrams remarked sourly.

Carrick was bitterly disappointed. He had thought, remembering all too clearly how Mallory had looked scared witless the last time he had seen him, that as soon as he was confronted with firm evidence he would crack. But he had insisted, ever more loudly, on his innocence. Nothing was the same as it had been on Saturday night, Carrick now realised. Even the pictures of the girls on the walls had lost their power to shock. His own heightened senses had been to blame, that and being exhausted, and the lights and the noise and the fact that the flat had been reeking of pot.

He tried again. 'Did you know Susan Fairbrother?'

'No. I don't think I even clapped eyes on the girl. I'm not here all the time, anyway.'

'So where do you go when you're not here?'

'The same places that other people go,' Mallory replied angrily. 'To the shops, the bank, the hairdresser's, to have something to eat.'

'The other night you told me you were in publishing. What does that entail?'

'I'm a freelance editor. But it's not the sort of thing you'd be able to make sense of,' Mallory said with a sneer. 'It's not a nine-to-five job.'

Carrick turned to Ingrams. 'I'm not sure what *that* is, actually. Do you?'

'Never in a million years, sir,' Ingrams obediently replied.

'Try me,' Carrick said to Mallory. 'I might understand if you speak slowly.'

Mallory had not expected this cutting sarcasm. He also suspected – something to do with the cadence of these last remarks – that Carrick might be Scottish. God, most of them would shove a broken bottle in your face as soon as look at you. (He had not read the article written by Cooper in that morning's *Bath Times*.)

'I work, mostly from home, for a small company. We produce what I suppose you'd call fringe journals. About the arts, music and so forth. Experimental stuff.'

'Hence Humpleschlacht?'

'Yes.'

'Surely that can't be exactly lucrative?'

'Not that it's any of your business,' Mallory countered. 'No. I don't have to support myself. My father gives me an allowance.'

'Lucky for some,' Ingrams mumbled, wandering away to have a look at the pictures.

'Where is this – er – publishing carried out?'

'In Bristol.'

'The address?'

Mallory gave it to him, adding, 'It's down by the docks.'

'I know where it is,' Carrick said peaceably. 'Is Benedict Cooper involved in the firm as well?'

'No, of course not.'

'But he does run a small business?'

'I've no idea.'

'I thought he was a friend of yours.'

'He is but I don't pry into his affairs.'

Carrick gazed around the flat as though seeing it for the first time. 'He helped you set this up, you said. I should be very careful if I were you, Mr Mallory.'

'What the hell do you mean by that?'

'I came to Bath from London. I used to work for the Vice Squad. One night we raided a house in Romford and seized about a ton of pornographic material of a type that raised the eyebrows of even the most hardened members of the team. Videos, magazines, books, films, you name it, it was there. We didn't catch the two men who were renting the house and they had used false names. According to a tip-off from a very reliable source, one of them was Cooper.' Carrick smiled. 'But I think you know all this.'

'You won't pin this murder on me,' Mallory said in a low voice.

'*These* murders,' Carrick corrected. 'I'm fairly sure there's a connection.'

'The Vice Squad,' Mallory jeered. 'Run by a crowd of narrow-minded bigots and maiden aunts, no doubt. Yet as soon as you get here you're the same as the next man and have your hand up the skirt of your little redhead assistant. Handcuff her across your desk, did you?'

For some reason Ingrams, watching Carrick, found himself thinking about spontaneous combustion. But, if anything, it seemed that the reverse might occur, and Carrick, turned to ice, would shiver into a thousand pieces.

'Don't say you weren't warned,' the Inspector said quietly on his way out.

Outside, he leaned on the wall, eyes closed, and said, 'Say something nice to me, Bob.'

It wasn't particularly difficult. 'He was trying to wind you up, sir. Perhaps even hoping that you'd assault him. I don't know how you kept your cool, I really don't. I'd have thumped the bastard.'

'How's the nose?' Carrick asked, straight-faced. But his mind was elsewhere, he was haunted by Jamie's description of the man leaving the building. It had to be Mallory. But where had he been going?

With a heavy heart Jack Moffat took down the key from its hook in the narrow hallway of his house and went out into the square. It was a fine evening, the sunset having left a pink pearly glow in the sky. The sight did nothing to lighten his spirits, however, and he plodded across to the garden, his shoulders a little stooped.

His wife was not well; the whole wretched business of the two deaths had upset her greatly. She was talking of moving house, alarmingly hinting of going on her own if he refused to leave. Alice, he had to admit, had never really settled in Bath and still yearned for her native Welsh valleys. Cities, she had always said, were oppressive. He himself thought the reverse. He had never been a country-lover, preferring the liveliness and bustle of towns. Given half a chance he would return to London. Things happened in London, interesting things, there was always something important going on. The countryside, in his view, was mostly empty and boring. Even more so in the winter; just mud, trees and sheep. Bath had been a compromise – a fine elegant city set in a beautiful landscape. But now everything had gone wrong. First, that miserable old Pryce woman had moved in next door and started to make everyone's life hellish – no wonder someone had lost their temper with her – and then that tramp had sneaked into the boarded-up terrace and had the temerity to live there. That had really worried Alice; she was still fretting about it, couldn't sleep with the thought of someone like that lurking about.

And now there had been another murder . . .

From habit he went into the garden and had a quick look round. That was why he locked up before it was quite dark, so he could see if any litter had been thrown down and pick it up. People were sloppy these days, chucking things about when all they had to do was walk a few yards to a waste bin. Grunting, he stooped to gather up a cigarette packet and then, a few feet from it, an empty beer can. Probably thrown down by that bastard of a tramp, he thought savagely. God, he'd really like to put the frighteners on him so he never returned. Then Alice could relax and wouldn't want to move.

'How the hell did that get in here?' he said out loud, picking up something else. He turned it over wonderingly in his hand and then recognised it. How very odd!

'What?' James Carrick said, answering the phone half an hour later. He was snatching a few hours at home before

112

returning to his office to read through the statements and other evidence collected after Susan Fairbrother's murder. It was quieter at night, with not many people about, and he could concentrate better.

'Looks like it, sir,' Ingrams went on, knowing that he was not expected to repeat the news word for word.

'Is he hurt?'

'Who, Tommy?'

'Who the hell else could I mean?'

'No, he somehow managed to grab him and hang on while someone went to a call box and dialled 999. I'm not sure why he didn't cut and run, his sort usually do. Cheeky devil said he'd done it because he reckoned he'd been attacked with the murder weapon.'

'And now you're saying that he might be right?'

'Well, there are stains on it that might be dried blood. It's down at forensic now.'

'Is Tommy still there?'

'Yes, I knew you'd want to talk to him.'

'I'll be with you in a few minutes.'

Ingrams was slightly offended when Carrick insisted on interviewing the malodorous witness alone.

'This couldn't have come at a worse time for me,' said the man as Carrick entered.

'I know,' Carrick said, drawing up a chair and sitting down. 'I'm extremely grateful.'

'I almost did a bunk.'

'We could give you a going-over if you like, and then kick you out the back door.'

'No, thanks. I'll take a risk with all the unwelcome publicity.' He gave Carrick a hard stare. 'You would, too.'

'Of course. Always ready to do the Drug Squad a favour – especially if it is the long-lost murder weapon. Tell me what happened.'

'There's not a lot to relate. I was coming back to base. I suppose it was about ten. I can't be absolutely sure because I don't wear a watch. I saw someone was in the little garden and assumed, rightly, that it was the Colonel. He usually locks up at dusk. He was bending down picking something up off the ground. I've noticed that he clears the place of litter so thought nothing of it.'

'Did you actually see what he picked up?'

'No. He was partly obscured by the bushes and stuff. And I could only see him through the railings, of course.'

'Sergeant Ingrams tells me that he was still tightly clutching a beer can and a cigarette packet when he was arrested.'

'It's possible. I didn't notice. I was too busy keeping hold of him. He's very strong for his age. So was his language.'

'According to someone who spoke to his wife he suffers from what she called 'blank-outs'. He thinks he's back fighting the Japanese. Apparently he was taken prisoner.'

'Poor sod,' Tommy said with feeling.

'Well, obviously we'll have to ask her what form these turns take but do you reckon that's what it could have been? Was he rational?'

'No. Not at all. But I wouldn't like to have to guess whether that was because he was spitting mad with me or off his head for another reason.'

'Your presence *has* upset a few residents of Beckford Square.'

Tommy shrugged. 'So what?'

'I'll put my cards on the table, Sergeant Armstrong. I had a word with your boss as to the suitability of your chosen squat.'

'I see,' said the other evenly.

'I don't think you realise the impact that a stinking, ostensibly drink-sodden drop-out can have on law-abiding retired people. I've fended off the complaints because I'm aware that there's a big drugs bust on Wednesday night, the culmination, I understand, of several weeks' work on your part. I'm always very impressed with undercover work. Frankly, I don't know how you do it. But please bear in mind in future that, in that guise, you can generate real fear in the old.'

'Okay,' Armstrong said. 'Point made.'

'And you may have caught a murderer for me. The interesting thing is that Mrs Moffat – she came out to see what all the noise was about just before the area car arrived – identified the hammer as one that belongs to them. They used it at one time for breaking up large pieces of coal. But now they burn smokeless fuel they don't need it. She said it was mislaid some time ago.'

'You believe her?'

114

'Yes, I do, actually. Except that if her husband told her he'd mislaid it she'd believe *him*.'

'So he might have killed the Pryce woman during one of his funny turns.'

'I'm keeping an open mind on it until I know more. One point that I must take into consideration is that the hammer might have been placed in the garden for him to find.'

'By the murderer? That's quite possible.'

'It was certainly put there by someone since Friday night,' Carrick said. 'Everything but the plants and the boulder were put through a sieve. There's no way it would have been missed.'

'It gets my back up when killers start crowing.'

'Yes, but we mustn't lose sight of the possibility that someone was merely getting rid of incriminating evidence.'

'Any chance of some greasy canteen chips?' Armstrong said after a pause.

'No, I think that would be hazarding your cover. Tell your tale to Ingrams. I'll get him to type it out now so you can sign it and go. By the way, I thought you said you'd moved out of the square.'

'Just for the benefit of long ears. It's not worth moving for two nights.'

'The best of luck,' Carrick said. 'D'you need any money?'

'Well, to be perfectly frank, sir, excellency, munificence, the expenses are a little slow getting through just now.'

He was handed a ten-pound note.

'I can see why you got the job' was Carrick's parting remark.

It was a subdued Jack Moffat in the next room when Carrick and Ingrams went in a while later. He glanced up at Carrick, pointedly ignored Ingrams and resumed staring at the wall opposite.

'Right, sir,' Carrick said. 'Be so kind as to tell me why you carried out an unprovoked attack on a man in Beckford Square tonight.'

Moffat fixed him with a hostile gaze and spoke testily. 'You ought to be ashamed of yourself bringing me here. If you'd spoken to my doctor he'd have told you that I suffer from mental blanks when I don't know what I'm doing. I can

115

remember going out to lock up and then nothing until that damned tramp was practically breaking my wrist. It's him you want to arrest for assault. The bugger *stank*. Stank to high heaven, the filthy blighter. It's him who chucks all the rubbish about.'

'You've complained several times about his presence in the locality. Perhaps you decided to take the law into your own hands.'

'Would that be so terrible?' the Colonel roared. 'If you won't act, then ordinary folk must do something.'

'I know about the man. He's quite harmless.'

'Nervous women like my wife don't know about that. They just see someone lurking about. He doesn't look harmless, the way he staggers around mouthing things at people.'

Carrick was inwardly cursing Armstrong's over-the-top histrionics by now. 'Tell me about the hammer.'

'I don't know anything about a hammer.'

'You ran at the tramp waving it as though you were going to attack him with it. Your wife has identified it as one that went missing from your garden shed some while ago.'

'Well, she should know,' Moffat harrumphed.

'How did it get into your hand? Did you find it?'

'I've no idea. I told you, I –'

'Did you take it out into the square with you when you went out to lock up?'

'No.'

'So you remember back that far then.'

'Now, look here –'

'You picked up a beer can and a cigarette packet in the garden. Is that when you had one of your turns? You said you didn't take the hammer out with you. But you might have done. You might have deliberately taken it – to attack the tramp and perhaps frighten him off.'

'You're trying to confuse me. It's a devilish way to behave towards an old man. I demand to be examined by a doctor.'

Carrick turned to Ingrams. 'See if the police surgeon's free.'

A look of alarm came over the Colonel's face as the sergeant left the room.

'You're quite within your rights,' Carrick told him. 'And I have to establish that you're fit to be charged. There's every likelihood that your hammer was also used to kill Mrs Pryce.'

'But –' Moffat began, all the colour draining from his usually florid complexion.

'Tell me the *truth*,' Carrick shouted, slapping the table with an open palm.

'It can't have been,' Moffat whispered.

'There are bloodstains on it and one human hair, grey, caught in a crack in the haft. It's still a little early to confirm that either came from the murder victim but forensic are working on it. I should know very soon.'

'But I didn't kill the woman!'

'Who knows what you do when you're not quite yourself?' Dropping his voice and speaking in quite the most chilling tone, Carrick went on, 'Now, are you going to continue playing the senile old fool or behave in a fashion more befitting to your rank so we can talk about this man to man?'

Moffat's prominent Adam's apple bobbed as he swallowed nervously and there was a long silence. Then he said, 'Sorry. Went to pieces there for a moment.'

'I can understand that. Now tell me about the hammer.'

'It's ours. I can't remember exactly when it went missing. Alice reckons that I used it when I was working on the car out the front and left it in the gutter. Someone might have picked it up. But, look, I –'

'What happened when you went out to lock up?'

'It was just like any other evening to start with. Well, perhaps I was a little later than usual – I'd been watching the highlights of the cricket on TV. I did what I always do, took the key from its hook in the hall and went out. I remember that it was very quiet, no folk about just then. I went right in the garden, always check for litter. Sometimes the boy leaves his bike or a ball in there. I take it over if he does in case he wants it. As you said, I found a couple of things. Then I saw the hammer. It was lying half under a bush but with the top sticking out so I knew immediately what it was. I took it to where the light was better and recognised it as ours. There's a wedge I put in it when the head flew off once. Then I heard footsteps. It was him, drunk as usual, staggering all over the place. I got very angry.'

117

'What did you do then?' Carrick asked when Moffat paused for a moment.

'I decided to try to scare the fella off. Drunks have always made me really angry. If they only knew how stupid they look, grinning all over their faces. It was his idiotic smile that did it, really – all I could think of was Alice scared stiff of the wretched blighter. But I wasn't going to hurt him. I thought that as he was tight he'd frighten pretty easily. I mean, all the winos are well on the way to DTs. So I just sort of ran at him, shouting things.'

'What things?'

'Well, I swore at him a bit.'

'What did you say?'

'You don't want to know exactly, surely?'

'Yes, I do. I want to know how much of this you really remember.'

Moffat cleared his throat and told him.

'I see,' Carrick said. 'I'm not sure he deserved that, but carry on.'

'There's nothing much to say. I pretended I was going to attack him. But he didn't turn a hair – just grabbed my wrist so that I dropped the hammer. I have to admit that I was thunderstruck. What was even more peculiar, he didn't seem to be drunk at all.'

'And you're quite sure you didn't have one of your –'

'No, no. It's mostly at night, when I've gone to bed. Nightmares. I sleepwalk and shout a bit. Dream I'm back in the army. The Japs took me prisoner, you know.' His large gnarled hands, clasped tightly in front of him on the table, were shaking.

'And at no time since the hammer was mislaid until this evening have you seen it?'

'No. I swear it's true. I couldn't –'

'I think you could. You hated Mrs Pryce. Did you think that if you ran at *her* shouting obscenities she'd move away?'

'I'm not the sort of person to attack a woman!'

'She took no killing,' Carrick said softly. 'Skull like an eggshell. You might even have done it by accident, just waving the hammer around.'

'No!'

118

'No? And tonight – after your little sortie – you thought you might be acclaimed the local hero if the tramp had upped and gone. Something to tell your cronies in the pub, eh?'

The bleary eyes looked up. 'I've served with Scots,' Moffat muttered. 'You are a Scot, aren't you?'

Carrick nodded.

'It's there, the accent, just now and then, when a little emotion breaks through. But you're as hard as stone. You know that? Like the granite your bloody country's made of.'

'Please answer the question' was Carrick's only response.

'I didn't kill Mrs Pryce. It wasn't something that would have occurred to me. I'm not a violent man at all, soldiers aren't, you know. When we're off duty we do gentle, domestic things: wash clothes, read, even knit and sew. If people start waving guns around in barracks, they get sent to a head doctor – fast.'

'I want you to think back to that night. I shall have to ask you again why you didn't lock the gate to the garden.'

'I forgot. I do sometimes. Alice'll tell you that I'm getting absent-minded.'

'So it was a complete coincidence.'

'Yes.'

'Nothing to do with the fact that Miss Mackenzie had been to see you and said she was investigating the theft of Mrs Pryce's plants?'

'You *know* about that?'

'Of course.'

Silence.

Carrick said, 'You might have seen her climb over the gate a previous night to keep watch and thought you'd be helpful and leave it unlocked. It's a good vantage point – as a soldier you'd be very much aware of that.'

Moffat sighed. 'Oh, dear.'

'She's very attractive,' Carrick murmured. 'Isn't she?'

'Inspector. . . .'

'If you're worried that the other people in the residents' association or your wife will find out from me, I can assure you that is not so.'

'Is it *that* important?'

119

'To the case? Probably not. I'm merely trying to find out what sort of a person you are. Whether you lie without turning a hair.'

'All right, damn you. Yes, I admired the girl. Thought she was extremely plucky. I didn't know she was going to keep watch, of course. But I got out of bed one night to open the window a bit wider as it was hot, and that's when I saw her. She jumped over the gate and into the garden and then hid herself. Impressed me.'

'Didn't Alice notice that you didn't lock up? I take it you mean you left it open for several nights.'

'No. I still went out, you see. Pretended to do it. I didn't want the girl to hurt herself climbing over. Spikes on the top, you know. Damned vicious things. Could have impaled herself.'

'God help me,' Carrick whispered. *'Did you pretend to lock up on the night Mrs Pryce was murdered?'*

'I did, actually. But I needn't have bothered. Alice was in the bathroom.'

'What time was it?'

'Pretty late again. Cricket highlights, the test match, had been on that night too. I say, you won't let on, will you? Alice gets very annoyed if I take notice of pretty girls.'

*'What* time?' Carrick asked again.

'It must have been about half past eleven – a bit before, perhaps.'

'Did you see anyone?'

'No, but I could hear Mallory's infernal music.'

'I want you to think very carefully. Picture yourself going outside with the key but not locking up. Did you walk right over to the garden?'

'Yes.'

'Was the gate open or closed?'

'Closed. Yes, closed. I'm sure of it.'

'Did you check for litter?'

'Yes, I opened the gate and went in.'

'And you found nothing?'

'No.'

'When you returned, was Mrs Pryce's front door open or closed?'

'I'm afraid I didn't notice.'

'But you'd have noticed if it was ajar and the light on in the hall.'

'Yes, but not if the hall light was out. It's pretty dark just there.'

'You noticed nothing unusual?'

'No.'

'Are you left or right-handed?'

'Right. Left's a bit wonky these days so just as well. Can't grip things any more with that hand.'

'Why's that?'

Moffat smiled in crooked fashion. 'Blame the Japs. Smashed all my fingers. Bastards.' He extended the hand for Carrick to see, the fingers misshapen, hooked like claws.

'I stand in awe of people who survived that kind of thing,' Carrick said quietly. He went on, 'I'd like you to have a quick medical check before you go, to make sure the excitement hasn't done you any harm.'

'But I thought. . . '

'Just don't leave Bath. I might want to talk to you again.'

'So you're not charging me?'

'With assault, causing a public disturbance, being in possession of an offensive weapon? No.'

'But surely he's pressed charges?'

'Tommy? He can't be bothered. People like that are kicked from pillar to post all the time. Just don't think of taking the law into your own hands again.'

After a short silence, Moffat said, 'I say, I feel rather bad about all this. I've been a fool. Poor bugger's living rough with no proper home to go to. Might even by ex-army. Some of them are, you know. Can't adjust to civvy life.'

'He told me he's leaving in a couple of days. You could mention it to your wife.'

'I will. But I understand how she feels. You're on the other side of it, really – not having to live with a woman who's constantly in fear of being next on some madman's list.'

No, quite, Carrick thought. Perhaps I ought to do something about it.

121

# Chapter Twelve

'Live with you?' Joanna said in surprise. 'But I've a perfectly good flat of my own.'

She had found a very impatient Carrick on her office doorstep at ten past nine the next morning, impatient mainly because she was a little late, impatient because he had made up his mind and once he had done that there had to be action and, well, impatient. He had hastened up the stairs behind her and then paced the office like a caged tiger, jingling the loose change in his pockets, almost fizzing with suppressed energy. Implored to seat himself, he had given her a swift résumé of the past few hours' activities at Manvers Street and then, hardly pausing for breath, had said that he thought she ought to move in with him.

Carrick said, 'I wasn't thinking that you didn't have room for a couple of wardrobes.' She had an infuriating way of being flippant at the wrong moment.

'I see,' Joanna said slowly, switching on the coffee machine.

'Promise me you'll think about it.'

'All right.'

'And you will be sensible, won't you? I don't want you going out on your own at night.'

'Yes, James.'

Satisfied for the present and ignoring, or having not heard, the sarcasm in her tone, Carrick seated himself. He watched her lay out cups and, when it was ready, pour the coffee, admiring the neat, fluid movements of her slim body.

Handing him his coffee, Joanna said, 'The Reverend Forbes wants me to find the Chantbury Pyx.'

'It's probably in Japan by now.'

'I'm prepared to make a full investigation.'

He smiled, stirring in two heaped spoonsful of brown sugar.

'I intend to start by having lunch with Declan O'Connor of the Arts and Antiques Squad after he's been to see you.'

Carrick discovered that some of his coffee was now in the saucer. 'The hell you are.'

'Oh, and the Reverend Forbes suggested I visit the injured security man from the Sheridan Gallery. He's much better and has remembered another couple of details about the robbery. It was the smaller of the two men who appeared to be the ringleader. He was the one who hit him with the hammer and then used it to break the glass of the display case. The robber was left-handed and the hammer looked old and dirty. He remembers that it had a wedge in the top of the haft.' She smiled brightly. 'Does that help at all?'

Slowly, a frame at a time, Carrick placed his swimming coffee cup and saucer on a corner of the desk. 'May I use your phone?' he asked humbly.

Joanna passed it over. 'All yours.'

After speaking to Ingrams and telling him to arrange for the murder weapon to be shown to a certain hospital patient, Carrick sat back, accepted a fresh cup of coffee and mentally endeavoured to marry up a theft and two murders. Things began to knit together rather neatly.

'Mrs Pryce met a robber,' he said, finally.

'Yes.' She had never been one to crow over victories.

'Someone who might have left North Terrace at a little after ten that night and returned at approximately eleven thirty. She met him on the stairs. She must have done. It *has* to be Mallory. He left his music on loud, went out and later came back hoping that no one was the wiser. He's left-handed, too.'

'But why would be kill Mrs Pryce? She could have had no idea where he'd been or what he'd done. The fact that he'd gone out and left the music on isn't an act that would mean that people would suspect him of a crime. And the Chantbury Pyx is so small it could just be slipped into a pocket.'

'Perhaps he dropped it.'

123

'Right at her feet on the stairs? That's a little fanciful, James. Ten to one she wouldn't have known what it was even if he had. Just a small rectangle of metal.'

'And he wouldn't have been stupid enough, surely, to be still wearing a stocking over his face.'

'What about Stacey?'

Eyes narrowed, Carrick thought about it. 'But why would he go to Beckford Square after committing a robbery? It would have been the last place he'd want to be seen, with his aunt living there. No, he'd have headed straight for home. His alibi's pretty watertight, too – we've traced his movements around various pubs in Bristol with a deal-cert sighting at around the time of the murder.'

'Are you going to pull Mallory in for more questioning?'

'Yes, it might pay off. He said he went out for a meal on Saturday night and then on to a club. Perhaps he lied about knowing Susan Fairbrother and took her with him. The problem with that is that no one knows of any plans she had that night.'

'Was she lured into West Terrace, do you think, and then killed?'

'There were signs of a struggle in the end house where her body was found.'

'It doesn't make sense or she was downright stupid. I wouldn't go into a building like that with a man I didn't know very well.'

'For sex? She couldn't take him back to the nursing home.'

'Mallory has a car, for God's sake.'

'Yes, you're right. He'd have taken her somewhere lonely, strangled her there and dumped the body somewhere. Her purse was taken too.'

'Then it was a deliberate ploy to make it look as though Tommy had killed her. Muggers don't hang around in a place like Beckford Square – they'd starve.'

'We keep coming back to the idea that she was killed because of the colour of her hair.'

'Can you think of any other reason?'

'No. Unless there's a jilted lover in there somewhere.'

'What does the matron of the home have to say about that?'

'There was nobody that she was aware of; her friends knew of no one either.'

They lapsed into silence for a few moments and then Joanna said, 'James, when do you think the murderer will realise he's made a mistake?'

'He might not.'

It was as if they were not talking about her but someone else, a complete stranger.

'Whoever it is lives in the square. I'm sure of it. How else would they know so much about what goes on there?'

Carrick got to his feet. 'Stay *right* away from the place. I'm going to pull Mallory in. If I get no joy with him I'll arrange police protection for you. And don't argue – if you were anyone else I'd probably have done it already.'

Joanna leaned back in her chair and looked up at him. 'What would you miss most, my fanny or my brain?'

'Pass,' Carrick said. Then he laughed and bent over to kiss her.

Joanna had arranged to meet Declan O'Connor in the Hare and Hounds. It was her own local and she thought he might enjoy the superb view after having to stare out across London, day in day out, from the fifteenth floor of New Scotland Yard.

''Tis herself of the spa,' he said by way of a greeting, gripping her hand firmly. 'You said you had red hair, my dear, but you didn't mention beauty that would drive a man clean out of his mind.'

He was older than she had imagined, probably in his forties, dark and slightly haggard as though he had recently been very ill. She discovered quite a while later from Carrick that he had at one time worked for the Serious Crime Squad and had been shot arresting a suspect.

'It's very good of you to spare the time to talk to me,' Joanna said. He had insisted on buying his own drink and had returned with menus from the bar.

He looked surprised. 'But you're in the trade, Miss Mackenzie. Can I call you Joanna? Good. I've learned over many years that we cops are too careful sometimes whom we talk to. We yarn with snouts and grasses and scorn those like yourself who are often striving to reach the same goals. No, I regard this as a working lunch and therefore, because I am loaded with expenses, I shall pay. I understand that your partner has been in an accident and is in hospital?'

Joanna, mentally reeling from this spate of words, delivered at machine-gun speed, decided that she liked him very much already. She said, 'Lance? He'll probably live. But I've a feeling that the business won't. No matter, we're not here to talk about that. Inspector Carrick said that you might have a lead on the Chantbury Pyx.'

'It is listed in a computer database, that's all. The real problem as far as a humble cop in the street is concerned is that I'm not quite sure what it is. Our usual reference books aren't at all forthcoming.'

Joanna produced the picture postcard given to her by the Reverend Forbes, which O'Connor fell upon delightedly.

'Yes, Carrick was talking about a reliquary and the fact that it was made of bronze with gilding,' he murmured after a while, reading the reverse. 'But all in all we're looking for a thing no larger than a notebook. But with a strange beauty,' he went on, flipping over the card. 'The kind of artefact that should never even be breathed on by thieves and dealers. May I keep this?'

'Of course. Tell me about your raid in Chiswick.'

His face lit up. 'A whole warehouse full of stolen property lifted from the Home Counties and beyond. We've had a man inside, you understand, and he gave us the nod that the gang were having a meeting. They were so well organised they had an AGM!'

'At the warehouse?'

'Yes. There was a small export company they used as a front and for getting the stuff abroad. There were even staff who worked in the office who thought it was a bona fide outfit. They didn't keep the real records at the office, though, they were safely stashed away in someone's house in Epping. I finally managed to break into the system – mainly by twisting the arm of the guy whose computer it was until he gave me the entry code – and hey presto!'

'Were there full details of all the stuff in the warehouse?'

'And more. I learned first of all that every item they had stolen – or arranged to have nicked, they'd contracted out more than half of the jobs – was given a category depending on how much it was worth, who the owners had been in some cases and who wanted it. They'd worked mostly to order.'

'Did you find out who wanted the Pyx?'

'Unfortunately, no. But I haven't had time to really get to grips with the thing yet. One contact is in Australia. He'd order a whole containerload of mixed items, some of the things stolen, mostly genuine stuff bought from wholesale dealers. As you know, that's how antiques are exported all the time. Now, the Pyx had been given a top "A" rating. But they didn't have it, it wasn't in the safe where they kept small, really valuable things.'

'Sold already?'

'I'm not sure. As I said, I've still not finished going through the info. Some of it's in a sort of code that I haven't cracked yet and chummy's not talking. But I've a feeling – though I might be right up the creek here – that they've never actually had their hands on it.'

'It had a full twenty-four hours to get from Bath to London.'

'I know. Plenty of time. Time to fly it over the North Pole.' O'Connor grabbed a menu. 'I'm famished. What do you recommend?'

'A T-bone steak. You look as though you need feeding up.'

'Perhaps I will. And you?'

'A roast-beef salad with no onions, please.'

When he returned from giving their order, Joanna said, 'The vicar of Chantbury told me that he'd been approached a few years ago by a dealer in Bath who was interested in buying the Pyx for a client in Japan.'

'Did you get the name of the dealer?'

'Yes, but it's a highly reputable firm.'

'I'm quite sure it is. And they might have the Japanese gentleman's name still in their records.'

'Do you reckon you caught everyone in the gang?'

O'Connor grinned. 'No. By no means. A couple of the big fishes slipped out of the net. We know who one of them is.'

'Only what I was thinking is that if the Pyx has not been handed over there's every chance that it's either still in the thief's possession or has been hidden somewhere.'

'Quite likely. More than likely, in fact.'

'Did Carrick tell you about our murders?'

'Yes, he did. And while I was with him someone reported that a man injured in the robbery had identified a hammer that had been found as likely to be the one he'd been attacked with. One has to be very careful with things like that, though. A hammer is a hammer, they all tend to look the same.'

'I agree. But this one was fairly dirty where it had been used to break up coal at one time, and had a wedge in the head end of the haft. The first murder occurred just after the robbery took place.'

'It's a good lead. You're thinking that the Pyx and the murderer are still in the area and he's biting his nails down to the quick as his fence is lying low and not answering the phone.'

'He could find another fence.'

'No doubt. But it's not easy when you're selling hot property.'

'This fish of yours that got away . . . Have you any idea where he is?'

'Probably at his villa on the Costa del Crime.'

'So there's nothing to stop whoever took the Pyx flying out there and handing it over.'

'Knowing the way he works I'd say it was unlikely. He's never taken work home, so to speak, always played the law-abiding citizen and good family man when not at the office. Definitely not kept open house for dodgy contractors.'

'Did Carrick have a man called Mallory in for questioning while you were there?'

'If he had he didn't tell me.' After gazing at her carefully O'Connor said, 'Why, or are we still talking about the same cases?'

'I'm a bit more involved with this now than I want to be,' Joanna admitted. 'I was in the vicinity of the first murder and saw someone walking away who turned and saw me. The second murder was of a girl with red hair who worked nearby.'

'And there's no other apparent motive for that killing?'

'Not that the CID have been able to discover so far.'

'And we're not talking about cops in the sticks here – Carrick used to be in the Vice Squad.'

'I'm in the position to know that he's good at his job. I used to be his sergeant.'

'Holy Mother. No, don't worry, I won't ask why you left. Has he arranged protection for you?'

'He said he would but in a way I'd rather he didn't. I like my freedom.'

'You like your sweet life too,' he said fervently. 'I'd volunteer myself but I'm a bit old for that kind of thing now.' He smiled wistfully. 'If you should be looking for a house-trained maid-of-all-work and bed-warmer, though, just give me a ring.'

'I'll certainly bear that in mind,' Joanna assured him, wondering what Carrick would make of *that*.

Later, when she went home she did not particularly notice a red car parked opposite the herbalist's or that it slowly pulled away from the kerb when she went to her own car parked just around the corner. She was far too worried about a message from the hospital to the effect that Lance was to undergo more surgery as a result of complications. Unobserved, the car followed her all the way home.

# Chapter Thirteen

'So, what have we got?' Carrick said at six thirty that night. Ingrams was with him in his office but Carrick had actually been addressing the files and folders that were spread over his desk, some of them with papers fanned out, most closed and stacked up untidily.

'There was no choice but to release him,' Ingrams said.

It touched a raw nerve. Despite exhaustive questioning, Paul Mallory had remained adamant that he had not left his flat on the night of Mrs Pryce's murder, nor had he heard her ring his doorbell. He had gone out on the Saturday night, however, and his already good alibi had been reinforced by a croupier at the club where Mallory had been entertaining friends. The man, just back from a two-day visit up north for a funeral, was sure that the party had stayed at the club until after three a.m. and also that none of the girls had had red hair.

'What about the address he gave you?' Ingrams wanted to know. 'The publishing place.'

'Bristol are looking into it,' Carrick replied. 'They won't find anything – Cooper's far cleverer than that.' He added, savagely, 'No doubt he's laughing now I have egg all over my face.'

'At least we have the murder weapon.'

'But it's not particularly helpful,' Carrick growled. 'The murderer knew it wouldn't be. That's why he gave it to us – to confuse the issue. God, I won't be played cat and mouse with.'

'You really think that's the reason?'

'Can you think of any other reason to leave it in the garden, almost at the same spot that the body was found?'

'Only to implicate the Colonel.'

Carrick did not reply. What he really needed right then was an assistant who did not possess a brain like suet pudding.

'I keep thinking about little Jamie seeing Harbutts at just on ten that night.'

'Yes, and shortly afterwards seeing another man leave the building. And later that night, but not much, the Chantbury Pyx was stolen by two men, one tall and powerfully built, the other smaller. I've been through it in my mind a hundred times. I'm beginning to think that –'

The phone rang, breaking Carrick's train of thought.

'There's a Dr Hendricks here, sir,' said Woods's voice. 'He's remembered seeing a man and woman walking in the square on Saturday night and he thinks the woman had red hair.'

'Show him in here,' Carrick instructed.

Hendricks was aged about sixty with silvery grey hair and a fresh complexion. He took a seat and said, 'I must apologise for coming forward so late. I don't come home all that often and was only calling in for a few things – clothes and so forth – as I was travelling to London on the Sunday.'

Carrick had not had to glance at Ingrams's diagram of the square. 'And you live at number 4 South Terrace?'

'That's right, Inspector. Not that I will be for much longer.' He smiled happily. 'I hope to marry soon and don't want to be in Beckford Square when the developers start work on West Terrace – which I believe is next month. Besides, my wife-to-be has a very pleasant house in Ralph Allen Drive.'

'Which is where you reside for most of the time now,' Carrick said, his expression that of a polite police officer merely getting the facts right. 'Please tell me what you saw.'

'I don't know why I noticed them. I usually tend to concentrate on driving. The square was quiet and it was pretty late, slightly after midnight.'

'Isn't that a rather strange hour to be dropping in at home, sir?' Ingrams said.

Hendricks looked a little irritated at being interrupted in mid-flow. 'Yes, I suppose it is, but doctors lead rather strange

131

lives. I had been very late getting back to Marion's from the hospital and after we'd eaten she reminded me that I had to go to London for the conference and asked me if I'd remembered to pack a dinner suit. I keep most of my clothes at her house, you understand. I hadn't, it was at home, hence the late visit. A nuisance, I can assure you.'

'Go on, sir,' Carrick requested.

'Where was I? Oh yes, the girl with red hair. I think I must have noticed her particularly because they were standing near a lamp-post. Beautiful hair, you don't see girls wear it long like that very much these days.'

'The man who was with her, what did he look like?'

'He was quite young – about her age, I should think. Very fair hair, but longer than yours, Inspector. He had his hands in his pockets. That's all I noticed about him, really. They were laughing together.'

'I've seen someone fair,' Ingrams said under his breath. 'Yes, I've got it. A young bloke works in the nursing home some evenings and weekends. Christopher someone.'

'Go and talk to him, would you?' Carrick said. 'Bring him in if you think it was him and he won't cooperate.'

'He's already lied about it once,' Ingrams pointed out. 'Said he hadn't seen her that night.'

'Did you see anyone else?' Carrick asked Hendricks.

'No.'

'What about when you were leaving? Were they still there?'

'If they were I didn't notice them.'

'About how long did you stay indoors?'

'Longer than I had intended. The place was in rather a muddle and there was the usual pile of circulars and other rubbish on the doormat. All my friends know I'm living with Marion, you see, so there was nothing important. But by the time I'd quickly sorted through it just in case and bagged it all up to take with me and put out for the dustman, I suppose half an hour had gone by. In fact I almost forgot what I had gone for, the dinner suit.'

'And you're quite sure there was no one in the square when you left?'

'I'm afraid I wasn't really looking for people, Inspector. It had been a very long day and I was tired. Such a terrible thing, though. I only wish I could help you more. Marion told me about the murder when I got home tonight.'

'Did you know Mrs Pryce?'

'The other poor woman? No, not really. I'm around at what are called unsocial hours. I couldn't say that I really know anyone in Beckford Square other than just to nod to, with the possible exception of Colonel Moffat. He's sometimes locking up the little garden when I pop home. Pleasant enough chap.'

Something clicked in Carrick's memory. 'What medical condition would cause a woman to have a gas heater going full blast on a hot day? Could it be something to do with the fact that she seems to suffer from agoraphobia?'

'Seems to?'

'Her behaviour suggests that she does.'

'You mean she gets panic attacks when she's out?'

'Well, if she does I don't know anyone who's witnessed it. No, she rushes about furtively.'

Hendricks guffawed. 'Got a screw loose, if you ask me.'

'That's the impression I got when I interviewed her. Thank you.'

'Anyone I might know?' asked the doctor lightly.

Carrick hesitated. 'In complete confidence?'

'Of course.'

'A woman called Bethany Cryon. She lives in the top flat at number 3 North Terrace.'

'Oh, *her*. Yes, I've seen her a couple of times but I didn't know which flat she lived in. I saw her early on Saturday morning, as a matter of fact, when I was walking by the Abbey. I'd come into the city centre to buy a paper and a few other things.'

'What was she doing?'

'Queuing up outside the entrance to the Roman Baths and museum, waiting for the doors to be opened.'

Carrick thanked him for his help and Hendricks left. Half a minute later the phone rang and it was Woods again.

'Sorry to bother you again, sir, but the Chief's just come in the back door. I thought you'd like to know.'

'Thanks,' Carrick said.

He had time to groan and remove his feet from the edge of his desk before the door was thrust open. Chief Inspector

Haine believed in catching people unawares, hence Carrick's early-warning system. There followed a fairly typical interview when he was expected to provide an up-to-the-minute report on every serious case outstanding, the pressure even more intense than usual as his superior had just returned from a meeting. Towards the end of this, Ingrams returned with a blond youth firmly in his grip, the latter sullen and grim. When released in an interview room, he fetched his captor a flying kick to the shins that felled him completely, banged the head of a constable against the wall and bolted.

Carrick heard Ingrams shout, ran out into the corridor and was in time to be right on the youth's heels. Woods, another constable, two dog handlers, one man reporting an accident, and a woman making a complaint about her neighbour's bonfires were then treated to a classic rugby tackle, the pair sliding for a considerable distance on the polished floor of the waiting and reception area. Carrick was more used to muddy grass.

'Keep your hands off me!' the youth screamed, following it with quite a bit more in the same vein.

Carrick kept sitting on him all the while, having waved away assistance. His voice cut through the other's effortlessly. 'You can stand up when you stop behaving like a three-year-old.'

Ingrams hobbled up. 'The little sod's got steel toecaps on his boots.'

'Bastard fuckin' police!' the youth shouted as he was permitted to regain his feet.

'Wants his backside tanned,' said the woman by the reception desk and sniffed. 'I bet he comes from Bristol, too.' she added as the subject of her scorn was hustled back the way he had come.

'All your theories in ruins, James?' asked Haine out of the corner of his mouth.

'I'll keep you informed, sir,' Carrick answered blandly.

'This is where you put the boot in,' the would-be escaper was saying in satisfied fashion to his disenchanted audience of three when Carrick arrived, Ingrams carefully rubbing his shins. The Inspector sent Woods back to his post and Ingrams for a plaster to put on his leg, which was bleeding, and sat

134

down. The only other remaining person was Willis, over by the door, with a sore head.

'Your name's Christopher Thorn?' Carrick asked.

Thorn mouthed an obscenity at him.

'Do I charge you with assaulting two police officers or do we talk about this sensibly?'

'Go to hell.'

'Or I suppose I could ask Mrs Lang to come along and box your ears.'

A slight flicker of alarm crossed the youth's features. As Hendricks had said, he was very fair, his hair cut fashionably short at the back but long on top so that it flopped over his eyes and ears. Occasionally he raked it back with his fingers.

'Even assuming that we have the man we want to interview,' Carrick continued. 'But I'm reasonably sure of that now. Sergeant Ingrams wouldn't have brought you here and you wouldn't have tried to run away if you had nothing to hide.'

'Piss off, cop.'

'What are you doing at university? Sociology?'

This seemed to cause deep offence. 'Am I *hell*!'

'My apologies. The Arts, then? History?'

'Engineering.'

'You astound me. I'm obviously out of touch. I never thought that engineers went hand in hand with left-wing crap.'

The other wriggled, impaled on an icy blue stare.

'Or is it just that you have some left-wing friends? Showing you how to be a man, are they, Christopher, taking you to all the right political meetings? Now there's a thought,' Carrick said, getting up. 'Perhaps we're talking about a group of morons who have been causing affrays outside pubs and, when the police arrive, attack them with weapons they just happened to have with them, chains, knives and so forth?'

'No!' Thorn shouted. 'I'm nothing to do with it.'

'You were seen talking to Susan Fairbrother late on Saturday night. Tell me about that.'

'I didn't see her. I wasn't there.'

Carrick paused in a slow perambulation of the room. 'You weren't where?'

135

'Wherever someone saw me.'

'You weren't *anywhere* on Saturday night? Now that's really different. Experimenting with the paranormal as well for your studies?'

'You know what I mean!' Thorn yelled.

'You were seen,' Carrick said softly. 'Now suppose you stop wasting my time. Someone saw the pair of you laughing and talking together. A reliable witness too, someone who admired Susan's lovely hair. Now she's dead, something that ordinary people find very tragic, and yet here you are, strutting and posing and openly contemptuous of those trying to find her killer.' Here Carrick leaned a hand on the table and spoke very close to Thorn's right ear. 'Aren't you sad about her death, Christopher?'

'Yes, of course.'

'She put up quite a struggle before he managed to strangle her. Then he stole her purse, probably to make it look as though the down-and-out had killed her. But Tommy didn't kill her – we're quite sure about *that*. And she hadn't been sexually assaulted so the motive wasn't rape either. Is that what you were talking to her about – sex?'

'No!'

'No? So you were genuinely fond of her then? You weren't trying to get her somewhere quiet for a quick –'

'Stop it!' Thorn shouted. 'You bastard! I won't have you talk about her like that. She wasn't like that. I really loved . . .' He bit his lip hard but had already lost the battle and burst into tears.

Ingrams re-entered the interview room at this juncture and was in time to see Carrick give the suspect a consoling pat on the shoulder.

'And what,' Carrick said, sitting down again, 'was that stupid charade all about just now?'

Christopher blew his nose. 'I knew you'd think it was me. Rod – one of my chums – said I was as good as banged up. I was the last one to see her alive.'

'Only if you killed her. The murderer was the last person to see her alive.'

'I *knew* you'd think it was me,' he said again. 'I've been in a bit of trouble lately. A couple of us were picked up for being drunk and fooling around. Rod said we were picked on. And once your face is known and you're labelled a trouble-maker. . . Look, I was bloody scared. Rod told me that the filth – er – police here in Bath keep the younger element right down. I don't come from round here so I'd no idea what went on.'

'And you share a flat with this character?'

Christopher nodded miserably.

'It's your life,' Carrick remarked. 'But if I were you I'd get some different digs before the new term starts.'

'I was going to anyway. Me and Susan. . . .'

'Were you lovers?' Carrick whispered.

'No.'

'But you were hoping you could get a flat and live together.'

'Yes, but it was only a dream really. We couldn't afford it on her pay and my grant. My mum helps me out but she wouldn't. . . .'

'Quite,' Carrick said dryly. 'Lots of mums won't help with what they regard as living in sin. What time were you talking to Susan in Beckford Square?'

Sniffing, Christopher said, 'I don't know the exact time. Before midnight until about half past. We'd had a bit of a row. My fault. I was going to apologise so I waited for her to come back to the nursing home. But when she came back she wasn't mad with me any more and we laughed about it.'

'Where had she been all evening?'

'To the pictures.'

'On her own?'

'Yes. We were supposed to have gone together but I went off in a stupid huff.'

'What had you argued about?'

'It was childish really. She teased me by saying that she thought Rod was good-looking. He isn't – he's an ugly bastard. I said that if she thought he was so great she could go out with him.'

'The trials of youth,' Carrick murmured, gazing at the ceiling. 'I once fell out with a girl who said I reminded her of a horse. What she meant was that it was a palomino the same colour as my hair. So, you chatted in the square. Then what happened?'

'Nothing. I said I had to go. I was bushed. I hadn't had much sleep the night before, we'd been out boozing. She said she didn't want to go in yet as it was such a nice night. She was a bit unhappy about the woman who'd been killed.'

'Surely in that case she wouldn't want to be out in the square alone?'

'No, I didn't mean it like that. She wasn't frightened. Susan was religious. She didn't say so but I think she wanted to be quiet in the square and pray a bit for her.'

'*Were* you alone? Did you see anyone else?'

'Just a few cars driving through, that's all. And a bloke who called at one of the houses for a while.'

'No one on foot?'

'I don't remember seeing anyone.'

'What size shoes do you take?'

'Nine and a half.'

'Sergeant Ingrams will take you home. Show him a pair of your shoes, the ones you wore Saturday night. He might want to borrow them for a while. The other thing I want you to do is stay out of trouble from now on. You could also apologise to my colleagues here for being a young idiot.'

'You really believe him, sir?' Willis said when Ingrams and Thorn had gone.

Carrick said, 'I have to admit to being strongly influenced by Mrs Lang's choice of staff. She said she had a good team and, let's face it, she has several hundred students to choose from. My only worry is that no one, the matron included, seems to have been aware of Chris and Susan's feelings for one another, unless – and this is a strong possibility – the feelings were all on his side. Hardly a strong personality, but if he went off in a paddy after being teased, what would he do if she'd suddenly decided to ditch him?'

'She was a strapping girl, though, and he's built like a broomstick. I doubt if he'd have been up to killing her.'

'My thoughts precisely. And did you notice his hands? Small and delicate like a woman's, his fingers were half the size of the bruises on the girl's throat. I ask you, what the hell's engineering coming to?'

Carrick was at home later that night when he realised that he had broken a promise. He reached for the phone, changed his mind, threw on a jacket and went out, walking up the hill.

It was only a small sound but unfamiliar and Joanna was instantly awake, listening. The house creaked, as all old houses do, and the water pipes made strange noises when people turned on taps. But this was more immediate, close by, a sound from within the flat itself. Without moving much she looked at the bedside clock; one fifteen, the green glowing figures shining like malevolent eyes. She had always hated that clock.

Someone was in the flat. She had not needed to check the time to know this, of course, it had merely been a small automatic human reaction while the brain assimilated the unthinkable. The sound she had heard was that of a garment brushing against a wall in the dark.

Joanna slid out of bed on the side nearest to the door. This was ajar, for she preferred fresh air to enter via an open window in the kitchen and along the passage to being disturbed by traffic roaring up the hill outside her bedroom window. Just then a car revved noisily in the road and she moved quickly under cover of the racket to stand behind the door, flattening herself to the wall and praying that whoever it was would not shine a torch through the crack at the hinges end and see her.

Soft footsteps approached. In the next moment he was right in the room, just a darker outline in the gloom. He stood still for a second or so and then moved soundlessly over towards the bed. Joanna balanced herself carefully on her toes and than ran at him, right hand raised to chop him across the back of the neck.

He heard her, twisted round, grabbed her and threw her over his head. She landed partly on the bed, partly on the floor, rolling away desperately as he lunged after her. Between the bed and the wall he caught her, his weight winding her completely as they crashed down together. Her arms were pinioned, there was no room to fight him off. He began to rip off her pyjamas, biting her, a hot, sweaty hand shoving between her thighs.

Somehow, Joanna found the strength to heave him up and get a knee in his groin, hazily remembering one of the more difficult judo throws. But he was already off balance and pitched forward, landing behind her. Hoping that he had broken his neck, she scrambled up and ran.

Halfway down the hall he caught up with her and hit her around the head. She staggered, snatched a picture from the wall and threw it at him. Amazingly, it connected and she heard him exclaim. But it hardly stopped him at all, the next second he had got hold of her again.

There was nothing for it but to stand and fight. Again, she repelled him, kicking him off. But her feet were bare, she could not inflict real damage. When he got hold of her again his hands were around her throat, pushing her down, crushing her to the floor with all his strength, gasping with exertion.

By this time they were right in the kitchen doorway. Joanna went limp, taking him by surprise, and managed to struggle free. On the kitchen worktop was her knife block. She threw herself at it. No, not the cheap bread knife or the chopping knife, fool, the new one, the Sabatier that would fillet a bison.

She couldn't find it. Her throat still felt as though he was choking her, and everything was going fuzzy. He *was* choking her, he was right at her side, his fingers around her throat, thumbs pressing into the carotid arteries. Killing her.

Joanna was floating in a weird world inhabited by black blobs that swirled and bounced like lost planets. One was right beneath her and she started to slide down into it. It was like a dark mouth that gaped endlessly and hugely. Deep from within its throat came a booming noise. The booming noise got louder.

As though someone was trying to break down the door.

She put all her remaining energy into a scream that, because fingers were tightly around her throat, wasn't a scream at all.

# Chapter Fourteen

Carrick was at the top of the flight of stairs on the second floor when he heard a clatter from the other side of the door facing him. Two long strides brought him right to Joanna's front door. From within came more sounds; a heavy thump, scuffles.

He took several steps back and shoulder-charged the door. It held. And again, and still the door held, bouncing in its frame. Swearing fluently, he aimed two kicks at the lock. Both found their target with great accuracy but the door still would not yield.

Then he heard a faint scream, choked off.

Afterwards he could not reconstruct the next few seconds, only that a kind of madness came over him. Suddenly the door was no longer an obstacle and he was staggering, off balance, in the dark of the hallway, the crash of splintering wood in his ears. There was a heavy collision with someone who gave him a savage shove and then ran, momentarily silhouetted against the light rectangle of the doorway. Feet pounded down the stairs.

Carrick's hand brushed against a light switch and he switched it on. Then he ran from room to room switching on other lights until the flat was blazing with light.

'Joanna!' he shouted.

She was in the kitchen, the last room he looked in, curled up in a pathetic childlike huddle on the floor, half-naked.

He could find no pulse and she didn't seem to be breathing.

When he rolled her over onto her back her limbs were limp and heavy. He shut his mind to the great fear that she was

141

already dead and gave her mouth-mouth resuscitation; three breaths and then a short pause while he applied heart massage; three breaths and rhythmically compress her ribs; three breaths . . . And again, and again.

Suddenly, her arms flailed, clouting him on one ear as he bent over her. He glanced around, all at once aware that they weren't alone, and someone who had been peering round the door bolted.

'Oi!' Carrick yelled. 'Come back!'

No one came but a door close by slammed loudly.

'Call an ambulance!' he bellowed. 'For God's sake call an ambulance!'

He glanced down and saw that Joanna was looking at him, extremely puzzled. He risked leaving her for a few moments, ran into her bedroom, snatched the quilt from her bed and wrapped her in it.

It soon became apparent that the neighbour had called the police before bravely venturing next door, hoping to catch a glimpse of what he assumed to be the aftermath of a drunken party. The crew of the area car answering the call, only one of whom knew Carrick by sight, immediately radioed for an ambulance when they arrived. It came, collected the casualty and then left.

Not even when his wife had died had Carrick wept. He did now, shutting himself in the bathroom, aware that the people outside the door were expecting him to take charge, evaluate the situation and issue orders.

He had used her repeatedly and, despite all the resources at his disposal, had failed to protect her from a killer.

'What would you miss most,' she had asked, 'my fanny or my brain?'

He accused himself that he hadn't fought to prevent her being forced to resign because then he would have had to admit that he couldn't function without her. And, for the same reason, when they had been thrown together a few days previously, hadn't he done all in his power to get rid of her only to turn up on her doorstep driven by lust?

Finally, he splashed cold water over his face, borrowed one of Joanna's soft, fluffy pink towels, took a deep breath and went out. His training and experience seemed to take over at this point for he managed to get through the next hour and a half without making any mistakes or breaking down again. Then, at five past three, the flat having been dusted for fingerprints – they all seemed to be those of the same person, probably the owner – every inch examined for clues, Benedict Cooper arrived.

'Heard there was a bit of bother,' he said, putting his head around the living-room door where Carrick and Ingrams were sitting, Ingrams making notes.

'How did you get in?' Carrick asked coldly.

Cooper made a play of looking at his feet. 'There didn't seem to be anyone on guard,' he said with a smirk.

Carrick stood up. '*How* did you hear?'

Leaning against the doorpost, Cooper said, 'You're calling into question my professional ability to scent a good story. Don't tell me, I've guessed already. The local Jock police inspector is so inept that he can't protect a witness to a murder even if she happens to be his screwing mate. I think I've a bit of a scoop there, don't you?'

Ingrams had already witnessed the speed with which Carrick could move but was nevertheless unprepared to see him, in the blink of an eye, grabbing a big handful of Cooper's shirtfront.

'I want to know,' Carrick said, whispering, 'who told you.'

'One of your little erks at the nick.'

'You're lying.'

'Assault, too?' Cooper sniggered. 'She won't think much of you now, sunshine. You can say bye-bye to all that delightful what I believe John Masters called in and out and round and round. It's perfectly possible, of course, that she'll regard this little episode as a heaven-sent opportunity to get rid of you – you probably aren't much good at that either. Let go of me, copper, you're spoiling a perfectly good tie.'

Slowly, very slowly, Carrick released him. 'It's never been made public knowledge that Miss Mackenzie witnessed anything.'

'Someone with a brain can put two and two together,' Cooper said, unaccountably angry. 'She's been asking questions in Beckford Square. Several people mentioned that to me.'

'Now give me the name of the person at the nick who told you about this.'

Cooper shook his head. 'Oh, no. I have to protect my sources. That's the agreement. I slip them the odd fiver and forget what they're called and they come up with useful info. Surely you didn't imagine you were leak-proof?'

'You're still lying.'

'Call yourself a man?' Cooper scoffed. 'Is that all you can say?'

One of the crew members of the area car that had originally answered the 999 call now appeared. 'Sir!'

Carrick went out into the hall with him and there was a whispered consultation. When he returned his expression was completely without emotion but his eyes, Ingrams noticed, were fever-bright. The sergeant, who had been present when Carrick had issued an order an hour earlier and contacted Haine, held his breath.

'You came here,' Carrick said to Cooper, 'hoping to goad me into taking you apart. You were desperate, Benny, and you've failed.' Almost lovingly, he took possession of the front of the reporter's shirt again. 'I sent someone round to take a look at your friend Mallory. As a matter of fact I asked Chief Inspector Haine to take a look at him. He's none too good and is suffering from a cut head and various other minor scratches and bruises. He seems to be blaming you too and is very angry with you. In short, Benny, he's singing his head off. About tonight, your little financial arrangement, the porn business based at Bristol. Everything. Bob, get him out of my sight.'

'I'll kill him!' Cooper raved. 'This was his idea, you know, the girl. He wasn't really going to hurt her, just muddy the waters of your investigation so –'

Ingrams steam-rollered the man through the door and out of the flat, taking him right to the top of the stairs before he arrested and cautioned him. So he was not present to see Carrick smash his fist into the wall near where Cooper had been standing and then remain still, sobbing with pain and rage, the tears pouring down his cheeks. And because Cooper's loud voice had reached every corner of Joanna's home, the others present left him alone for a while.

Haine, wisely deciding that Carrick was too emotionally involved, took charge and sent his subordinate home with orders to get some rest. Carrick went to the hospital instead, where he was told that the assault victim was asleep, in no danger and that he could see her at midday. There was no choice but to plod back out to his car and do as he was told.

He was woken by the phone ringing at eight, thrashed out of the twisted sheet and almost knocked the lamp off the bedside table.

'It's me,' said a faint croak on the other end of the line. 'Glad I found you in.'

'Joanna!'

'Bob Ingrams is waiting to interview me but I'd rather you were here.'

'I'm there,' he pronounced, trying to free himself from the rest of the sheet.

'And, James?'

'Yes?'

'Have you got the keys of my flat?'

'No, they're at the nick, but I can get them for you.'

'Please would you call in and bring me a few things? A clean nightie? And my toothbrush and flannel?'

'No problem.'

'Oh, and my handbag.'

In the end he packed a small weekend case with things, including underwear, clean jeans and a cotton jumper for when she was discharged, a light dressing gown, most of the little jars and bottles from the top of the chest of drawers in her bedroom and a bath towel. We didn't take flowers, he hoped she wasn't going to be there for very long. Besides, Ingrams was waiting, Ingrams with his big ears and coarse red neck. Damn Haine for sending him.

She looked dreadful. One eye was half-closed and the left side of her face livid with contusions. The marks on her throat. . . .'

Carrick sat down quickly, thankful that he had asked his sergeant to remain outside for a few minutes.

'James, what on earth is the matter? You look ghastly.' Her voice was still very husky.

'I'm an arsehole. I forgot to send someone to keep an eye on you. I'm sorry. And for everything else – for not sticking by you, for putting my own career first, for being an utter *shit*.'

After a longish silence Joanna said, 'Did you look in the fridge?'

'Your fridge? No, of course not.'

'There's a bottle of champagne in there that I bought the day I left the job. To be opened in the event of hearing one word of regret from you.'

'But you nigh-on seduced me the other night!'

'That's another matter entirely. I'd go a long way by bus and train to go to bed with you, James Carrick.'

'It was Mallory,' he said when another eternity had gone by.

'Poser's aftershave. It would figure.'

'Quite. El Bandito. He reeked of it every time I saw him.'

'James, that was *clever*.'

'You're a cow. He's selling Cooper all the way down the river, too.'

'Wait a minute, though. How do you know what he smelled like?'

'Ah,' Carrick said. 'Well, as a matter of fact it was me who broke the door down and –'

'You came round? But you said you forgot.'

'I remembered too late.'

'I must know the truth. I had a dream that I was lying on the floor in the kitchen and you were making love to me.'

'No.'

'No? *What* then?'

'You'd stopped breathing,' he said, a tremor in his voice.

'I'm a cow after all,' Joanna murmured. 'And Cooper?'

'He arrived when you'd been taken away in the ambulance and did his level best to make me lose my temper with him. He was desperate, knew we were closing in on him and that he'd made an appalling mistake in getting involved with Mallory for his money.'

'But it solves nothing – you still haven't caught a murderer.'

'I don't know how I ever thought I could manage without you. No.' Out of the corner of his eye Carrick could see Ingrams hovering hopefully. 'Can you tell the story? Do you feel well enough?'

146

'I want to get it over with,' Joanna replied wearily.

'Leave out the bit about the dream of me making love to you on the floor, there's a good girl.'

He let Ingrams get on with it; the sergeant's pen kept busy writing as a trained memory recounted in detail what had occurred. She seemed to be taking it very well, Carrick thought.

At last, Ingrams snapped shut his notebook. 'Right. Thank you, Miss Mackenzie. Sir, I'm still worried about Harbutts. There's a discrepancy between his account of his movements on Friday night and what Jamie told you later.'

'Yes,' Carrick said. 'The time. He said he left at ten thirty and according to the boy it was ten because he was counting as the clock struck. Is it right, by the way?'

'Yes,' Joanna said.

'He said he arrived at a quarter to,' Ingrams said. 'It's a bit suspicious. I think we ought to talk to him again.'

'They don't waste much time, according to Mrs Moffat,' Joanna recollected. 'That's also according to Karen Williams according to Miss Braithewaite. He arrives, there's much bonking and shrieks from the woman and then he goes away again.'

'His wife's an ex-beauty queen,' Ingrams commented morosely. 'Got form, too – shoplifting.'

'An ex-beauty queen?' Carrick said in disbelief. 'Are you sure?'

'Yes, guv. Miss Chipping Farrington 1990. A bit of a pin-up by all accounts, baring all her charms on a calendar put out by Upper Piddle Lubricants.'

A nurse arrived to send away the visitors and found the patient hooting with laughter, holding her aching ribs.

'D'you want me for anything?' Ingrams asked outside.

'No, not at the moment. Take Miss Mackenzie's statement to Haine, he'll probably want it.'

'What about Harbutts? Are you going to talk to him again?'

'Eventually.'

He went back into the ward and sought out someone in authority. Then, with permission to speak to the assault victim for a further one minute only, he returned to her bedside. She seemed to be asleep.

'Joanna?' he whispered.

'I thought you'd gone,' she said without opening her eyes.

'You can be discharged this evening if someone will look after you for a few days.'

'I can't bother my friends with things like that.'

'You can bother me if you want to.'

Her eyes opened wide, even the swollen one.

'I mean it. And there'll be someone nearby for when I'm not around.'

'But I'm a wreck. I won't be able to do anything.'

He kissed her forehead. 'No, you're to stay in bed and be waited on.'

'I won't be able to do anything in bed either,' Joanna pointed out grimly.

'That's all right, I never fancy black and blue women.'

She turned over and commenced to snore gently, an action that he read as an affirmative.

'I can't say that I remember anyone of that description,' said the well-spoken woman on the entry desk at the Roman Baths and museum. 'And I was here on Saturday morning.'

'It would have been first thing,' Carrick said, 'just as you opened.' He stepped back as a party of American tourists approached and there were several minutes of complete pandemonium while it was established that they wanted tickets for the nearby Museum of Costume as well; directions were given to the Pump Room, the toilets and the gift shop and, finally, it was made clear to them that photographs could be taken.

'No, I've just remembered,' the woman said as the chattering crowd departed in the care of a guide. 'Sonia was here for a while – I was a little late, the car wouldn't start.'

'Is she here now?'

She looked at her watch. 'No, but she will be in about half an hour.'

'In that case I'll wait.'

'Take a walk round, Inspector.' She smiled coquettishly. 'On the house.'

Carrick had visited the Baths before but was now looking at these well-preserved remains of Roman Britain from quite another viewpoint. He wandered past the locked cabinets containing offerings thrown into the sacred spring for good luck – carved gemstones, an earring, coins, silver, bronze and pewter utensils – sparing a glance as he progressed at the life-sized bronze head of the goddess Minerva, found by men digging a sewer in 1727. And then down and into the past, the sound of gushing water getting louder, the air warm and steamy. Here Romans had lolled while slaves scraped and oiled them and then moved through to the Circular Bath for a cold plunge. This area, the hypocaust rooms, was built up on five successive occasions to avoid the ever-present threat of flooding.

It was like a labyrinth, with literally hundreds of places to hide a small item.

At the lowest level a steaming torrent of water – a quarter of a million gallons a day at 117 °F – poured through a Roman archway. This was the overflow from the reservoir, water that had started off as rain on the Mendip Hills some ten thousand years previously.

It was all very well hiding something small in a place like this, but getting it back safely was what mattered.

The Great Bath, used by the Romans as a swimming pool, was open to the sky, everything above shoulder height built by the Victorians. In the alcoves that lined the bath were stone seats, the remains of pillars, a section of the original roof, doorways, archways. . . . Carrick sat down and stared at it all. He would need an army.

Sonia, when he found her, or rather when she found him, was a woman in her sixtieth year, a little out of breath. 'I understand you want to speak to me, Inspector.'

Carrick rose politely and asked her to sit with him. When she had settled herself he said, 'I want you to think back to early Saturday morning, when you first opened. You were on duty selling tickets. Can you remember a woman wearing glasses? She's about five foot six inches tall with dark hair. Rather an odd sort of person, looks a bit furtive.'

'Straggly hair tied back?'

'Yes.'

'Her clothes were quite long, shapeless really. They looked as though they'd all been put in the washing machine together

149

when they were new and the colours had all run into each other.'

'Perfect,' Carrick said. 'What did she do?'

'Just bought a ticket and went in.'

'Did she join one of the tours?'

'No, there wasn't one just then. I'd say, if anything, she would have avoided one. As you say, furtive.' She laughed. 'Bath might be one of the most beautiful cities in the world but it has its eccentrics like everywhere else.'

'Did you see her leave?'

'No, I was really supposed to be helping in the shop that morning so when Elsa finally arrived I went in there.'

Carrick gazed across the green, steamy waters of the Great Bath. 'Did you notice if she was carrying anything?'

'Just a big handbag. Clutching it to herself as though someone might try to steal it.'

'And I assume it was pretty quiet just then, not many people about?'

'Only about half a dozen. We find that on Saturdays most of the tourists seem to have a lie-in.' She uttered another tinkling laugh. 'Taking after the Bathonians – they never get up in the mornings either.'

'Whereas you, dear lady, are from Bristol,' Carrick said, smiling and deliberately pronouncing it "Bristle" in the local vernacular.

'Clifton. I've lived there all my life.'

'And yet you travel to Bath to work.'

'Labour of love really. I'll still come to look at these lovely buildings after I've retired.'

Carrick lingered, going into the elegant eighteenth-century Pump Room for tea. Under the rather frosty gaze of the statue of Richard 'Beau' Nash – the man who set the social and dress standards for Georgian Bath – an American couple sampled a brimming tumbler of the waters from a fountain, warily eyeing one another as though they expected to be poisoned. On a stage, a string quartet played Haydn.

Why had Bethany Cryon visited the Roman Baths? Was he really being fanciful in wondering if it had been to hide the Chantbury Pyx? His training told him to go and see her again and try and get the truth out of her but instinct whispered caution. There was another man, the one Jamie had seen leave the building. Probably a murderer.

When he had eaten a Bath bun with a pot of China tea, Carrick went to find the person in charge and told him that he wanted to make a thorough search of the entire complex.

# Chapter Fifteen

It was rather a shock to Carrick when he realised that Joanna was to be taken to his car in a wheelchair. But, as she explained, it was only because she was 'wobbly'. Before his arrival she had argued against the decision, all too aware that the doors of his ground-floor flat had been specially widened so that his wife, confined to a wheelchair for the last eighteen months of her life, could move around. To remind him of that, in such circumstances, was more than unfortunate.

As it happened, everything went smoothly, a nurse doing the pushing, chatting to them happily. When they reached the car Joanna was able to get in unaided and when they arrived at their destination she just had to walk a short distance on the level to the door. Being brave once safely inside was beyond her.

He had expected something like this and held her tightly when she burst into a storm of tears. His main concern was that she might not have told Ingrams everything.

'What's that?' she gulped when he had steered her gently towards the big sofa and fetched them both a small bracer.

'Brandy.'

'Do you have any ginger?'

'Sure.'

This provided, she said, 'James, how did he get in?'

'You left the big kitchen window open. The fire escape isn't that far away and there's a big set of drainpipes on the wall in between that and your little balcony. Easy.'

'I wouldn't have thought he was fit enough to do that.'

'Me neither. He seems to be more scared of Cooper than of breaking his neck.'

Joanna took a large mouthful of her drink. 'No amount of training can prepare you for the real thing.'

'No. But you're safe here. All the windows have locks on them and a probationer called Russell will be here for a while tonight –'

'You're going out?'

'Someone saw Bethany Cryon queuing to go into the Roman Baths. I forgot to mention it earlier.'

'She *is* bananas, though.'

'Have you met her?'

'No, that's just hearsay.'

'Oh, she's bananas all right. Just the sort to get mixed up in something dodgy.'

'You think Harbutts and someone else are using her?' Joanna drained her glass. '*Super* anaesthetic.'

He gave her a drop more.

'So you're going to talk to her again tonight?'

'No, I've arranged for a very low-profile search of the Roman Baths and the museum.'

'Surely they have security checks? They'd have found anything that shouldn't be there.'

'No doubt they do. But they can't always check everywhere – not among all those piles of wee slabs in the hypocaust, for example.'

'It would be a lot easier to put the frighteners on Harbutts.'

'I'd like to take him to a piece of waste ground and pulverise him,' Carrick admitted. 'That's the only way with people like that. But I can't and there's no real evidence against him. I've never worked on cases with less evidence.'

'There's only the hammer as the common denominator, too.'

'Don't remind me. It might not be the same hammer either, wedges notwithstanding.' He stood up. 'Bed, you. I've made the spare room all pretty for you. I don't think I'll be late but if it looks as though I will be I'll give you a ring. If not, I'll cook us something when I come in.'

'And young Russell will be outside?'

'Across the door like a ridgeback. He doesn't have a key so no one will be able to thump his head and take it away from him. He does have a radio, though. All right?'

'Yes. Thank you.'

'Do you want anything from your place? I'm going up there to check because I can't remember whether anyone shut that kitchen window. No point risking burglars getting in.'

'No, I'm fine.'

'Joanna, I have to ask you this. Did he. . . I mean. . . . You didn't have much on when I found you.'

'No, but I think he thought about it.'

'I'd have killed him if he hadn't run,' Carrick said, wrenching open the door and plunging out.

Joanna picked up her overnight case from where he had put it just inside the front door and took it into the spare bedroom. He had indeed made it 'all pretty' for her, the bed made up with lace-trimmed sheets and pillowcases, yellow freesias fragrant in a delicate vase. They both knew that she was not a frilly sort of person, but when you have been subjected to a vicious attack, such little luxuries are food for the soul.

She was fully aware too that he hated himself for not taking Cooper's threats more seriously. She supposed that Carrick had assumed that the threats, as such, were directed at him personally. His vow to put the crime reporter behind bars had been no secret at the Manvers Street CID offices, even in the days when Joanna had worked there; in fact, it had been something of a diversion, 'Carrick's vendetta'. That the affair had sunk to such personal, acrimonious levels was rather shocking.

Part of the problem was that Carrick was such a private person, even now she felt that she hardly knew him. Even quite ordinary queries from his staff about his wellbeing had met with a stony response. The only times he had thawed had been the odd occasion when several of them had gone for a drink together. After two or three whiskies she had known him to become quite chatty. Perhaps then he had forgotten for a little while that he had to return home to a dying woman.

And now he had saved her life. It took quite a lot of getting used to.

Catching a glimpse of herself in a mirror, Joanna paused in her slow pacing of the room and sank onto the bed. She could still see her reflection, though, and the image that stared back at her, looking horrified, was of a stranger; green eyes almost hidden by the puffiness of her face, her mouth swollen, bruises everywhere, no trace of what a lovesick boyfriend had once called 'Degas beauty'. Her hair, definitely her best feature, was tangled and in dire need of washing. Like a robot she went into the bathroom, vaguely searched for shampoo but again found herself face to face with her own hideous reflection in another mirror.

What sort of relationship was there to be had with a man who only wanted to pick your brains and use your body? It was true that when he was with her he was tender, amusing in his way and quite good company. Then he went away until the next time. He had looked quite ghastly at the hospital, though. He obviously *cared*. He had clearly been deeply in love with Kathleen.

In a kind of dream Joanna wandered into his bedroom, not even sure what she was looking for. But she found it; a picture of Kathleen on his bedside table. It was a carefree snap of a young woman hugging a huge shaggy dog in someone's garden.

She could have been Joanna's twin sister.

Carrick was deliberately not thinking about Joanna as he drove the short distance up the road to her flat. It was dark now, which took him by surprise: he had spent longer with Joanna than he had thought. There was plenty of time, though; he had asked Ingrams to arrange to start the search at ten. He wanted it done thoroughly but quickly, using personnel borrowed, if necessary, from Bristol, and had emphasised that everyone was to use an inconspicuous emergency exit made available by the museum authorities. A member of staff would be present.

He still had the keys to the new lock in his pocket, his violent entry having necessitated the services of a carpenter. Mind on a hundred and one other things, he inserted the key in the lock, opened the door, snapped down the hall light switch and went in, pushing the door closed behind him.

The light did not come on.

'Shit,' he whispered.

He turned to open the door again in order to let enough light in to see by and someone leaped on him from behind, clutching him around the throat. He grabbed both the hands, yanked them off, twisted round and struck out blindly. His fist connected, but uselessly, striking a leather-clad shoulder. Anticipating retaliation, he ducked down, dived right past his attacker and then used both feet. There was a howl of pain.

Then someone else gripped him from behind.

In the dark he tried to fight them off. He was fitter than most and extremely agile, his main asset to his chosen sport that of being able to dart and weave and run like a hare. But he was lightly built, no match for two mauling thugs. One of them, he soon discovered to his cost, was armed with a pickaxe handle.

Once or twice he broke away and, hitting walls, furniture, doors and hard surfaces in all directions, endeavoured to hide. But he was on unfamiliar territory; if the attack had happened in his own flat he would have had more chance. They always found him again, hands in his hair, grasping his clothes, pinioning his arms.

Soon, semiconscious, he slipped to the floor, left only with the instinct to curl up and protect his head with his arms. Then they switched on a table lamp, to enable them to see what they were doing.

All in all, it went on for far too long.

Ingrams waited until ten past ten and then ordered the search to commence. He watched for a few minutes and then went out of the side entrance to his car, parked discreetly with a couple of unmarked minibuses that had brought the search team.

'Is Inspector Carrick with you, sir?' he asked when he had radioed to locate the DCI.

'No, I thought he was helping you with your archaeological dig,' Haine said impatiently, expressing his opinion of the exercise.

'He said he'd be here at ten, that's all,' Ingrams went on lamely.

'Wasn't he collecting that girl from hospital first?'

'Yes, I believe so, sir.'

A dirty chuckle came over the air. 'Call yourself a detective, Ingrams? He's more than likely decided to slip in a quick one first. Roger and out, eh?'

There was a guffaw of laughter cut short by a click as he replaced the mike.

'Very funny, I'm sure,' Ingrams muttered. 'Right, my lad, we'll get you back to work.' He called in again and asked to be put through to the man keeping watch on Carrick's flat.

'No, sir, he went out,' said Russell.

'When?' Ingrams barked.

'About three quarters of an hour ago.'

'Did you see which way he went?'

'Only that he drove up the hill.'

'But he's supposed to be –' Ingrams bit off what he had been about to say. 'Shall I ask Miss Mackenzie if she knows where he went?'

'No, I'll –'

'Hang on, sir, she's here.' His radio must then have been removed from his grasp for the next voice Ingrams heard was hoarse and did not give the impression that the speaker was particularly awe-struck with him.

'What's the problem, sergeant?'

Ingrams came straight to the point.

'He said he was off to find you. But first he was going to call in at my flat to check that the window had been closed. Why, have you *lost* him?'

'He's not here.'

'Then for God's sake get someone up to my flat! Number 7 Hillcrest House, Landsdown Road. Have you got that?'

Ingrams rather thought that he had. In fact he went himself, leaving a uniformed sergeant in charge of the search and commandeering an area car and its crew who were in the locality.

The door of the flat was wide open, a draught of air fanning into their faces. Apprehension wrenching at his stomach, Ingrams led the way at a run. He did not have to search for very long. Carrick was in the living room, conscious after a fashion, and trying to get to his feet. He saw Ingrams, appeared to give up the struggle and pitched forward to lie still.

Ten minutes later, the siren of the ambulance still audible, Ingrams forced himself to concentrate. Whoever had attacked Carrick had broken in through the same window –

157

which had been closed – by smashing the glass near the catch. The Sergeant did not enter the kitchen as he waited for the scene-of-crime team to arrive, just stood in a state of stunned disbelief, staring at the slivers of glass glittering on the floor, the scuff-marks of shoes on the draining board and a couple of long scratches on the white paintwork of the window frame.

'Well, it wasn't Mallory,' he said as he heard someone approaching behind him.

'What the hell's happened?' asked a woman's voice.

Ingrams whirled round. 'You shouldn't be here.'

'I brought Russell with me,' Joanna snapped. 'He didn't have a lot of choice, actually, so don't bawl him out. What's *happened*? I heard the ambulance.'

'He walked into some kind of ambush.'

'Meant for me?'

Ingrams shrugged.

'Well, is he dead?' she shrieked.

'No, no,' Ingrams hastened to say. 'He was conscious when we arrived but passed out. Pretty badly beaten up, I'd say.'

Her gaze flicked around the kitchen. 'Have you spoken to the neighbours?'

'Not yet.'

She turned to face him. 'Perhaps you better had.'

'Don't try to teach me my job,' he said coldly.

'Someone has to, sergeant. Otherwise, when Haine rolls up in a few minutes, you're going to be caught with your short trousers down.'

'Bitch!' he spat at her as he walked out.

With determination Joanna walked into the living room. 'Don't touch *anything*,' she said to the crew of the area car who were in there.

Some of the furniture was overturned, ornaments smashed, one of the dining chairs had its back splintered but it still stood upright, jammed under the table. She suddenly felt sick. The attacker, or attackers, had not just used their fists.

Moments later the flat was full of people, probably the same people who had been there the previous night, Joanna thought. Then Haine arrived, greeting her with exactly the same remark as had Ingrams.

'It's *my* flat,' Joanna reminded him, flicking her damp hair away from her face.

'There's no doubt this was intended for you,' Haine said, after issuing orders. 'You seem to have made a hell of a lot of enemies.'

'So you don't think there's a connection with the Pryce murder case, then?'

For some reason he was peering in corners. 'I'm keeping an open mind about it until I know more, something that appears to have been in lamentably short supply lately. I've never gone along with the idea of linking two murders and a robbery and all on the strength of one hammer. I intend to take over these investigations personally and shall continue to direct them when Inspector Carrick is fit enough to return to duty. In the meantime, Miss Mackenzie, I'd be grateful if you'd get yourself out from under my feet.'

On the way out she said, 'Oh, by the way, those scratches on the window frame weren't there before.'

Russell was still outside. He towered over her, gimlet-eyed, ready to take her safely through hellfire and worse. She warmed to him.

'I shall have to borrow your arm,' Joanna said apologetically.

Russell assessed the situation for himself. And carried her.

Joanna's immediate ambition to re-acquaint herself, briefly, with the brandy bottle and then go to bed and sleep for a week had to be postponed because when they got back to Carrick's flat the phone was ringing.

''Tis yourself, my dear,' said Declan O'Connor's cheery voice. 'Now that's really strange, I tried to reach you at your flat not thirty minutes ago and here you are at the next number on my list.' He chuckled.

Joanna explained that there was a bit of a crisis at her end of the line.

'Holy saints! And I thought Bath was the kind of place where it made the headlines if someone fell off a bus. Is the man all right?'

'I've no idea. He's only just arrived at the hospital so I don't suppose I could find out yet.'

'Well, I won't keep you. I was ringing about that antique dealer you told me about. Squeaky clean. And they didn't keep a note of the name of the Japanese man so no leads there, I'm afraid.'

159

'Inspector Carrick organised a search of the Roman Baths tonight but it's too early to know if they found anything.'

'For the Pyx? That's really imaginative. Any idea why?'

'Someone saw a woman called Bethany Cryon queuing up to go in early on Saturday morning. It's all a bit tenuous but she's a sort of girlfriend of a man who was in Beckford Square the night of the first murder. He's got form.'

'The tenuous bit being the famous hammer, I presume?'

'Yes, but shortly to be discounted. You'll have to contact Chief Inspector Haine from now, he's taken over the cases.'

'No leads on the woman?'

'No. And she's Canadian – or says she is. Mad as a hatter, according to Carrick.'

'There's nothing like a little inspired lunacy for keeping at bay people who might ask awkward questions,' O'Connor said just before he rang off.

On a notepad at the side of the phone Joanna scribbled a reminder to herself to make enquiries about Cryon to the Canadian authorities.


Carrick had just received a 'suicide' pass from a flanker and, despite accelerating, took the full consequences, slammed face down in the mud, at least five men piled on top of him. He kept hold of the ball. This shrunk and was now an apple, the one he had picked when seven years old from a tree growing over the garden wall. The person trying to take it from him was his grandfather, a ferocious old man, an Elder of the Kirk, who threatened to 'thrash the De'il oot of ye' for not only stealing but stealing on the Sabbath.

Thrashed he certainly was, the 'breeks' removed right there and then in the garden and a leather belt wielded with strength and self-righteous ire. He screamed, the pain quite insupportable. Suddenly his mother was there, breathless having run from indoors, shouting at her father to stop. Carrick slipped off the bony knee and was sick, wallowing in his own misery and vomit on the grass. But he still had the apple tightly clutched in his hand.

Only it wasn't an apple now but a smooth metal bar. He was lying on his stomach on a hard surface and although his eyes were shut he knew that the lights were very bright. Hands were touching him all over and so was the pain. He gripped the metal bar more tightly but it didn't help and he foundered, writhing. Then a needle pricked his arm and he floated off into nothingness.

Waking from this was like being reborn. Before had been a void; now all at once he was lying in bed in a hospital ward, reality bursting in on his senses in the shape of a large woman in a purple dressing gown laughing loudly. He closed his eyes firmly again for a moment and then opened them. No, he had not been dreaming, he really was in a mixed ward. She saw him looking at her.

'Sister! Your policeman's awake.' She beamed at him. 'Better now, lovey? You looked so peaceful lying there. Maisie and me had a bet on the colour of your eyes. She said green but I knew they were blue.' Coming up close she peered at him. 'Blue. That's a quid she owes me. Don't take any notice of me,' she added with another laugh. 'And you're not on your own. There's old Mr Jeffers over there come in to have his waterworks seen to. There can't be anything worse for blokes than to have their waterworks play up. I mean, it's all in an important sort of area, isn't it?'

He was noting with some surprise that he did not seem to be hitched up to any medical hardware, drips or monitoring devices. Somehow he had expected to be.

The sister came bustling up. 'Well, Inspector, how are you feeling?'

'I'm not quite sure,' he answered truthfully.

'We've given you sedatives and pain-killing injections and let you sleep. You'll be very bruised and sore, of course, but nothing's broken. Dr White says there's a chance you might have internal injuries. In view of that we would like you to remain here under observation for forty-eight hours.'

He stared stolidly back at her.

'It's in your own interest.'

'I'd be the last person to disagree with that.'

'Good,' she said over her shoulder with a smile as she went away.

At ten thirty that morning White did his rounds, this being very informal as he was standing in for the consultant who was on holiday.

161

'You're very fit,' he said to Carrick, after introducing himself.

'And keen to get out of here.'

'Quite badly beaten, though. We'd like to keep an eye on you for a couple of days.'

'I've come off worse playing rugby.'

'Been out of bed yet?'

'No, but I could do with a short walk.'

White leaned both hands on the end of the bed frame. 'Okay,' he drawled. 'If you can get to the john under your own steam and everything works and you don't pass blood I'll think about it.'

Carrick's arms felt like boiled spaghetti as he lifted the covers off and got out of bed. He suddenly realised that he was wearing only a hospital night-shirt that was fastened at the back with tapes. It felt slightly draughty, as though some of them might have come undone. To hell with it.

'I'll go with him,' offered the lady in the purple dressing gown, who had been eavesdropping.

'A *nurse* will go with him, Mrs Donnelly, thank you,' White said.

There was something about White's manner that Carrick found interesting, something perhaps the smallest bit hostile. 'Been stopped for speeding lately?' he asked as he stood up.

'You won't make it,' White said, smiling gently. 'Your arms and legs took most of the punishment. Beat you up in the dark, did they?'

Carrick didn't reply, concentrating on walking in a straight line.

'He's got a nice bum,' he heard Mrs Donnelly say as he turned the corner.

The slightly surreal, glad-to-be-alive feeling soon dissipated, however, and when he was taken home that afternoon he found that some kind of delayed reaction had set in and he shook like a leaf in a gale. Haine, who had collected him from the hospital and taken the opportunity to make his feelings forcefully known on several subjects, delivered his parting salvo.

'Oh, by the way, they found nothing at the Baths. Nothing except a few apple cores that people had lobbed over the railings into the hypocaust and a dead pigeon. Perhaps that was what your daft woman was trying to get rid of.'

The front door slammed.

'You can come out now,' said Carrick, who had let them both in using his own key. He sat down, it was imperative.

Joanna came from her temporary hiding place, the bathroom.

'Courage, child,' he said softly. Again he was appalled by her appearance, the bruising and swelling of her face.

'Lance is dead,' she whispered. 'He died suddenly last night – there were complications.'

He held out his arms to her and she sat with him on the big sofa and cried.

'I wanted to put some hemlock in his tea,' Joanna said after a while. 'I feel really awful. I feel really awful about you too. I'm so sorry, James.'

He smiled at her. 'Men are better survivors of this kind of thing. Don't be sorry. I feel that I can look you in the eye now.'

'It's all part of the job.'

'And because of everything else,' he elaborated.

'Atonement? But I'd be the last person to –'

He laid a finger to her lips. 'Tea? Shall we draw straws for who's going to crawl into the kitchen and put the kettle on?'

'You stay right there. Do you want some water first to take pills with?'

'Brilliant woman,' he murmured, closing his eyes.

There was a knock at the door. It was someone from Carrick's team, wanting a statement.

For several days it was as if they each lived on their own. They were in the same flat and yet they hardly communicated. Whoever was in the kitchen when the other entered prepared food or hot drinks, whichever one of them got up first checked on the wellbeing of the other. They respected one another's privacy and yet at the same time did not lock doors or worry overmuch about appearing half-dressed.

Carrick, in fact, spent two days in bed, alone with the consequences of checking that a window was closed, and taking painkillers only when he wanted to sleep. He was

163

aware of Joanna looking in on him occasionally and thanked her for the light snacks that she sometimes brought. He wasn't particularly hungry but ate them all the same. If he ate and slept he wouldn't start drinking.

On the third morning he got out of bed, slowly, his own bruises well in evidence, and made his way to the shower where he succeeded in getting soap and water over most of his person and drying nearly everywhere off. That small triumph behind him, he made a pot of tea and, while it brewed, picked up the phone.

'They don't seem to have made any progress,' he reported when Joanna appeared a few minutes later, a towel around her head, having just washed her hair.

'Were you talking to Ingrams?'

'Yes.'

'I'm sorry they didn't find anything at the Baths. I thought that idea had quite a lot going for it.'

'That's life.'

She sat down. 'You never told me that I looked so much like Kathleen.'

'I didn't?' he replied woodenly.

Joanna went away to dry her hair.

With orders to stay on sick leave for at least a week there was little Carrick could do. It was not possible for either of them to attend Lance's funeral because his family lived in Newcastle and he was to be buried in the cemetery next to the parish church. The surviving partner of the business continued to grieve and feel deeply guilty.

'I'm sure you shouldn't be doing that,' Joanna said when she took him in a cup of tea on the fourth morning and found him doing bend and stretch exercises.

Carrick groaned, not a reaction to her comment by any means. He straightened slowly. 'I'm sure too.'

'You look as though you've been hit by a train,' she said when they had both subsided onto the floor with their tea. 'They must have known who you were, surely? I mean, if you're waiting to attack someone and somebody else turns up, you don't –'

The phone rang.

164

'Many apologies for not ringing before to find out how you are,' said Declan O'Connor. 'I hope you didn't have to run to the phone – you sound a mite breathless.'

'No,' Carrick said. 'Just discovering that I can't touch my toes any more.'

The Irishman burst out laughing. 'Ah, well, there's nothing like fifty press-ups to start the day,' he said, adding 'sir' as an afterthought. He went on, 'I'm not too sure how much in touch you are with developments at your end but I felt that it might be my duty to inform you that there was a break-in at your Roman Baths last night.'

In his excitement Carrick swore in Gaelic. 'What happened?'

'A chappie broke in – climbed over the wall by the Great Bath using grappling hooks and ropes. But he was spotted over the security cameras and chased. Got away. Ran like a mountain goat, according to one of the guards. I think we might be talking about some kind of military training here.'

'D'you mind telling me who told you about this?'

'Well, it was your good sergeant. It would seem that he was as disappointed about the search drawing a blank as no doubt you were. Haine's not interested.'

'I'm indebted to you. Thanks.'

Deferentially O'Connor went on, 'And it isn't for me to ask but have you tried the Mounties about your crazy Canadian woman? I know the DCI's dropped the idea but –'

'Joanna left me a note about it,' Carrick interrupted with a wry smile. 'God,' he said when he had hung up. 'I wish he was working for me.'

'I heard most of that,' Joanna said. '*What* was it you said when he told you about the break-in?'

'Filthy Gaelic – I wouldn't even begin to translate it into English.'

'I didn't know you could speak Gaelic.'

'I can't, just swear in it. It's –' He broke off and got up abruptly.

'What's the matter?'

When he did not reply Joanna rose and wrapped his towelling bathrobe around his shoulders, perceiving that he was shivering.

165

'I've just remembered something,' he said after a little while. 'They switched a light on. At least, I think they did. I wasn't taking too much notice by that time. I saw their feet. One of them was wearing brown lace-up shoes. Old, scuffed. I'd say they were probably a size eight.'

'With a plain sole?'

'As far as I could see. But I could have imagined or dreamed it when I was out cold. I did have some weird dreams.'

'That kind of footwear would be very impractical for the activities he was undertaking.'

'Yes. Perhaps he's superstitious.'

'Lucky shoes?'

'Something like that.'

Joanna wrinkled her nose. 'Dressed to kill?'

# Chapter Sixteen

It was an ethereal, timeless scene that the tiny camera had recorded: the water of the Great Bath steaming gently into the night sky, the archways between the stone columns in utter darkness. Carrick half expected to see a procession of high priests and acolytes emerge from a hidden doorway and make their way, chanting and leading animals for sacrifice, to the pagan altars in the lower levels.

Then, like a wraith, a figure appeared on the balustraded walkway above and abseiled down until he stood right at the water's edge. He was dressed in dark clothing and was hooded, with holes cut for eyes and mouth. After standing motionless for a few moments he began to walk slowly towards the camera, apparently listening. He was carrying something in his right hand, possibly a flashlight. Then he stopped suddenly and ran back, rapidly climbing back up the rope and disappearing from view. As he did so, two security guards came into the range of the camera, running. One looked for a moment as though he might follow the intruder, using the rope, and then changed his mind.

Carrick switched off the video recorder. He had viewed the short scene several times and was no nearer coming to any useful conclusions.

'O'Connor was right,' Sergeant Ingrams said. 'There's something SAS-style about him.'

'If only they'd watched him for a bit longer,' Carrick grumbled. 'They knew we were interested in the place. There was every chance that they would have been able to grab him too.'

Ingrams asked the important question. 'You think there's a connection with our cases and that it's not just some prank?'

'He doesn't look like a prankster, does he? But I know what you mean. He could also have been intent on breaking into the gift shop hoping to raid the tills.'

'You don't seem too convinced about that.'

'I'm not. It's fairly obvious these days that important tourist attractions are protected with security devices. He took the risk and I don't think it was just for money.'

'What for, then – the Chantbury Pyx?'

'Are you sure they looked everywhere?'

'Every nook and cranny, sir. It took all of four hours.'

Carrick took the tape out of the machine. 'I'll borrow this if I may. I'd like Miss Mackenzie to see it. One thing: did he leave any equipment behind other than the rope?'

'Just the grappling hook attached to it.'

'No fingerprints?'

'No.'

'I'm forgetting – you need gloves for abseiling. It must have been the same rope he used to climb up to the walkway first. So how did he get down if he left it all behind, jump?'

'Must have done, sir. But there might be projections a good climber could use – drainpipes and so forth.'

'I can't remember any. We might be looking for someone with two broken ankles.'

'Shall I make enquiries at the hospital?'

'Excellent idea.'

Haine barged in. 'Oh, there you are, Ingrams. There's something I'd like you to do for me.' He looked at Carrick in surprise. 'Are you fighting fit? Been cleared by the doc?'

'No, sir,' Carrick answered, knowing what was coming. Illness irritated Haine, he loathed being surrounded by what he called walking wounded.

'I don't want to see you here until you're fully recovered.'

'There's nothing wrong with my brain,' Carrick countered, annoyed anyway.

The Chief Inspector seemed to be in a very bad mood. 'And what brilliant deductions have you come to since your arrival?' he enquired sarcastically.

'That something's been hidden in the Roman Baths and no one's found it yet.'

Haine's face creased into a patronising smile. 'You're talking about the spiderman, I take it. Forget it. Someone did a parachute jump inside St Paul's Cathedral but there was no criminal motive. Nothing was stolen, no damage was done. Don't tell me you're still banging on about the Chantbury Pyx. It's on the other side of the world by now, James. Let the Arts and Antiques Squad worry about it. The Baths were searched. Exhaustively. You'll be saying next that you want us all to go swimming.'

Ingrams discovered that an extremely chilly gaze had come to rest upon him.

'Did you?' Carrick asked.

'Go swimming?' Ingrams said, losing his wits for a moment.

'Get a frogman to check the pools, idiot!'

'No, but you can see right into them.'

'Not into the Great Bath you can't. The water's green and five feet deep, dammit!'

There was a silence broken by Haine saying, 'No, I can't justify authorising it. There's no evidence – nothing to go on at all.'

'One man for about an hour, that's all,' Carrick said.

'Bring me some more *evidence*,' Haine said. Then, infuriated even further by the look on his subordinate's face, added, in the guise of half-joking, 'Remember what happened at Culloden, James.'

Carrick, the menfolk of an entire branch of whose family had been wiped out at that historic battle between the Scots and the English, walked out. There was nothing that smacked of capitulation or petulance about this, any more than the troublesome tribes of the north have ever been finally subdued, for he quite quickly returned. With him was Joanna Mackenzie. They both went into Haine's office, inscrutable as a pair of stuffed owls.

The Chief Inspector was writing a report; it was this exertion that had caused him to be in such a bad mood in the first place. He was rather regretting his comment, for he had high regard for Carrick's capabilities. Haine had had little to do with Joanna Mackenzie, however, since she had left two weeks after he had been posted to Bath from Taunton. He had heard, from others, that they had worked very well

169

together as a team. It came as rather a shock to him to realise, as they entered, that nothing had changed. Here, it was obvious, were like minds.

'It's him,' Joanna said without preamble. 'The man who broke into the Roman Baths is the same one I saw leaving Beckford Square when Mrs Pryce was murdered.'

Haine invited his visitors to be seated. 'Are you sure? *Can* you be sure?'

'I'm almost a hundred per cent sure. There's something about his walk – I can't really describe it. A slight bounce in the step, perhaps. And something I'd forgotten about: he holds his head slightly on one side.'

There was a short silence during which Carrick shifted slightly in his chair, wincing.

Haine shoved the report to one side. 'James, while you've been recovering I've studied every aspect of these cases – the Pryce murder, Susan Fairbrother's death, the theft of the Chantbury Pyx. I agree that there might be connections but when it comes to some of the witnesses I think you've overlooked things.'

'Such as?' Carrick asked.

'Jack Moffat for one. I dug a little more deeply. He wasn't invalided out of the army – he was cashiered.'

'What for?'

'It was hushed up, of course, and officially he resigned his commission. He was only a captain when he was captured by the Japanese in Malaya and went on, after the war, to serve in the Royal Engineers at Elgin. In the late fifties he took a Defence College course and was posted to Whitehall, by this time colonel. The incident happened shortly after his arrival. He attacked someone who worked in the department with him, a civil servant. The man ended up seriously hurt in hospital.'

'You say shortly after he arrived. How shortly?'

'Within a year. Eight months, I think. I can dig all the facts out again if you like.'

'Weapon?' Carrick wanted to know impassively.

'Fists.'

'What was it all about?'

'No idea. But I intend to ask him.'

Carrick sighed. 'I believed his account of finding the murder weapon.'

'You might well have done. He possibly believed it himself. But on his own admission he gets funny turns. He might have started having them in London and that's why he went for someone. He could have conceivably placed the murder weapon in the garden in Beckford Square and not remembered doing it afterwards. You're forgetting, he attacked Sergeant Armstrong with it – no provocation. Don't shake your head at me, James. Those are the facts.'

'His wife's not at all strong. And Armstrong, frankly, was right over the top. In a word, disgusting. I can understand what Moffat did.'

'I'm going to pull him in and talk to him.'

'Do I get my diver or not?'

Haine just looked at him.

Carrick said, 'Moffat's right-handed. His left's a real mess after what the Japanese did to it. Mrs Pryce's killer was left-handed.'

'You can't absolve him on those grounds alone. He could have used his right hand from another angle. No, I think we hang fire on the baths.'

'Then at least put a couple of our people down there in case the intruder returns.'

'I'll think about that' was all Haine would promise.

Carrick bumped into Ingrams on the way out.

'No one admitted to hospital with broken ankles,' the sergeant said. 'One broken leg – a woman fell off some kitchen steps reaching up to a top shelf.'

'Did you try the hospitals in Bristol?'

'Two guys badly smashed up after a car crash, a five-year-old with a broken arm, a teenage girl with a broken wrist. That's all. Oh, and Benedict Cooper's here – he wants to talk to you.'

'Tell him to go to hell.'

'He said it's important.'

'Is he on bail?'

'Yes.'

Carrick called to Joanna who had gone on ahead and she returned. 'Cooper's here. He wants to see me. Do you mind waiting for a while?'

'Shall I wait in the car?'

'I'd rather you didn't go off on your own.'

'What does he want?'

'No idea.'

'Can I be a fly on the wall?'

'Can you face being in the same room as the bastard?'

'Definitely.'

Cooper was in number 2 interview room. Without the habitual sunglasses – they were tucked into the top pocket of his jacket – he looked quite different and somehow ordinary. At his feet was a bundle, a black plastic refuse sack tied with string.

'Come to gloat?' he said when he saw Joanna.

Carrick said, 'Miss Mackenzie is under police protection. She expressed an interest in what you have to say.'

'So correct and precise,' Cooper mocked. 'The pair of you are positively unsettling, you're so inhuman.'

'And yet you've been trying to prove for years that I'm as human as the next man. Get on with what you have to say – I'm busy.'

Cooper nudged the parcel at his feet. 'Present for you.'

'What is it?'

'Take a look.'

'*You* open it.'

Cooper bent down and untied the knots. 'I'm not touching it in case there are prints on it. Here.' And he slid the bag across the vinyl floor.

Carrick very carefully rolled down the bag so that he could see what was inside.

Cooper said, 'Believe it or not, there is an element of the criminal minority in this lovely city of ours that doesn't take kindly to people half killing coppers. As you almost certainly know, in my job as crime reporter I meet all sorts, some of them downright shady. I can't reveal my source but you may depend on it that that half-burned leather jacket was worn by one of the men who attacked you.'

'Where was it found?'

'On some waste ground at the Longacre industrial estate.'

'Are you sure it didn't belong to the man who told you he found it?'

'Positive. He's knee-high to a grasshopper and never had the nerve for rough stuff. Housebreaking's his line of business.'

'No one said anything about size,' Carrick murmured.

'The jacket's big, though.'

Peering over Carrick's shoulder, Joanna said. 'Those studs on the shoulders and upper arms could have made the deep scratches on the window frame.'

'So did your source seek you out and tell you about this or did you ask around?' Carrick enquired.

'Why should I ask around?' Cooper said with something of his old sneer back.

Calmly Carrick replied, 'Okay, he came to you. I'm still not sure why.'

'He was hoping for a few quid, I expect.'

'Why *you*?'

'Perhaps he thought I could do a deal with you and you'd put in a kind word with your pals in Bristol. But I know when I'm flogging a dead horse.'

'If you hadn't put Mallory up to that vicious attack on –'

'That was his idea.'

'He hasn't got that kind of brain. I think you'd better get out of my sight. I'm glad, really glad, that Bristol and Haine are handling this between them and I don't have to get involved.' When Cooper still sat there he said, 'You don't have to make amends to *me* but to this young lady here. You wrecked her career and you tried to –' He broke off. 'Get out.'

'Make amends?' Cooper said as he went towards the door. 'All's fair in love and war.'

'Do you believe him?' Joanna asked when Cooper had gone. 'About his source, I mean.'

'I don't believe anything he says.' Carrick picked up the bag. 'I'll let forensic have this straight away.'

Joanna was staring into space. 'That was the sort of thing Lance would have said. "All's fair in love and war." He was always trotting out hackneyed phrases.'

'D'you miss him?'

She smiled sadly. 'Yes, I do.'

'What will you do with the business?'

173

'I don't know yet. Only half of it's mine. I don't even know if he left a will and I don't suppose anyone he left his share to would greet the news with glee – it would probably be regarded as a liability.'

'Not a going concern then?'

'Early days really. We were bumping along. You need to make a name for yourself before things really pick up.' She shrugged. 'I don't know. I might even sell up.'

'Forget that for a moment. Imagine that you're in your office right now. What would you do, bearing in mind events that have recently come to your notice?'

She ran a hand through her hair. 'What an odd question!' Then she grinned. 'Yes, I know. I'd get on the phone to the Reverend Forbes and ask his permission to hire a diver to search the Great Bath, the insurance company paying, of course.'

Carrick grabbed her hand and towed her into his office. There, he thrust the phone at her.

Appalled, she stared at him. 'Really?'

'Lost your nerve?' he asked roughly.

'But what about Chief Inspector –'

'Sod Haine. *You've* been hired to find the Chantbury Pyx.'

Her hands were shaking as she dialled.

Leather does not burn very easily and the person who had tried to destroy the jacket had doused it in petrol first. Newspapers and cardboard boxes had also been heaped on the pyre, traces of ash from burned paper still visible on the charred remains of the jacket. The forensic department had produced an amazing amount of information. The wearer had either put on weight recently or the garment had changed hands, because there were splits in the seams under the arms and across the back. His hair was long and greasy, there were still traces on the collar. Other grease on the cuffs was thought to be motor oil and sundry hairs on the lining of the collar and inside the jacket generally were human, dog's and cat's. The entire garment was, in fact, a pathologist's nightmare for besides all this detritus there was sand, sawdust, iron filings, earth and minute pieces of copper and steel, possibly swarf from machine tools. Most interesting of all were the traces of white paint on two of the metal studs on the right shoulder.

'Conrad Stacey's a garage mechanic,' Ingrams said to himself, having read these findings. He decided to drive out to Camerton, taking the jacket with him. Going to Stacey's home first was deliberate, Ingrams wanted to have another look round the outside of the cottage while the owner was at work.

First Ingrams called at the farm next door. The contrast between the two properties could not be more extreme, the cottage seemingly unlived-in for years, the farm with its newly whitewashed buildings, neat yard with not even a stray wisp of hay in sight, the windowboxes on the house crammed with geraniums and trailing lobelia. From the open front door, as Ingrams approached, wafted the smell of baking. His stomach groaned. When had he last tasted a home-made cake? He knocked.

The woman recognised him. 'Hello, sergeant. You're just in time for coffee.'

He followed her into the large airy kitchen. Stretched out in front of a dark green Aga was a golden retriever. It opened one eye dreamily, decided he represented no threat and went back to sleep again. Ingrams then noticed that curled up close to it was a Siamese cat. This was awake and regarded him stonily with sapphire eyes, somehow reminding him that he was on business.

He said, 'There's a jacket here I'd like you to take a look at, if you wouldn't mind. I'd like to know whether you've seen it before.'

The farmer's wife, whose name was Mrs Hanley, gave him a shrewd look. 'You mean have I seen my neighbour wearing it?'

'Or anyone who's a friend of his,' Ingrams replied urbanely. He shook the garment from the bag onto the floor, an action he immediately regretted as the quarry tiles were immaculately clean, the jacket most emphatically not. Mrs Hanley appeared not to mind.

After gazing at it for several long moments she shook her head slowly. 'No. It's not really Conrad's style at all. I mean, I know he's a bit scruffy but he doesn't wear this kind of thing. It's a biker's jacket really, isn't it?'

To hell with Carrick, Ingrams thought, he would go and confront Harbutts with it.

175

'You could ask his wife, though,' Mrs Hanley was saying. 'I think she's at home.'

'I thought she'd left him.'

'Oh, she's left him several times. Poor Jill tries to shock him into treating her better. The irony of it is that I think he's really fond of her. Just lazy and prone to drinking too much.'

'Is it just that? Does he knock her about when he's had a few?'

Mrs Hanley took mugs from a dresser and spooned instant coffee into them. 'I don't *think* he does. I've never seen her with black eyes or anything like that.' She shrugged. 'Who's to know what some men will do when they've been on the beer?'

'Does he go out drinking a lot?'

'Most weekends. Friday usually. Sometimes he doesn't come home until the next day. I blame that aunt of his in a way. I know she's dead but she could have made things easier for them – he's had a lot of time off work with chest infections. He's never been very strong. I feel sorry for them really.'

'Do you think he might have killed his aunt?'

'Don't ask me things like that. Anybody is capable of doing things when they're drunk that they wouldn't contemplate sober. Even you, sergeant, even you.'

Ingrams drank his coffee in silence, then thanked her and went next door.

The description 'poor Jill' did not really fit the woman who answered his knock. She looked very self-assured and, right then, angry. When Ingrams introduced himself she became very angry indeed.

'You never leave people alone, do you? It was bad enough having the police banging on my mother's door and upsetting her just to tell me about Conrad's old bitch of an aunt dying, without you coming round here as well. What did you expect me to do, come running back to hold his hand? Conrad couldn't kill anything – not even set a mousetrap.'

'How long have you been back?' Ingrams asked.

'Since yesterday. But I'm not staying, I've just come to pack up some more of my things. Then I'm off, for good.'

'May I come in? I'd like to ask you –'

She interrupted him with a loud laugh. 'Like hell you will.'

176

Ingram removed the jacket from the bag and held it under her nose. 'Recognise that?'

She hardly glanced at it. 'No.'

'Is it your husband's?'

'No. That's a real man's jacket.'

'When did you leave him?'

'When?'

'That's what I said.'

'Well, if you mean *this time*, on the last day of August. The other lot asked me that too.'

'Communications failure,' Ingrams snapped. 'So you weren't in the area on Friday 4 September.'

'No. How the hell could I have been?'

Turning to go, Ingrams said, 'I'm surprised you're going now he's come into all that money.'

'Money's not everything,' she said and slammed the door.

He sat in the car for a while, trying to make sense of everything and really needing to talk to someone in authority. After a few minutes' deep thought he jabbed the key into the ignition and drove off, having come to two conclusions. First, that he had been overhasty in his condemnation of Conrad Stacey and second – this with a sinking feeling – that he would have to admit that he was stumped to Carrick who was, no doubt, still with the Mackenzie girl.

As it happened, Carrick was in his office, Joanna having gone home with Russell riding shotgun to put her flat in some kind of order. The Inspector glanced up when Ingrams entered, then subjected him to a longer steady look.

'Sit down, Bob,' he said.

Ingrams sat and there was a little silence. He knew that he ought to say a lot; to apologise for his boorish behaviour, to admit that Carrick's previous sergeant but one was light years ahead of him in every way, to confess that his cherished ideas of his own usefulness were far from the truth. All he succeeded in doing – and Carrick actually found it rather touching – was to sit there looking like a schoolboy who had been sent to the headmaster for cribbing homework.

'I took the jacket over to Camerton,' he said at last.

'Wasn't Stacey at work?' Carrick said.

177

'I didn't ask him about it. I went to see his neighbour. To cut a long story short, she'd never seen it before. But Stacey's wife was at home. Packing up to leave for always. She said she hadn't seen it before either and that it was a "real man's jacket". To my mind he's well rid of her.'

'Did Haine get anything useful from the Colonel?'

'He's interviewing him now.'

Carrick steepled his hands, regarding Ingrams across the tips of his fingers. 'I assume that your instinct tells you to take the jacket to Bill Harbutts and confront him with it.'

'Yes,' Ingrams said, 'I think he's in this up to his neck.'

'So do I. But I want to leave him to stew for a bit longer. The other man, the one who Jamie saw leaving the flats, is far more important. Cryon's in it too – I'm convinced of it. I've faxed the RCMP about her.'

Ingrams went off, whistling tunelessly. Carrick remained at his desk. He supposed that his despair originated in the deadly tiredness and the fact that he hurt all over. But some kind of decision would have to be made.

# Chapter Seventeen

The search was again conducted at night, and whereas the previous one had been really low key, this took place under the utmost secrecy with an absolute minimum of lighting and noise. Only five persons witnessed it; Carrick, Joanna, the museum curator, the diver and his assistant. As far as Carrick was concerned it was a private matter, he himself was there in the capacity of the instigator's companion.

'Everything above shoulder height is modern,' he murmured to no one in particular as he gazed over the calm surface of the water to where the diver, Jon Gavin, from a Bristol-based company of salvage experts, prepared to commence. The lights surrounding the bath had not been switched on, at Carrick's request, and they were working by the soft glow from several lamps set in the alcoves. Gavin was using a torch to check his air bottles and had another, more powerful, to use underwater.

'The Romans trod these slabs,' Joanna said from somewhere in the gloom behind Garrick. 'It gives you a spooky sort of feeling.'

'This is all new to me,' said Gavin when they strolled round. 'I've worked in some strange places but this beats them all.'

Joanna said, 'There have been curative springs on the site since the year dot. A King Bladud erected a temple here in gratitude for being healed of leprosy. When the Romans arrived in AD 43 they turned it into Britain's first health hydro, called the place Aquae Suilis and dedicated the temple to Minerva, their goddess of healing.'

'Must have been a bit parky in the winter even with the water hot,' Gavin commented with a chuckle.

'It was roofed,' Joanna said. 'With special box tiles that prevented condensation.' She looked around. 'You can stand here and almost feel that they're watching you – the builders, the centurions, senators . . . ghosts.'

'It isn't a body you're looking for and you're trying to wind me up?' asked the diver with a grin. 'I've come across quite a few of those.'

'No,' Carrick assured him. 'A small packet of some sort. And be careful – I'm not too sure about underwater projections.'

'Don't you worry. I wasn't about to jump off that,' Gavin said with a wave of one hand in the direction of the large diving stone. A few minutes later he slid into the water and swam down one long side of the bath. The lamp he was holding cast a weird green glow.

'This might take quite a while,' Carrick said, seating himself on a stone bench. 'And water flows in at one end and out through a drain at the other so one must assume there's a slight current. Something fairly lightweight dropped in might move over a period of days and weeks.'

'Have you shown the video to Jamie?' Joanna wanted to know.

'No, but I intend to.'

'Do you really think the Pyx is here?'

'If it isn't I have a real problem.'

'It's a good try though.'

'I'm not thinking about professional competence, although that does come into it as well. The whole business of solving these cases hinges on it being here. I haven't told you this yet but before we came here I went with Bob to question Bill Harbutts. I wanted to leave him a bit longer but the pressure's really on now. He wasn't at work, supposedly off sick. He wasn't at home either. So we took the jacket round to Bethany Cryon's flat. She was out too.'

'This is a woman who hardly ever goes out.'

'Yes, quite.'

The green glow was making steady progress over the bottom of the pool.

'See what you think of this, then. The Canadian authorities have never heard of her.' Carrick smiled bleakly. 'Now even a man who's been knocked around a little can work out without too much trouble that that means she's either a Brit and pretending to be from Canada or has a criminal record and is travelling on a forged passport. Either way and whatever happens here tonight I intend to find out.'

'Didn't you ask to see her passport when you first interviewed her?'

'She actually offered to show it to me but I declined. A bad mistake, I know, but at the time she was the last one I was suspicious of. All I wanted to do was get out – her flat was as hot as hell. That might have been deliberate on her part – to make sure I didn't stay too long.'

'That rather does point to her falling into your second category.'

'Yes.'

'Does she have big feet?'

'God knows, with those trailing skirts.' Carrick discovered that he was being smiled upon gently. 'You think she's the murderer?'

'Why not?'

'Jamie saw a man.'

'*Thought* he saw a man. It might have been a skinny woman.'

'Joanna, I wasn't beaten up by a woman.'

'You're assuming it was the same people because of the shoes. You might have dreamed that bit – you said yourself you had weird dreams.'

Carrick took a deep breath. 'Yes, you're right. Retain the professional attitude even when taken apart. I'm beginning to think she's been hiding a man in her flat.'

'If they were waiting for me – and there was no reason why they should have known I'd been attacked by Mallory the previous night – but saw you get out of your car and enter the building, they might have decided to put you out of action if you were making for my flat. They might have panicked, thought you were on to them, realised they might not have had time to escape the way they had come, anything like that.'

'I still don't think I was done over by a woman.'

There was a silence before Joanna, without perhaps evaluating the wisdom of the words, said, 'Sometimes I wish I was back on the job.'

'Could you live with the discipline again?'

'Perhaps not,' she said after due thought.

'Did you ever think of appealing?'

'I might have done. If you'd encouraged me to.'

After a short silence he said, 'The accusation that you threw at me was quite accurate. I was selfish and only worried about my career.'

'It was an unfair remark. You had your wife to think of.'

'Yes,' he acknowledged softly. 'But she wouldn't have minded.'

Horrified, Joanna saw the real meaning of his words. 'You *told* her?'

'Kathleen and I told each other everything,' he said simply, adding, 'On very rare occasions she used to lose her temper and throw things, sometimes at me. If I wasn't there she might chuck plates at the wall. But she always used to tell me about it – she was one of those people who hated her own weaknesses. And I used to tell her about things I'd done – gone through a traffic light at amber or whatever. When she became really ill she said on several occasions that she didn't expect me to stay faithful to her now she found lovemaking painful. I think that although she was hard on herself she understood failings in others, almost loved them for it, really.'

'She must have loved you,' Joanna whispered. 'Very much.'

'Yes.'

Joanna was silent. Was this the reality – would she be no more to him than the look-alike woman whom he had gone to when he needed help and whose entire persona was superimposed by that of an understanding, dying wife?

After ten minutes the diver surfaced, got his bearings and went under again. He had already covered half the bottom of the bath, working much more quickly than Carrick had estimated.

Strictly speaking Sergeant Ingrams was off duty but had lingered, thumbing disconsolately through files, wandering up and down the office, the business of two murders and the theft of church property bothering him enormously. He was

182

in no rush to go home either; his wife had gone to a hen night and would not be back until late, very late probably. Finally, he bad-temperedly slammed his way out and crossed the road, thinking vaguely of a couple of pints of bitter followed by fish and chips. No, perhaps one pint, he was driving.

He turned right, walking in the direction of Pulteney Bridge. It was not far, he could collect his car later. That was the beauty of Bath, all the best pubs were close to each other; you could have a wonderful time and not walk more than a quarter of a mile.

In the summer months tables and chairs were set out in front of the White Hart. The weather had remained so warm and fine that even in the middle of September they had not been taken in and on this particular evening were crowded with tourists as well as local residents. Ingrams fought his way to the bar through the even greater crush within and then returned to the fresh air. There were still no tables free but one had only a single person sitting at it, a man whom he recognised as he approached.

Jack Moffat looked up. 'Hell's bells, you haven't come to drag me back into your Kremlin!'

'No, sir. I didn't even notice it was you until I got close. May I join you?'

Moffat gazed around at the throng. 'I suppose you'll have to.'

'Can I get you a drink?' Ingrams asked, noticing the empty glass.

Moffat thawed slightly and said, 'Good of you. Whisky and a thimbleful of water.' When Ingrams returned he said, 'Well, all the dirty washing's out on the line now. That's the trouble with you lot – you think that because a man's stepped out of line once he'll do it again.'

'I'm afraid it's a case of the boss having different ideas,' the sergeant said.

'Haine, you mean? I thought Carrick was your boss.'

'Haine's Carrick's boss so as far as I'm concerned he's God.'

'So where's Carrick?'

'On sick leave. Someone beat him up rather badly.'

Moffat looked appalled. 'What's the world coming to? Is he badly hurt?'

'No actual damage. But he's the sort of bloke to try to carry on as though nothing's amiss.' Ingrams took a large swallow of his drink. 'Colonel, I know you've had enough of questions but this isn't about you at all. Have you ever clapped eyes on Conrad Stacey's wife?'

'No. No, hang on . . . Yes, once. He came to see his aunt a while back and she was in the car. She didn't go into the house but got out of the car to clean the windscreen with a cloth. The vehicle was filthy, it usually was.'

'Did you get a good look at her?'

'Not really. I mean, Alice and I try not to be nosy. I just remember that she had blond hair – looked as though it was out of a bottle, if you get me – and was rather thin. Awkward sort of woman actually, she tripped up the kerb.'

'Any idea how long they've been living in the area?'

'No. All I know is they haven't been married all that long. I believe Mrs Pryce mentioned it in the days before we fell out with her.'

'And judging by her daughter-in-law's behaviour Mrs Pryce had fallen out with *her*.'

'Must have done. It wasn't difficult, though, as you know.' Moffat placed a hand on Ingrams's arm and spoke earnestly. 'For God's sake find the bastard who did this dreadful thing, sergeant. And then everyone can be left in peace to live out what remains of their lives. I told your Haine over and over that I didn't kill the woman. I know I tore into a clerk at Whitehall. But I knew what I was doing – I didn't have my funny turns in those days.'

'Why *did* you go for him, sir?'

Moffat drained his glass before speaking. 'They call it sexual harassment these days. No woman in the office was safe from him. And he didn't just pinch their bottoms either. The man was an utter pest.'

'You could have reported him to his boss.'

'He was the boss. Not my boss, you understand, but the chief clerk. And *his* boss knew about it and turned a blind eye. No, I'm afraid my temper snapped one day and that was that. It probably cured him – his face wasn't the same afterwards.'

Ingrams was beginning to see Haine's point of view. No funny turns, perhaps, just a violent temper. He said, 'It was a big sacrifice to make, though.'

184

'Me?' Moffat said with a dry laugh. 'I'd had enough. I'm not a desk-wallah – never have been. Give me a job to do in the fresh air and a bunch of blokes and I'm happy.'

'So what do you do with yourself these days?'

'Alice and I go out quite a bit. She likes to get out into the countryside in the summer. We take picnics. I belong to the bowls club, it keeps the old bones from creaking too much. We go to concerts, read a lot. We're quite busy really. Let me get you a drink.'

'No, not for me, sir. I've got to drive.'

Moffat slapped a hand on the table. 'I *knew* there was something I was going to mention. Forgot what with that Haine fella getting a bit unpleasant. It's this. I pop round to the Pear Tree most evenings. Don't drink a lot, you understand, never have done. Company and all that, have a few cronies and we yarn together. One of them, chap by the name of Harry Porter, said to me on Saturday night that he'd seen that poor girl who was murdered talking to the odd woman who lives in the top flat opposite to me.'

'When?'

'That's the trouble. Harry can't remember. It's no good you putting pressure on him either because he's a bit vague, is Harry. It's worse than that really – he's slightly off his trolley these days and it's getting worse. But I thought I'd mention it to you.'

'Any idea where he saw them talking?'

'In the square.'

'About what time?'

'Pretty late, according to him. He was on his way home one night – he cuts through the square.'

'*Could* it have been on the night she was killed?' Ingrams was ignoring the implications as to the closing times of the Pear Tree; it was well known that the landlord invited 'friends' to stay on after the doors were locked.

'Haven't a clue. You could *try* asking him – he's better some days than others.'

'Is he likely to be round there now?'

'Almost certainly.'

Ingrams stood up. 'Would you mind coming with me? Then you can point him out to me.'

185

'Gladly. It's only just round the corner from where I live, too.'

Harry was there. Not only that, he had remembered.

The diver surfaced right in front of them, removed his face mask and leaned both arms on the edging stone. 'Nothing but a few coins that people have thrown in.'

'What about gaps in the stones and nooks and crannies?' Carrick asked.

'It's lined with lead. Nothing like that.'

Carrick put his head in his hands and tried to think.

'I can go over it again if you want me to.'

Joanna said, 'Not doubting your vigilance but would you notice a packet if it was roughly the same colour as the bottom or there was just a bit of plastic wrapped round a metal rectangle? It's quite small.'

'This light's absolutely ace,' said Gavin, bringing it out of the water with a splash and switching it off.

'And where the water drains out?'

'There's a grid.'

'Could something small go through it?'

'It might do. It's just a hole with bars across – they're quite wide apart.'

'Could you check that again?' Carrick requested.

'No problem.' With a swirl of water he was gone.

'No luck?' said a voice behind them.

It was the curator of the museum.

'No,' Carrick said. 'I think my luck's run out as far as this case is concerned.'

'I didn't want to get under your feet so I stayed out of the way. Has he checked the drain? Things that blow over the wall do sometimes end up stuck in that.'

'He's looking at it now.'

'Make sure he looks right inside. There is another grid – a more modern one with a small mesh about a foot inside the pipe. I presume the Victorians put it in when they discovered the bath in the 1860s. It was completely covered by buildings, you know – it was found when they were investigating a leak in the King's Bath.'

The three of them walked round to a spot directly above where Gavin was working. He must have seen them for when

186

he surfaced, almost immediately, he came fountaining up-
wards like a grampus, making them rather wet.

'There's something in there but I can't reach it. I'll need
some tongs.'

'Tongs,' Carrick said thoughtfully.

'Tongs?' Joanna wondered.

'Yes, tongs,' said the curator and went away. He returned,
very shortly, from the direction of the Pump Room with a set
of brass Regency fire irons.

'Fantastic,' Gavin said, in receipt of the coal tongs.

'It's probably a soggy fag packet,' Carrick muttered.

'A photo of someone's Aunt Maud,' Joanna said.

'What the hell's he doing?' Carrick agonised after ten
seconds silence.

Then, like a hand bearing aloft Excalibur, the tongs reap-
peared, gripping a small packet. Carrick leaned out for it and
without speaking offered it to Joanna.

She shook her head. 'I can feel one of my all-fingers-and-
thumbs funny turns coming on,' she whispered.

Whatever was inside was well wrapped in thick plastic with
sticky tape wound round and round to seal out the water, the
first proof that the contents had not been intended to get wet.
Carrick was one of those men who carry a Swiss army knife
and used the tiny scissors on it very carefully to slit one end of
the packet. Opening it like an envelope he extracted another
packet wrapped in thinner plastic, holding it just on the
edges. No more unwrapping was necessary, what was inside
was clearly visible.

'I think I'm going to cry,' Joanna said.

'Is that it?' Gavin asked.

'Yes,' said Carrick and the curator as one voice.

The pool in the pagan temple had been forced to give up its
little Christian relic.

187

# Chapter Eighteen

Bob Ingrams stepped back several paces, eyeing distance, and then ran forward and shoulder-charged the front door of Bethany Cryon's flat. (They had a search warrant but had forgotten the sledgehammer.) He would much rather Carrick was performing the task but clearly Carrick was not fit enough so all he, Ingrams, could do was pray that he would not ignominiously bounce off. His prayers were answered and the door yielded.

'Take care!' he heard Carrick say urgently behind him. 'No, on second thoughts, I'll go first.'

All was in darkness, the air stuffy and smelling of last week's cooking. Carrick groped for and found a switch and light flooded the narrow hallway. The first room on the right was the kitchen and he switched the light on in there too, satisfying himself with a quick glance that no one was in there.

'She's done a runner,' Joanna said, just to his rear.

'Stay back,' he ordered.

The room he had been into before, the living room, was strewn with clothes and other belongings as though someone had thrown out of suitcases all but the bare essentials. Some of the clothes were men's.

'I knew it!' Carrick exclaimed, picking up in quick succession a shirt, a tie and a pair of jeans with a thick leather belt still threaded through the loops on the waistband. 'She had someone hidden away up here.' He turned to Ingrams. 'Get on the radio and organise some bods to take this place to pieces.' He stalked into the single bedroom.

Here, as in the other rooms, the curtains were closed, looking as though they had been yanked across the windows in a hurry, and there were more clothes on the floor and on the bed. The wardrobe door was open, the rail within holding only hangers. Carrick peered into a fitted cupboard but that too was empty, the shelves lined with newspaper yellow with age.

'I don't think there was much here to start with,' he said as he emerged from the bathroom. 'Even though the flat was probably let furnished.'

'Do you want me to put out a description of her?' Ingrams called, his head round the front door.

'Yes,' Carrick replied. 'And then stay here and take charge of the search.'

Joanna, who had obediently gone back out onto the landing knowing that she should not really be present at all, said, when she saw Carrick emerge through the front door, 'I'll go and give the Reverend Forbes the glad news.'

Carrick looked at his watch. 'I'd give him a ring if I were you, it's a bit late to call on him tonight. Besides . . .' He broke off and smiled.

'You'd rather I didn't go on my own and you can't really spare anyone?'

'That's about it. I'd come with you myself but I ought to –'

'What can you do, though? Aren't you still supposed to be on sick leave?'

Surprisingly, he nodded meekly. 'I suggest you go back to my flat and get some rest. You're not exactly in the pink yourself. I'll come as soon as I can.'

There was no point arguing.

Joanna was crossing the square to her car when she saw Monica Lang. The woman called a greeting; she could not wave, she had her arms full of Doolally.

'I'm keeping a much closer eye on him now,' she said as she got closer. 'If the scoundrel thinks he's going to spend every night out on the tiles he's got another thought coming. Besides, he still isn't quite his old self.'

'I know the feeling,' Joanna said.

'I'm actually a little worried about Tommy, the tramp who was trying to make a home for himself in West Terrace. I haven't seen him for some days now. I hope he's all right.'

'He's left the area,' Joanna told her, scratching behind Doolally's ears.

Mrs Lang looked at her severely. 'You mean the police threw him out.'

'No, nothing like that.' Observing that she would have to be a little more specific in order to put Mrs Lang's mind at rest, she added, 'Inspector Carrick had a soft spot for him – Tommy told him he was leaving.'

Hefting the cat over her shoulder, Monica Lang said, 'Well, all the same, it is a bit odd. I do a little voluntary work and I was coming back here quite early this morning when I heard a crash over in West Terrace that sounded just as though someone had fallen through the floor. That's what set me worrying about Tommy. But if you say he's moved away . . .'

'What time was this?'

'About six thirty.'

'I know for a fact that Tommy isn't there.'

The woman gave her a broad smile. 'Oh, well, it's nothing then. And for goodness' sake, the entire building is on the verge of falling down, it's not surprising if things go bump in the night.' She laughed.

They took their leave of one another. By her car Joanna paused when she had inserted the key in the lock. What if . .?

Carrick was still where she had left him, on the third floor of number 3, looking fit to drop.

'James, I've just been talking to Mrs Lang. She said there was a loud noise somewhere in West Terrace early this morning.'

'I expect a ceiling fell down,' he responded wearily.

Back in the days when she had worked for him he had given no quarter when his staff were tired. She saw no reason why she should give him any now.

'Suppose Cryon and Harbutts are hiding over there.'

He levered himself off the banisters with visible effort. 'And suppose Pulteney Bridge has fallen down.'

A few seconds elapsed during which the air seemed to crackle between them. Finally Carrick said, 'For what possible reason could they have gone to ground in there?'

'They don't know we've recovered the Pyx. It's as good a place as any to hide if they're hoping to have another go at getting it out of the Great Bath.'

He grimaced. 'It's a dangerous place to ask men to look over and all on a whim.'

She turned. 'OK, I'll wander over and have a look myself.'

His hand clamped onto her shoulder like something made of steel. 'You'll bloody well stay out of there.'

'A small, quiet-as-mice operation,' Joanna said calmly. 'The Territorial Support Group with Tommy as site adviser – he must know the place from top to bottom. Who does he work for, the Drug Squad?'

'Sunk without trace,' Carrick murmured, allowing his hand to slip from her shoulder. 'Who the hell's safe working undercover with women like you around?' He sighed. 'I'd prefer to have a bit more to go on before I order something like that.'

'Contact Tommy, or whatever his name is, and ask him about things like attics and cellars.'

In the square below vehicles were arriving.

'Look,' Joanna said, going to Carrick's side as, once again, he leaned both arms on the banister rail. 'I know it's a very long shot but –'

'I know,' Carrick interrupted. 'There's no need to spell it out to me. All right, we'll do it even though I think I'm agreeing only for the very bad reason of not wanting to be accused afterwards of failing to look there.'

Tom Armstrong was wearing black cords and a matching T-shirt with a white skull and crossbones emblazoned on it. This was not surprising in itself as he was not only off duty but on leave, after a successful raid on a house on the south side of the city and the arrest of a couple from London whose activities he had been closely monitoring for some weeks. No, what shook Carrick slightly was that without the stubble on his chin, the dirt and the dreadful clothes, Armstrong was unrecognisable. The first intimation that his helper had arrived was a grin being worn by a tanned face on the other side of the circular bar in the Pear Tree; Armstrong, owning to a huge thirst, refusing to meet Carrick anywhere else.

'This might not be too good for your cover,' Carrick commented, walking round.

'I'll be working over at Bristol for the foreseeable future,' Armstrong said. 'What's this about my squat?'

Carrick had not gone into details over the phone. 'A couple of suspects might have gone to ground in there. There might even be three of them. And seeing that you must have your Brownie badge on the place . . .'

'It's a deathtrap,' Armstrong said succinctly. 'Leave 'em in there long enough and the deathwatch beetles'll chew off their legs at the ankles. *Then* you can grab them.'

'Seriously,' Carrick said amiably. He had realised at their first meeting that Armstrong was different.

'Plenty of attics,' said the other. 'That's where I'd head for. You can get from one house to another up there – there's only a low brick wall between them. Fires used to spread like crazy in the days when they were built.'

'Someone heard a noise like a person falling through a ceiling this morning. I'm afraid that's all I have to go on. One of the people we're looking for might be Susan Fairbrother's murderer so I suppose that might be a link too if they've been in the building before. I've circulated descriptions and certain homes are being watched and I'm desperate enough to want to search West Terrace again.'

'Low-key, eh?'

Carrick nodded. 'We found the Chantbury Pyx low-key.'

'You want me to brief people or go in as well?'

'Both if you've a mind to.'

'Presumably now rather than later?'

'Absolutely.'

Armstrong drained his pint tankard and placed it back on the bar with great regret. 'Let's get on with it then.'

Despite his air of reluctance the Drug Squad sergeant had wasted no time in driving from his home at Keynsham; in fact, he had exceeded the speed limit all the way. His haste was partly due to the arrival of his mother-in-law, a woman who made no secret of thinking her daughter's choice of partner left a lot to be desired. One day, Tom had vowed, he would return from work in his most malodorous disguise during one of her visits. But tonight he could escape and do Bath CID a favour.

'The thinking behind this,' Carrick began as they approached West Terrace from the rear, 'is mostly based on circumstantial evidence but right now that's all I have to go on. With hindsight I should have brought one of the suspects, Harbutts, in earlier but there was nothing that I could have confronted him with other than that he gave his time of leaving the square on the night Mrs Pryce was murdered as ten thirty when a witness assures us it was ten. But the witness was wee Jamie and although I'm sure he is not a liar a defence lawyer would make mincemeat of him. Now, Mrs Pryce went across to North Terrace at slightly before eleven thirty that night – in such a paddy that she left her front door open – to complain about loud music coming from the flat on the first floor of number 3. We know that because, unable to gain access, she then went up to the floor above and tried to get Miss Braithewaite to bang on the floor. That lady, rightly, refused and the ladies had a bit of an argument on the landing which culminated in a little pushing and shoving, followed by Miss Braithewaite going back into her flat and slamming the door. Minutes later Mrs Pryce was dead, killed with a single blow from a hammer to the back of the head.'

Armstrong said, 'After which the body was dragged into the garden in the square and dumped. Your Miss Mackenzie then appeared on the scene and saw someone leaving the square. The next night Susan Fairbrother was murdered, a girl who also had red hair.'

'That's right. And the only clue was an imprint made by a size-eight plain-soled shoe. Now that morning, the Saturday, Dr Hendricks, who lives with his lady friend for most of the time but has a house in South Terrace, saw Bethany Cryon, a woman who has a flat at the top of number 3 North Terrace, queueing up outside the Roman Baths waiting for the doors to open. We found the Chantbury Pyx in a drain in the Great Bath.'

'And her boyfriend is the yob with the motorbike.'

'Correct, Harbutts. Jamie saw him leave the square on the night of the first murder at ten – as I said just now – and shortly afterwards, as Jamie was sneaking back home, *another* man leaving by a back way. There were items of male clothing too small to belong to Harbutts in Cryon's flat and –'

'Any size-eight shoes?'

'No shoes at all unless they were well hidden. The search team's still there taking up the floorboards.'

'Meanwhile all your birds have flown.'

'Yes.'

'So you reckon Cryon, Harbutts and another bloke stole the Pyx.'

'There were two raiders, one tall and well-built, the other of slighter build.'

'Yes, of course, that's what it said in the papers. So Cryon stayed at home and Harbutts waited for the other bloke somewhere round the corner. They then went on his bike to the place where they overpowered the guards and stole the van. Afterwards – what?'

'It's all guesswork, but I think the second man came back to Beckford Square with the Pyx in his possession and on his way up to Cryon's flat somehow got involved with Mrs Pryce. She ended up dead, possibly killed with the same hammer that he'd used to break the glass of the showcase, a hammer that at one time had been the Moffats'. He dragged her body outside and then made a run for it. He saw Joanna as she noticed him and assumed it was the girl he'd seen going in and out of the nursing home. If he'd been living with Cryon he'd have had plenty of time to stare out of the windows.'

'Did anyone notice a man looking out?'

'If they did they didn't mention it.'

'Why the hell did they need Harbutts?'

'God knows. Transport perhaps.'

'They could have stolen a motor. Besides which he's hardly the sort of bloke you'd associate with stealing works of art.'

'I know. This has all gone through my head thousands of times. You've been listening to a theory – and, as we all know, theories have a way of turning out to be gold-plated cobblers.'

Armstrong made no further comment. You're not noted for cobblers, he thought, giving Carrick a quick sideways glance, the grapevine was quite sure about that.

'I don't *think* they're armed,' Carrick said as they came to a halt at the entrance to the overgrown lane that led behind the gardens to the rear of the terrace. 'At least, not with firearms. But there's one pickaxe handle for sure. We must be prepared for knives and other hardware.' He grinned at Armstrong's puzzlement. 'Another theory. Yours truly walked into a little reception committee probably intended for Joanna.'

194

Well, that explained the air of vengeful malice anyway, Armstrong decided.

It was quite dark, the two men hardly able to make out one another's outlines. They had stopped in the lee of the overgrown hedge and, after waiting for a few seconds, Carrick whistled softly. There was no response.

'Funny,' he muttered. 'They should have been here by now.'

'The heavy brigade?'

'Yes. A few lads able to take care of themselves from B Relief. They should have been in position here several minutes ago.' He swore under his breath and then said, 'Hang on a moment and I'll go and radio from my car – it's only round the corner.'

Armstrong waited impassively. He was used to it, waiting was about 95 per cent of the job. He had been standing quietly by the hedge for a few minutes, strictly speaking among the foliage, when a man ran right at him in the dark. It was a heavy collision and Armstrong staggered, momentarily winded. One of his flailing arms connected with a sweater-clad shoulder, his hand clutching involuntarily to save himself from pitching headlong into the hedge. The man hit him on the jaw.

That changed things somewhat for although Armstrong could be polite, he didn't insist on it. The blow had not forced him to relinquish his hold of the other man's clothing so he made a quick guess as to a likely target and lashed out. His fist connected. Afterwards, events became a little confused.

Clarity emerged, finally, when his opponent apparently walked into a lamp-post. Although what a lamp-post was doing there Armstrong wasn't sure, picking himself up doggedly from a blow, and not for the first time. Something whistled past his ear and there was the sound as of several sacks filled with bones being thrown into a cellar.

'Are you all right?' asked the lamp-post, yanking him to his feet.

There was no time for Armstrong to reply, for both of them had to give their full attention to their opponent, and there was a little very one-sided violence that finished up by Carrick handcuffing the man's arms behind his back and shining a

195

torch in his face, both of which police-issue items he had brought back from his car.

Bill Harbutts scowled up at them.

'God, if I'd known it was him I'd have hit him harder,' Carrick said disgustedly. 'Where did you find him?'

'Just came blundering along,' Armstrong said, gently feeling his face to see if everything was still there.

'He's mad,' Harbutts muttered.

Together, they hauled him up.

'Mad?' Carrick queried.

'I was making a break for it before I end up dead.' The big man started walking, towing Carrick and Armstrong along like two ships in his wake.

'Whoa,' Carrick said, bringing Harbutts to a stop by the simple expedient of a hand in his hair. He rounded on them furiously.

'Ever wondered why you're still alive, cop?' he almost spat in Carrick's face. 'Why you weren't crippled that night? Why you didn't end up with every bone in your body broken? Well, you can thank me. I was doing the hitting and I didn't hit you very hard. I'll tell you why. It's because I know what happens to people who cripple the filth. Another thing is that I'm not going to get banged up for ever on account of someone who's stark raving mad.'

It occurred to both policemen simultaneously that Harbutts was utterly terrified. And not of them.

'Where is he?' Carrick whispered.

'Inside. Hiding in one of the lofts.'

'On his own?'

'Yes.' Astoundingly there was a catch in Harbutts's voice. 'Get me away from here, for Christ's sake. If I'd known this bloke here was a cop I wouldn't have given any trouble.' He set off again and Carrick permitted him to.

'A killer then, eh?' Carrick asked quietly, he and Armstrong with a hand on each elbow.

'He killed the girl.'

'And you both stole the Chantbury Pyx?'

'Will you put in a word for me if I cooperate?'

'If you turn Queen's evidence it'll be better than that.'

After a pause and when they were actually in Royal Crescent, where Carrick had parked his car, Harbutts said, 'Yeah, we nicked it.'

'And murdered Mrs Pryce afterwards.'

'No.'

'No?'

'I had nothing to do with either of the killings. That was him. But he didn't top the old woman. She was already dead or something. He wouldn't talk about it so I didn't ask.'

They halted by Carrick's car. 'You believe him?'

Harbutts nodded dumbly and then said, 'Like I said, he's got most of his pages stuck together but he's no liar.'

Armstrong said, 'Er, your reinforcements, sir?'

Carrick was busy with another set of handcuffs fastening Harbutts to the listed iron railings. 'Took a direct hit from a motorbike. No one in the van was injured but they had to give assistance and the vehicle is badly damaged. I am assured that my urgent request for personnel is being attended to but people are thin on the ground because of the football match in Bristol where trouble is anticipated and an incident in the centre of Radstock, no details as yet. I suggest therefore, that we get on with it.'

'What about your sergeant?' Armstrong persevered.

'Bloody useless.' Carrick dived into the car and reported the arrest, adding that he proposed to make an initial surveillance himself. Emerging, he said, 'Are you game?'

Armstrong had established that his face was merely numb in places. 'It's nice to be asked,' he said, with a grin, meaning it.

Carrick gave him a mad grin in return, this illuminated by the headlights of an approaching car. It proved to be an area car. Carrick ordered one of the crew of it to caution and arrest Harbutts belatedly and took the other man with them, positioning him at the entrance to the lane with instructions to apprehend anyone who tried to escape from the building. He also acquired another torch.

'He'll hear us coming,' Armstrong pointed out in a low voice as they entered by the rear door where he had originally gained access, most of the planks now wrenched out of position by Harbutts's panic-stricken exit.

'I've no intention of creeping all over this bloody ruin like a Red Indian,' Carrick said, not bothering to speak quietly. He walked straight through into the hallway of the house and shouted, 'This is the police. The house is surrounded. We have Harbutts under arrest. I want you to –'

'Watch out!' Armstrong yelled.

A large chunk of concrete crashed onto the hall tiles on the exact spot where Carrick had been standing a split second earlier.

Silence but for a few small pieces pattering down. Then, distinctly, the same sound that had alerted Armstrong – floorboards squeaking above their heads. He ran forward, keeping to the side of the hall. Carrick, who had leaped into the open cupboard beneath the stairs, joined him and they raced up to the first floor. In the twin torch beams they caught a glimpse of a flying figure on the next staircase. Then a door banged resoundingly.

'Which one?' Armstrong muttered, gazing in despair at several closed doors in turn. Carrick made no reply, opening the door nearest to him, noisily, Armstrong thought, shining his torch into the room. But he was walking backwards, on tiptoe, along the passage towards an open doorway, the room beyond just a gaping blackness.

At the last second, when Carrick was right in the opening, he swung the torch round to shine into the room. There was a flash and he disappeared, the light going out. But there was a solid shape in the darkness and it moved, lunging towards Armstrong as he stood a short distance away. Momentarily a crazed image filled his vision before he threw himself to one side, dropping the torch through the banisters as he did so. It smashed on the stairs below and everything became very dark. He suddenly remembered that there was a large hole in the floor around here somewhere.

'Carrick!' he hissed, fear almost choking him.

Ahead of him, blessedly, there was light.

'The bastard does have a knife,' said Carrick's voice. He came down the passage. 'You all right?'

'He missed,' Armstrong replied, picking himself up. 'Mind that hole.'

'Well, at least we know there's only one of them after all,' Carrick said, setting off up the next flight of stairs.

'You were expecting two.'

'Cryon and a bloke. Only Cryon *is* a bloke. End of mystery.'

It occurred to Armstrong that he had never been in a situation like this before but he did not question why Carrick was suddenly so laconic, nor notice that the inspector's shirtsleeve was suddenly crimson.

Ahead of them the streetlights shone through the dirty windows of what had been Armstrong's living quarters. From the room a voice spoke.

'You lied, Carrick. There's no one out there.'

Carrick gave Armstrong his torch, halting in the doorway. 'It makes no difference. You're under arrest.'

Cryon was standing by the window, gazing out over the square. He was wearing jeans and a sweater, the straggly hair scraped back into a ponytail. He turned to face them, taking a fresh grip on the knife.

'Just put that down and don't be a fool,' Carrick said softly.

'I'm coming through that door,' the other said. 'Whether you're there or not.' He took three paces towards them.

Armstrong heard Carrick sigh. It was a sigh of regret, not submission.

'I mean it!' the man shouted. 'Out of the way!'

Carrick stooped quickly and picked up by the neck one of the several bottles with which Armstrong had chosen to decorate his home. A quick flick of the wrist and it was broken against the doorknob. 'I'm afraid this is the chosen weapon of some members of my race,' he said.

Armstrong remembered to breathe, seeing the jagged ends of the bottle catch the light, glittering, as the hand holding it made a sudden movement.

'Drop the knife,' Carrick whispered, walking forwards. 'Or you'll have so many stitches in your face they'll run out of suture thread.'

'You're not allowed to do things like that!' Cryon raged.

'Or no face at all?' Carrick continued, no louder, still advancing.

Then, in a blur of movement, it was over. Cryon yelped once with fear and pain and dropped the knife. He had been so transfixed with horror, staring at the bottle, that he had not seen Carrick's foot come up to kick him on the wrist. In the next moment he had been slammed up against the wall and was being searched for other weapons.

'Do we have another set of handcuffs?' Carrick asked Armstrong in conversational fashion, but breathing hard.

'No, but . . .' Armstrong searched around and found a short piece of thin rope he knew was in the room somewhere. Not so long ago he had used it to keep up his trousers. 'Where did you learn things like that?' he asked, binding Cryon's hands together.

'From a man in a pub in the East End,' was the reply. 'A Scot from Rotherhithe. He said it was time I learned how to defend myself.'

# Chapter Nineteen

A week later a service of thanksgiving was given in the parish church of Chantbury for the safe return of the Pyx. The ancient building was full for the affair of the theft and recovery had caught the imagination of people throughout the West Country. In fact the Reverend Forbes, resplendent in a chasuble borrowed specially from a friend for the occasion – his own being rather faded and threadbare – had not had such a large congregation since the wedding of a film star who had lived in the area in the early seventies.

A true organiser, the elderly priest had arranged for the choir of Bath Abbey to sing, a local ladies' flower-arranging group to augment the sexton's wife to decorate the church and, last but not least, humbly requested his bishop to preach. The result, quite the most sublime and magnificent offer of worship that the district could remember, touched hearts. And through the presence of a television news team, the producer of which decided the story deserved a proper programme, soon the entire nation was made aware of the precarious state of the fabric at Chantbury's church. Cheques started to arrive.

This was in the future, though. Now, on a fine morning in late September, the congregation left the church, Handel ringing in their ears – all spare money had gone to maintaining the organ for, as the Reverend Forbes had said on more than one occasion, not *everything* could be neglected – and spilled out onto the gravelled walks of the churchyard. A few of the locals glanced at the slender red-haired girl and her companion and wondered who they were, the most common guess being that they were from the media.

They had not arrived together; Joanna had been rather surprised to see Carrick there. She had moved back into her own flat the morning after the arrests. He had not tried to stop her, and said very little on the subject and had made no effort to see her since. In the church he had suddenly appeared at her side and had smiled briefly before kneeling.

'I thought you'd be a son of the Kirk,' she said as they strolled.

'I *was*. My granddad drove me into the arms of the Episcopalians.'

'What does that make you?' she asked, not knowing about such things.

'An Anglican, thank God.'

'It sounds as though your granddad was strict with you.'

'He was terrified that as I had no father – he was drowned at sea before I was born – the Devil would get his hands on me. So he thrashed me at every opportunity. My mother moved us away from her parents' home as soon as she could and we went to live with her aunt at Crieff. Then, when I was ten years old and she had married again, we moved south.' He appraised her. 'How are you?'

'Mended, thank you. I won't ask if you've recovered – it's obvious you're in rude health.'

They sat on a wooden seat and gazed out over Somerset, the distant hills blue in the sunshine. Carrick had had the stitches out of the long gash on his arm that morning.

'I went to see the Moffats yesterday,' Joanna said. 'Alice told me that a few days ago a man knocked at the door and gave her a huge bunch of flowers. He just smiled, said he was sorry and went away. The wording on the card was, "From the smelly tramp who didn't mean to frighten you."'

Carrick chuckled.

'Cases all sewn up now?' she asked in off-hand fashion.

'Almost. Harbutts didn't stop talking as soon as we got him to the nick, hoping to save his own skin. Cryon's real name is Bart Ryan and he's not Canadian at all. His father was a small-time crook killed in a shoot-out in London in the sixties. His son swore to get even and to make a name for himself in the underworld of crime. He didn't do at all well, apparently, and was shot himself, causing injuries so severe that he was never the same again. But he had a bit of a reputation as a cat burglar so someone gave him the job of stealing the Chantbury Pyx. He seemed to think that if he succeeded it would be his return to the big time. But it was all in his mind, really – the man's more than slightly crazy. That won't stop him from going to prison for a long time for murdering Susan Fairbrother, though. We found the girl's purse under the floorboards at Cryon's – Ryan's – flat.'

'Why rent the flat in Beckford Square?'

'Just as a front, really, and to act as a base for new operations in the West Country. He'd decided to get out of London after this job.'

'And Harbutts?'

'They met in a pub. Ryan decided to use him as a bodyguard-cum-heavy. It was all part of his self-delusion – he saw himself as a master crook with his own band of armed thugs.'

'A good actor, though – he fooled you, James.'

'I know. And Harbutts was all part of that deception too, of course. The boyfriend who visited and much bouncing of bedsprings. Nothing like that, needless to say – actually they loathe one another. Especially now Harbutts is singing like a canary.'

'Did you discover how he lured poor Susan into West Terrace?'

'He told her the tramp had been taken ill and asked her to look at him. He realised he'd killed the wrong girl when he saw you talking to me in the square the following day. Harbutts says that Ryan really lost his head then and saw us both as the biggest danger to his successful new criminal career.'

'So I saw Ryan leaving the square after killing Mrs Pryce and then he presumably cut round the back and went in that way. Why did he kill her?'

'They both insist that neither of them did. Harbutts says that Ryan dragged her body into the garden after he'd found her dead. But he refuses to go into details.'

'What does your intuition say?' Joanna asked.

'Mine?' Carrick thought for a moment. 'It suggests that someone else was involved. Which brings me to something I was going to ask you. How about a weekend in Tintagel?'

She gazed at him rather severely. 'I take it you're going to remain mysterious about the reason for the venue until we get there, when all will be revealed.'

'Naturally.'

'I shall have to be back first thing on the Monday.'

'For work?' he asked, inscrutable as an Egyptian cat.

She smiled broadly. 'Lance left me his share of the business. I still haven't recovered from the shock.' She glanced at her watch. 'Look, I must dash. I'm seeing a client about a job in the Western Isles. He seems to think his family's done him out of his croft but can't go himself because his baby daughter's very ill.'

'You might need a little local knowledge for something like that,' Carrick said eagerly.

'Too right. There's a firm of solicitors in Oban who deal with that sort of thing. I shall call on them as soon as I arrive.'

'Well?' he said when she had got to her feet.

For a moment she gazed at him blankly. 'Oh . . . yes. All right.' Another smile. 'Why not?'

'Shall I pick you up at about seven thirty on Friday night then?'

'Fine.'

He watched her hurry away. Sadly.

Great waves like molten green glass were breaking on the rocks at the foot of Tintagel Castle, throwing spray high into the air that looked as though it was trying to snatch the sea birds that wheeled and hovered on the updraught. The woman leaning against a low wall, once part of the curtain wall of the castle, could feel the vibration beneath her feet as each wave thundered against the sheer cliff. She had come here on most days since her arrival in the town to be mesmerised by the roar of the sea and the endless screaming of the gulls. She had discovered that the everlasting power of nature could blot out the misery of her human awareness of self.

The idea that this might be the final solution had crept into her mind the previous day. And now the nameless urging was giving her no peace. She had lain awake all night while that part of her that used to be a religious, responsible woman argued ineffectively like the useless bleating of a doomed sheep in a slaughterhouse. Worse, it seemed to her that what she would have regarded at one time as criminal behaviour, now assumed the guise of a new responsibility, the only course open to an adult with a conscience. And, deep down, it mocked her with the truly wicked thought that if it was not to be, then she would be prevented from doing it. For after all, taunted the inner voice, Christians are God's chosen, aren't they?

Miss Braithewaite put her hands over her ears, trying vainly to block out such iniquity. What was wrong with her? Was she going mad?

As always, she was drawn to look at the sea and its ceaseless and unrelenting surge a hundred feet below in and around the rocks that resembled the stumps of blackened teeth. She leaned out a little farther.

'Do take care,' said a man's voice.

She had not heard his approach. 'James!' Such was the shock that the familiarity was out before she could prevent it.

'So you do remember me from schooldays?'

She took a deep breath. 'Of course.'

'I thought that when . . .' He smiled.

'It wasn't appropriate for either of us to mention that we knew one another – not under the circumstances.'

'You must have taught English to thousands of children.'

'But you were head boy for a year until you left – and I seem to remember you and me working together on a school play.' Miss Braithewaite gazed, unseeing, at the horizon. She felt very weak, her emotions in tatters but also oddly at peace. It was over; he was not here by accident.

'Would you like to have lunch with me?'

'I don't think that would be right, do you?'

A warm brown hand covered one of hers as it rested on the top of the wall. 'You're freezing.' Astoundingly, he took the hand. 'Coming?'

'Where are we going?' she asked, convinced that she knew already.

'To a pub.' He drew her arm through his. 'Forget spit and sawdust. The Steam Packet is quite respectable.'

He was teasing her but his expression was very grave.

Miss Braithewaite wavered. 'I don't know how I can look you in the eye.'

205

'Loss of self-esteem proves a healthy conscience.'

They faced one another for several long moments and then Carrick said, 'You did try to tell me, didn't you? You mentioned Cryon's sweet tooth and the thanks you'd received for the syrup tart. Most unusual in a woman, you said. When did you guess that she was a man?'

'Almost straight away. To be honest, I wondered if he was a transvestite. I didn't say anything to him, of course, and it *was* just a guess. But afterwards I knew. He was very strong for a woman, you see.'

'And you've stayed on here with your sister, hating yourself because you read in the papers that he'd been arrested for theft and murder.'

'There's more to it than that,' she whispered.

'I know. Come and have lunch.'

All too aware that Miss Braithewaite had probably never been in a public bar in her life, Carrick carefully ensconced his guest in the small area of the Steam Packet that was set out as a restaurant, fetched menus from the bar, a pint of bitter and a dry sherry.

'This is really quite pleasant,' said the lady, somewhat hesitantly, looking around.

'It's the other pub that has the bear pit,' Carrick said. 'Your health.'

'Now you're laughing at me,' she remonstrated gently.

'Revenge for the five hundred lines you once gave me when I was in the first year.' He picked up one of the menus. 'I can recommend the fish chowder.' Looking at her over the top of it, he went on, 'I have no great desire to be the first policeman in the history of this planet to arrest his English teacher, so for the love of subordinate clauses tell me what happened on the night Mrs Pryce died – *after* you thought you'd pushed her down the stairs and gone back into your flat.'

The play had been one that she had written herself, based on a novel by Dorothy L. Sayers, she had forgotten which one. She was reminded of it now for here before her was Lord Peter Wimsey; Carrick as he had appeared on stage all those years ago. With his fair colouring and sharp, rather bleak features he had been just right.

'I'm afraid you will have to arrest me,' Miss Braithewaite said sadly. 'For I did kill Mrs Pryce.' After the weeks of worry the admission was balm. She closed her eyes for a few moments and heard the soft sound as he laid the menu back on the table.

'She attacked you with the hammer?'

'I *thought* she was going to attack me. She'd met Bethany Cryon downstairs, who for some reason had this hammer. Reading about the arrest in the paper since, I've realised why she – he – had it, but at the time I supposed it was for protection. I heard raised voices and immediately thought that Mrs Pryce had fallen heavily on the stairs and that people had found her. So I went outside onto the landing again. But it was *her*, shouting.'

'Take it easy,' Carrick said softly, for Miss Braithewaite was shuddering violently.

'I have *never* been so frightened,' the elderly woman continued. 'Opening the front door I beheld her running up the stairs towards me waving the hammer. She was quite beside herself. To me she looked almost mad. She ran straight at me. I realised afterwards that she'd only meant to go into my flat to bang on the floor with it, for that was what she'd originally wanted, wasn't it? I grasped her by the wrist and twisted and was very surprised when she let go. The hammer dropped on the floor. My one thought was to get it and throw it down the stairs or something. She screamed at me. I picked up the hammer and . . . Oh, dear.'

'What sort of scream?'

'Rage. Her hands were like claws. She threw herself at me. So I . . .'

'Yes?'

'I took a sort of wild swipe at her with it. I thought that if I hit her somewhere she'd come to her senses. But she'd slipped somehow on that grating in the floor and I hit her right on the back of the . . .' Here she fumbled in her bag for the bottle of small pills, her face chalk white.

Carrick fetched her some water and a stiff brandy.

'I shouldn't drink alcohol at all,' she said weakly a couple of minutes later when she felt a little better.

'Listen,' Carrick said, taking her hand for the second time that morning. 'If she had intended to use the hammer to bang on anything, she would have belted Paul Mallory's front door. He was the original subject of her anger, wasn't he? But she went right past that and came on up the stairs. Miss Braithewaite, you *were* her target and there's no jury in this land that will find you guilty of murder when what happened was an accident anyway.'

'Bethany helped me,' she said when she had dried the few tears. 'She picked up Mrs Pryce and carried her downstairs. I didn't ask what had been done with the body, I felt too ill. I thought I'd had a heart attack, I felt so dreadful.'

'What was Cryon wearing?'

'A tracksuit with what looked like men's brown lace-up shoes. That was what I found so strange. She knocked when she came back to see if I was all right. That was when I really knew she was a man, the way she spoke. He said he didn't want anyone to know he'd been out dressed like that at night and if I kept quiet about it he wouldn't say anything about Mrs Pryce. The way I felt just then, James, I would have agreed to anything. The woman was dead and there was nothing either of us could do to bring her back. All I wish now is that I'd told you the whole story when I went to the police station.'

Carrick thought how Susan Fairbrother had died as a result of Mrs Pryce's body being dragged into the square. But Miss Braithewaite could not be blamed for that. If the man who had stolen the Chantbury Pyx had not returned home just then, there would have been no hammer to snatch. And if Mrs Pryce had not been such a horrible woman –

'I shall never forget that sound as the hammer . . .' Miss Braithewaite was staring at him fixedly but, he thought, not seeing him at all.

'You're left-handed,' Carrick said, mostly to himself. 'I should have remembered.'

# Chapter Twenty

Joanna switched on the telephone answering machine, had a brave attempt to tidy her desk, gave up and fixed herself a cup of coffee. Out in the small reception area a man was installing an intercom so that she would not have to leave the outer door open all day. When Lance had been there a lot of the time, personal security had not been important.

'Perhaps I'm getting nervous,' she said to the geranium on the window ledge.

As she had come to realise, too late, the weekend in Tintagel had been a mistake. Carrick, obviously, had had his mind on the person he had gone down to find, and the circumstances of where and how he had found her had hardly made the experience an enjoyable one. In fact, he had arranged straight away for Miss Braithewaite's sister to return with the three of them to Bath because he did not feel that his quarry should be left on her own at home. Luckily the sister was also retired and, after arranging that someone would look after her cat, had been able to leave immediately.

'She'll be all right,' Carrick had said to Joanna more than once.

Joanna was sure she would be, at least, from the point of view of not being sent to prison. She was sure too that he was hating himself and his job right now. The third certainty was that a relationship based almost solely, as far as he was concerned, on physical attraction had no future whatsoever.

'You're a fool,' she said to the geranium. 'To think that the man might actually grow fond of you.' While it was true that he had asked her to live with him, his motive was unclear.

Joanna had a nasty feeling that it had a lot to do with company in bed and being able to discuss his cases with her. And here he was, she could hear his voice, talking to the workman.

'I didn't think you'd be here,' Carrick said, accepting a cup of coffee. 'The Western Isles and all that. Which one, by the way?'

'Lewis. I'm off tonight. How is Miss Braithewaite?'

'Better now she's made a full statement. The trouble is these things drag on so. She's far more important as a witness when Ryan and Harbutts come to court.'

'Will *she* come to trial?'

'I wouldn't have thought so. For one thing Ryan saw what happened and that Miss Braithewaite acted in self-defence. It's hardly in his own interest to change what he's already said.'

'Did Mrs Pryce snatch the hammer from him?'

'Yes. According to him he had just reached the bottom of the stairs, having come in the back, and had taken the hammer from his plastic bag to – as he said – rewrap it more tightly. She wrenched it off him and ran back up the stairs. Naturally, he followed, smartly.'

'Is he denying any of the charges?'

'Trying to blame Harbutts for most of it. Who is trying to pin it all on him, of course.' Carrick placed his cup down on the corner of Joanna's desk and stretched. 'No, we have them well sewn up, I think.'

There was a little silence and then Carrick said, 'Have you thought at all about what I asked you?'

'The answer's no, James.'

'Look, I know I shouldn't have thought we could sort anything out by going to Cornwall for the weekend but –'

'Lance used me,' Joanna said quietly. 'You use me. Yes, I know you apologised when I was in hospital but nothing's changed, has it? I think you're quite keen to come to Scotland with me but it seems that might only be so I can have your support on your home ground. I'd be using *you*. I don't want relationships with people to be like that – just providing services for one another. There's more to life than that.'

'That's a bald way of putting it. I was under the impression that life revolved around people doing things for one another.'

'What about feelings?'

'Feelings?'

210

'Yes, or are you suggesting that we draw up some kind of agreement whereby I'll help you with your cases in exchange for you coming running when I need help?' Joanna's tone had become increasingly scathing as she uttered these words, mainly because she had suddenly realised that that was precisely what had been going through his mind.

'I don't think there's an awful lot wrong with the idea,' he said at last, looking a bit baffled.

'And when you fancy a roll in the hay, does that go down as overtime?' she stormed.

'That's hardly fair – you said yourself you –'

Bitterly, Joanna interrupted. 'You were only drawn to me in the first place because I reminded you of your wife – of how Kathleen used to be before she became ill. The fact that I already worked for the CID was a bonus. No, I'm sorry, James, I'm not going to come and live with you just so you can have a thinking woman on tap.'

'But you're not a domestic sort of girl,' he said faintly after another silence. 'I've never met anyone more efficient and professionally minded. It seems that you'd think it the most colossal cheek on my part to suggest . . .' Quite uncharacteristically he floundered to a halt. Then he said, 'I thought that's what you *wanted*.'

Joanna stared at him, thunderstruck.

'I mean . . . I was quite prepared to keep everything on a businesslike level and –' Again he broke off and shrugged helplessly.

'You mean you'd prefer not to keep things on a businesslike level?'

'No, of course not. Not that I'd expect you to have my dinner ready or warm my slippers or bloody stupid things like that. No, you'd have your career and I'd have mine and . . .' He grinned sheepishly. 'I'm not putting this very well, am I?'

'James, what are you *saying*?'

He groaned. 'I thought that if you came to live with me you'd soon realise I love you and might just . . .'

Joanna, becoming aware that her mouth was hanging open, closed it.

'I – I lied, as a matter of fact,' he stammered. 'I can speak Gaelic quite well. Not that there aren't any English-speakers on Lewis.'

211

## Biographical Note

MARGARET DUFFY, born in Essex, England, now lives in Beith, Scotland, with her husband of twenty-nine years, Gordon, and their daughter, Hayley Ann. Before becoming an author, she was a civil servant with the Ministry of Defence. Her many interests include reading crime novels, cooking, and underwater archaeology; however, the majority of her time is spent gardening in her six-and-a-half-acre woodland garden. Duffy attributes her ability to tell stories to her paternal grandfather, who regaled her with many of the wonderful folktales of his homeland, Bohemia. Noted on many occasions for her mastery of action scenes as well as character development in her seven previous crime novels, including *Who Killed Cock Robin, Rook Shoot,* and *Brass Eagle,* Margaret Duffy continues to please fans with her unusual characters and unique plot twists.